If dreams present a way to live a fairytale life eternally, why wouldn't you want to live in one forever?

THE JOURNEY TO WHITESTONE
A PARANORMAL ROMANCE
&
BOOK ONE
IN
THE DREAM MASTER SERIES
BY
Johnny Ray
Copyright © 2012
SIR JOHN PUBLISHING
ISBN # 978-1-940949-13-0

ALL RIGHTS ARE HEREBY RESERVED
BY
JOHNNY RAY

This paranormal romance, the first in this Dream Master series, is set in Atlanta, Georgia and the Great Smokey Mountains of Tennessee.

As Jacquelyn Parker struggles with her life spinning out of control, resulting in a bitter divorce, and her career ruined, she is sucked into a sinister world of late-night sleazy bars. It is her last minute prayer that fortunately finds its way to the Dream Master who controls the gates to Whitestone, a side door to heaven, and the next step in enlightenment. From her dreams she learns that she only has one chance to reunite with her one true love and advance to the next level of enlightenment.

In order for Jacquelyn to master the four steps of enlightenment and find her true love, the Dream Master summons the assistance of other enlightened ones who teach Jacquelyn various philosophies from the Tai chi to the Kama Sutra to guide her path.

After centuries of missing her true love in time and space, Jacquelyn has only one last chance to get it right, and live the ultimate happy ever after life. If she is unsuccessful, however, she will have to live with the tragic failure forever.

JOHNNY RAY is an award winning novelist who won the Royal Palm literary award for best thriller and is quickly making a name for himself as the master of the romantic thriller. He loves social interaction with his readers and can be found on

Twitter
www.twitter.com/sirjohn_writer

Facebook
www.facebook.com/authorjohnnyray.

He can also be reached by e-mailing at sirjohn@wwisp.com,

Or you can just follow him on his blog at www.sirjohn.us for updates and future releases.

Johnny Ray's other novels include:

DRONES
Published by Sir John Publishing in 2013

A WAR HERO RETURNS
Published by Sir John Publishing in 2013

JOHN RAIN – THE HAWAIIAN AFFAIR
Published by AMAZON DIGITAL in 2013

MODELS AND LOVERS
Published by Sir John Publishing in 2012

HER HONOR'S BODYGUARD
Published by Sir John Publishing in 2012

FOR LOVE AND VENGEANCE
Published by Sir John Publishing in 2012

SCANDAL – THE DEATH OF A LEGACY
Published by Sir John Publishing in 2012

THE SALSA CONNECTION
Published by Sir John Publishing in 2012

STALKING LOVE
Published by Sir John Publishing in 2012

CHAPTER 1

With her door closed and the Atlanta office quiet for a moment, Jacquelyn Parker slipped off her shoes and arched her petite body deep into her executive leather chair, crushing her shoulder length blonde hair into the headrest. All concerns and worries quickly faded as her mind wandered to a place where the world rejoiced in peace and beautiful scenery filled the world around her. She envisioned a mountain scene with water cascading down streams, and where the fragrant smell of flowers saturated the air.

A dark haired man walked beside her for a while before reaching for her hand. The tenderness and warmth of his touch spread through her body as she sank deeper into her world of dreams. Yes, she felt sure such a paradise could only be created in her dream world, but the images brought her so much relief from her problems in the material world.

Her beautiful daydream suddenly vanished as she heard shouting, and then more yelling as others entered into the fray developing into an all out brawl outside her office. The additional sounds of furniture being crashed sent her heart racing. *What in the hell is going on?*

"Get out of here," a female voice yelled as the commotion outside Jacquelyn's door grew while she heard more furniture being smashed.

Jacquelyn jumped out of her chair and quickly put her shoes back on before she rushed toward the door. With her heart now skipping beats, she hesitated at the door to listen.

"Vincent, stop right where you are. You know there's a restraining order against you, and you're not allowed in here," Andrew, the office manager, yelled additional commands, but they were not clear enough for her to fully understand.

"Oh my God," Jacquelyn whispered. While Vincent, her ex-husband, had pulled many stupid stunts before, she had never expected him to crash into her office, and especially in front of everyone. She pumped her fist before she slapped the wall with her open hand. *What am I going to do now?* If she confronted him here, it might cost her job.

"Get out of my way, asshole," Vincent shouted. "Where is she?"

"Call the police," Andrew ordered someone.

As sounds of the fight in the office outside her door escalated, she hid behind the door, but she knew it wouldn't take long for Vincent to find her. After all, her name was imprinted on the door.

Another shattering sound of glass breaking thundered like a lightning bolt throughout the building as the fight intensified. A secretary screamed as Jacquelyn heard Vincent cussing louder. Her hate quickly boiled over, overtaking her fear of coming face to face with him. He had disobeyed a court order restraining him from all contact with her.

After swinging open the door, Jacquelyn marched to the outside office and confronted Vincent. The office turned silent as several secretaries moved between Vincent and Jacquelyn. As Andrew retreated to one side with a cell phone in his hand, no one moved, with everyone waiting for someone else to make the first move.

Vincent's face flushed and his eyes darted around, giving him the appearance of a mad man. Seconds later, he focused on Jacquelyn. "You know, I'm getting damn tired of you not returning my calls. We still have items to work out, and I'm the best man you'll ever find," he snarled. "You need help, and I'm still willing to get that for you."

"Vincent, it's over. You need to get that through your dumb head. That's why I divorced you."

Andrew maintained his focus on Vincent. "Don't worry, Jacquelyn. The police are on the way, and this time he'll spend some time in jail."

Vincent's face remained defiant. "Jacquelyn, I hope you're happy with all you've done to me. It didn't have to be like this."

"Vincent, I'm not the one who needs help."

Apparently realizing the extent of just how much he was outnumbered, and how he might be going to jail, Vincent shot Jacquelyn a finger and ran out of the room as he shouted, "You'll not get away from me this easily. I'll see you later, when you don't have all of these damn idiots around you!"

Brenda, one of the office secretaries, yelled after him as he fled, "Get out of here, you crazy bastard."

Andrew shouted on the phone to the police. "He just left here." With his face flushed in a bright red, reflecting his anger, he continued, "Yes, we want you to pursue him. I want him arrested, and I'm sure Jacquelyn will want charges filed against him as well." After a short pause, he added, "We'll be here waiting for you."

With papers and broken furniture scattered all over the floor, the office looked like a bomb had exploded inside it. After glancing around the room at all the damages, Andrew yelled to everyone around him, "I want no one to touch this mess until the police arrive, since it'll be good for them to see what happened."

"Are you okay?" Jacquelyn asked as she approached Andrew. She grimaced at the blood coming from a small cut to his hand.

"Not really, but I'll be better in a minute. You know you really married an asshole. Somehow you have to get this taken care of. We can't have these sorts of incidents happening here."

"What can I do? I already have a restraining order against him. The police need to do their job."As several secretaries hurried over to Jacquelyn, she continued to fume. She knew the secretaries in the office used to love the way she always encouraged the group to laugh and have fun at work, but that was earlier. She quickly recognized how much her problems had affected them also. She knew she had lost her *love of life* and had become this new character she still couldn't fully understand.

She remembered being the one who always wanted to spread love around to everyone, but the stress had changed her. This wasn't the first time, and she knew it wouldn't be the last. She knew from the looks in their eyes how sorry they felt for her. Oh damn, how she remembered when she used to be the best employee in the company, and how her hard work had paid off. This had resulted in one promotion after another. Of course, that was all before she met Vincent.

As Brenda held her tight and supportively while she helped her back to her office, her world around her became a blur as she staggered to a chair in her office. "Thank you, I'll be fine," Jacquelyn muttered while still in shock at seeing Vincent and witnessing his outburst. While in the past he had been mentally abusive to her, she now knew that he was capable of being physically abusive as well. *What am I going to do?*

"I see the police in the parking lot. They'll be here soon," Laurie, another secretary, yelled as she entered Jacquelyn's office.

"Did they catch Vincent?"

"I don't know, but they should soon."

"Oh, my God! Will this ever end?" Jacquelyn put her head on her desk and cried softly.

With other office secretaries quickly surrounding her, Brenda started rubbing her back. There wasn't much else they could do but offer her a small sense of protection. These good friends knew what she had been through.

Jacquelyn remembered having fun with these girls earlier when life was great. She was the one who lit up a room when she came into it, and she had used this charm to her advantage so many times in obtaining new clients, or keeping old clients and employees happy. In her position it was her job to keep everyone's spirits high since the salesmen under her only performed well when she properly motivated them.

During the last six months of going through the divorce with Vincent, the sales in her department had fallen drastically. She knew management only allowed her to keep her job due to the potential they saw in her. Her boss told her many times that he hoped soon this ordeal would be behind them, and she would again be his superstar. The company had even arranged for her to see a therapist to help her work through the nightmares of the divorce.

Laurie entered Jacquelyn's office and closed the door behind her while carrying a glass of water and a wet cloth over to her. "Here. Take some water and let me help you with your face a little. The police will be here in a minute."

"Thank you." Jacquelyn said as she accepted the cloth and drank some of the water. She needed to gain control. It wasn't good to let her staff know she had become this fragile. The cool cloth felt good on her face and did help to bring her back to reality—at least to some extent.

Still, the last six months of battling with Vincent over the divorce had changed her so much. As she reflected on her hair which needed to be cut and styled, she knew that even the shine in her hair before wasn't so evident anymore, and while her eyes retained a beautiful shade of blue she was always proud of, she knew the circles under them told a heartbreaking story of what she had been through. As she washed her streaked makeup off and looked into a mirror at her pale dreary skin, she wondered where was the woman she remembered who had such a great vibrant glow.

After hearing a knock on the door, she heard Andrew yelling on the other side, "Jacquelyn, the police are here." After looking around the room, she arched her back, and tried to regain her posture. She had to act like the manager she knew they hired her to be and get through this situation somehow.

"Great, I'll be out in one second." She worked on removing the last of the makeup before turning to one secretary who offered a sign of approval.

Brenda walked to the door and opened it for her. "Good luck." Jacquelyn walked out, and hurried to meet the police without saying a word.

Andrew, who was standing next to two uniformed police officers, turned to face her when she joined them. "This is Jacquelyn. She used to be married to the man who crashed in here."

A tall, lanky, bald-headed officer glanced at Jacquelyn with the stern look of a military commando, which was much like she would expect from an officer in charge. At a time like this, she felt thankful for having someone who looked so professional to handle this case. The deeper she studied him, the more masculine he appeared.

While he appeared to be analyzing Jacquelyn for a minute, he showed no emotions. Then as if his mind was clear as to what to say and do, he walked over to her and extended his hand. "I'm Officer Abbott, and this is Officer Johnson."

Officer Johnson, a large, stocky, black lady with a stern but compassionate face glanced around the room. "This is terrible, but don't worry, we'll catch him soon."

"Then he escaped? You didn't catch him before he got out of here?" Jacquelyn asked.

"I'm afraid he vanished before we arrived. I assume you'll want to fill out a warrant to have him arrested."

"Yes, I would." *Damn yes, and maybe with him in jail I can get some relief.*

Officer Johnson turned to Andrew. "I assume you'd like to file a complaint also?"

"You damn right I would. This kind of outrage can't be tolerated in this office."

Jacquelyn quickly added, "Perhaps we need to go into my office to discuss this and let everyone get back to work." She motioned for the officers to follow her into her office.

"We'll be glad to as soon as the site team arrives and secures the area. We'll need to take some photos and gather some evidence." Officer Abbot noticed the blood on Andrew's hand. "Do we need to get you some medical help?"

"I'm fine. It's only a small cut."

"Just the same . . . we'll have someone look at it. We'll also need to take photos of the cut."

"Yes . . . that would be good, I think." Andrew produced a quirky smile.

"I have a restraining order against Vincent," Jacquelyn volunteered.

"Really! I think some guys just don't get the message, but this time . . . I think this guy will. We'll pick him up soon so don't worry." Officer Johnson nodded her head while maintaining a firm smile.

As a team of paramedics arrived, they looked around to assess the situation. Andrew held out his hand for the men to examine. "That's a bad scratch, but I think you'll live," one of the medics said with a smile to help make Andrew feel a little better.

Several other officers arrived and went to work documenting the damaged office as Officer Johnson glanced around. "Okay, let's go into your office and take care of some paperwork." After walking into Jacquelyn's office, Officer Johnson went straight to business. "I need to ask you some questions. Are you sure you're up to talking now?"

"Yes, I want to get this over with as fast as possible."

"I understand this was your ex-husband, and you mentioned you have a restraining order against him. Do you have a copy of it with you by any chance?"

"I do. It's in my purse."

"Can you give me a description of him?"

"I'll be glad to. Vincent's thirty-three years old and has light-brown hair he keeps short, and almost in a butch cut. You know, kind of like a football player would wear his hair, or a military man. His eyes are a light gray, and I'm sure you'll be able to see the evil in them. He had a kind of muscular build, but now sports a large beer belly. He normally wears all black clothing, which is what he had on here a few minutes ago."

"How tall is he?"

"He's around five feet and ten inches, and he weighs around one hundred and eighty pounds. Like I said he also has a good size stomach. That comes from drinking a lot of beer." Jacquelyn reflected on how she didn't know this about him when they first met, or how he could pull her into a life she could not have imagined earlier.

After she finally located the copy of the restraining order, she handed it to Officer Johnson who scribbled some notes on her pad. As they collected the rest of the information, Jacquelyn's mind stayed in a daze, making it hard to comprehend all of their questions. The officer eventually handed Jacquelyn the pad for her to sign. While she knew she should've checked it, she felt too drained.

As if in deep thought, Officer Johnson finally asked, "What do you think made him go off the deep end like this?"

She remembered her therapist, her lawyer, and her friends asking this question many times before. "Sometimes, you think you really know someone, but you don't. At the Baptist church where he goes, everyone thinks he's the pillar of the community and can do no wrong. To them, he's *Mr. Perfect*."

While Jacquelyn held back many times from telling anyone about Vincent's dark side, she now felt mad enough to tell all. "Vincent is very controlling and manipulative. In trying to be the perfect little wife, I went along with many of his crazy ideas. The emotions I took as passion, I now know consisted of nothing more than lust and abuse by him. You'd not believe all of the hell he has put me through."

"I'm so sorry." Officer Johnson nodded as if to console her.

"Being a small girl, he knew it was easy to get me drunk. He'd bring me drink after drink, so he could use me as his personal sex slave any way he wanted to." Jacquelyn couldn't believe she was divulging all of this.

"Have you told all of this to anyone?"

"Not all of it. It's so hard to admit what all he had forced me to do." Jacquelyn lowered her head to her desk for a moment before redirecting her attention on the officers. "You know I often daydream of finding a fantastic guy who loves me and respects me, and even after all that has happened to me, I still believe in true love, but until I have Vincent out of my life, I feel like that will never happen."

"Well . . . this time, I think you'll see the last of him for a while." With that, the officer closed her pad and smiled before they left the room.

Brenda came in after the officers left. "Is there anything I can do for you?"

"Thanks . . . but just shut my door and let me get my thoughts together." Brenda smiled as she left, leaving Jacquelyn to think for a minute.

After about twenty minutes, she heard a knock on her door as Andrew opened it and walked in. "How are you?"

"To be honest, I feel like a piece of shit. I'm so sorry this happened here."

"I just talked to the district vice-president. He has already received word of this, and wants to know what happened. Let me say that he's not very happy at all."

"What can I say, Andrew. I married a crazy person." She knew she had problems handling work right now, and her mind couldn't pull it all together.

"Jacquelyn, you know your job has been on the line here for some time now. This may be the final straw. I'm hoping you can show some improvements in your sector's performance this month."

"After a day like this, what can you really expect?"

"We *expect* you to be the executive we hired."

"I don't think I can do any super selling right now. You know how much my ex-husband has been harassing me. It's impossible to concentrate. Give me a little time and I'll have it all together soon."

"I'm not sure I can do that."

"What?"

"I know they're discussing who they could hire in your place right now. It's out of my hands. It's a terrible time to tell you this, and this incident today is extremely bad timing. You've become a liability in the eyes of the board of directors. These kinds of stories not only reflect badly on you, but on the company as well."

Jacquelyn fought the shock settling in as she fought back tears. What would she do without her job? "I know I can turn the sales around if—"

The cell phone in Andrew's pocket started to ring. "This is Andrew." She studied the seriousness in his face as he listened intensely. "I understand, but I don't agree. Yes, sir. I'll take care of it now."

Jacquelyn didn't need to ask what the call concerned as her worst nightmare unfolded in front of her. "I was told to tell you the president of the company isn't happy with you. They're going to evaluate your contract and get back with me. If you ever needed to close some major sales, the time is now."

CHAPTER 2

After arriving at her apartment building, Jacquelyn climbed the two flights of stairs to her place. While not in a bad side of town, the apartment she moved into after the divorce was a little old and needed some repairs, but with little income and living on her own the apartment supplied all she really needed at the time. Soon, as much as she hated it, she might be talking to her mom about the possibility of moving in with her. As soon as she could turn her sales around and get on her feet again, she hoped that she could rent a better place to live.

While the inside of the apartment looked plain and simple, it was at least clean. Jacquelyn dropped her purse on the table and stumbled toward the bed where she spent most of her time lately. With her depressing life making it too hard to function normally, she became accustomed to going to bed early for no reason at all except to try to escape from life. Today, she felt no different.

While resting on the bed with her clothes still on, she silently prayed. If she could only survive one more day, or one more night, she hoped eventually life might turn around for her. She fell asleep a few minutes later.

Jacquelyn soon dreamed of a place she had visited several times before. It felt like she had actually lived there earlier with the scenery along the oceanfront appearing so familiar to her. The deep-blue sea radiated so vibrantly beautiful, as the white beach she walked on extended for miles and miles with no ending in sight. She felt a warm breeze blowing in her face, offering her a fresh but slightly salty sensation.

A man slowly materialized as he walked toward her. While he had the sun behind him and she couldn't see his face, she knew that she was deeply in love with him. The feeling resonated so strong that she couldn't deny it.

"Good morning, love," she heard him say as he finally stopped in front of her.

"Good morning to you too," she answered back as she wrapped her arms around him.

She tossed her head to one side to try to see his face, but she was unable to do so because of the intensely bright sun. He looked muscular and tall, and most importantly, he made her feel extremely secure. His cheek next to her own felt moist and warm and sent an intimate sensation of heat throughout her body. As he pulled her closer, their bodies grafted seamlessly together. "I've been looking for you," he finally whispered in her ear.

"I know," she responded. His hands softly cupped her face as he worked his fingers to the back of her neck. He kept his thumbs under her chin as he tenderly lifted her face upward. With his lips so close, she could hear him softly breathing. She waited for him to touch his lips to hers, but he continued to wait patiently while massaging her neck. His first kiss felt soft and warm and with only a slight hint of heat infused behind it. The second kiss felt much warmer as she tasted the moisture in his lips kissing hers. Soon the intimacy of his kisses and the exploration of his tongue into every part of her mouth without hesitation sent waves of hot, tingling sensations throughout her body.

She wanted him with all of the strength within her as the attraction produced a feeling much stronger than she could ever describe in mere words. As he ravished her lips and caressed her skin, creating a deep, passionate heat that made even breathing hard to accomplish, his kisses intensified, showing no intention of slowing. His tongue tasted so sweet, and like a delicate flower, she felt it blossoming inside her and consuming her soul.

As if to catch a breath of air, he slowly removed his tongue before kissing her softly on the lips. He then rested for only a moment before he whispered, "We need to talk."

"I know we do. The doctors have told me what to expect." Tears flowed down her face.

It was not only her tears, but his as well that flowed as he continued. "What are we going to do? I love you and want to be with you forever."

"I don't know. If there's anything that can be done, you know I would. I don't want to lose you." She sobbed as her heart ached with a new level of pain.

"They say I might only have a week to live. That's not enough time. We're supposed to live together forever." He was not supposed to die. As tears soaked her face, images around her glowing from the brightness of the sun on the white beach quickly overpowered her.

"We've loved this beach and the ocean. Please remember this one promise—I'll always love you. One day we'll be together again. We both always wanted to live in the mountains. I wanted to take you there, and I will if I ever receive the chance," he whispered, as she felt the hand of a man holding her own who was supposed to be strong enough to lead her and protect her for eternity. *But why is this happening. He can't just die and leave me.* She knew that he was her true love; a love with no restraints or limitations of any kind.

The sun faded as Jacquelyn woke from her dream. As she stretched she remembered the events in the dream as if they had just happened to her in real life. All the details remained so vivid—so clear. Even if it represented only a dream of a perfect life, the memories helped Jacquelyn feel much better and ready to face another day of the problems facing her. Still, the thoughts of a lover dying also left her sad to some extent. *Would we meet again in the future?*

She soon drifted off to sleep again, where she rested peacefully for the rest of the night.

***

As the alarm shattered her last few moments of sleep after a long night, she needed to hurry. She reluctantly threw the covers back and rushed to the shower, since she knew she needed to increase her team's sales. She had this one and only chance this morning.

After quickly dressing she rushed to meet Fernando at a small café close to her house. He was wearing a business suit with a clean pressed white shirt and a nice tie. While he looked professional and ready for a great day, his face failed to hide his disappointment in her appearance. She knew that as his boss she should look better, but she simply didn't have enough time, or energy.

"How are you today?" He extended his hand with a small but polite smile.

"I'm sorry that I'm late. Do you have all the material we'll need for this presentation?"

"I think I have everything. Thanks for coming out to help me close this one." He looked sincere, but nervous.

Jacquelyn knew how much rode on the outcome of this presentation. He was behind on his quota and was struggling to learn the new technology. It felt strange to have to teach someone almost twice her age the basic facts, since her generation had no problem grasping the new advancements. Fernando's comprehension unfortunately left much to be desired.

"Okay, let's do it." She glanced through his case to make sure all the required material was in order.

"He's going to meet us here in a few minutes," Fernando offered, referring to their prospective client. "He doesn't want some of his people knowing that he's thinking of a change."

"But . . . he's the one who makes the decisions, right?"

"Ultimately yes, but his boss will have the final say."

"Fernando, you know this will result in a waste of time for us. You should have told me this earlier."

He lowered his head. "I need your help. Sorry. I need to add some sales on the board, and no one can work magic like you." Jacquelyn hung her head, but she said nothing while Fernando acted nervous as he attempted to lighten the moment by redirecting the conversation. "We've missed you at church lately, and—"

"Don't even get me started. I know how my name's bounced around the church."

"I'm sorry. I didn't want to make you upset." His eyes dart around and his face flushed with embarrassment.

Jacquelyn glanced at her watch. "He's late."

"I'm sure he'll be here soon."

"I'll let you wait for him. I have other people to see, and especially since he's not the main person we need to be talking with."

"I'm sorry again." He closed his eyes briefly. "I'll try to reach him and work the sale out."

"I hope so. This is going to hurt our monthly reports." She stood and looked down at him. "Yes . . . I remember a time I enjoyed many friends at the church, and I loved to be around everyone. I guess I learned a little too late just how much I was taken in by Vincent."

"If you want to come back, I'm sure members of the church will welcome you with open arms."

"I doubt that'll ever happen." She moved toward the door. "Good luck." Jacquelyn knew he had little chance of closing this sale on his own, and she felt sorry for him and his family. She had also counted on this sale.

When his phone suddenly rang, he glanced at it to identify the caller. "This is Fernando." He smiled and lifted a finger to ask Jacquelyn to hang on. Jacquelyn waited and struggled to keep smiling as the throbbing in her head grew. She didn't feel good and was looking for any excuse to go back home and sleep.

She watched Fernando smile as he talked on the phone. "That's great. I'll be here waiting for both of you. Thank you for calling me. I'm sure you won't regret it. I know we can provide you with better service and hopefully save you some money."

As she watched him hang up, she knew his client must be close. "I assume that was the guy we were supposed to meet with."

"They're running a few minutes behind, but the good news is that he's bringing his boss with him. He even mentioned how his boss is excited about the program." Fernando's smile radiated, and his eyes look like those of a small puppy dog asking for a little praise.

"I heard." She walked over and settled in her chair at the table.

"I didn't mean to upset you a few minutes ago, but I think I know a little about how much you've been through with Vincent."

As she recognized the sincerity of his comments, she decided to relax for a minute. "I do appreciate what you're saying, but it's still hard to accept how so many people took his side."

"I'm not one to take sides, and I know that many times there're two stories to everything. I know he's always asking about you around the church."

Jacquelyn leaned back in her seat and sucked in a deep breath. "I understand you know Vincent from the church, but do you have any idea about his other life?"

"I've heard some rumors, but that's about it." He leaned forward as if he really wanted to listen to her.

Jacquelyn knew Fernando was a little more open minded than most of the other church members, who didn't want to hear the truth. "When we first met, I had been going to the church for years, and I had enjoyed the activities and the friends I thought I had."

"I remember seeing you at church outings for a long time, and I also went to your wedding. It was very beautiful and I remember how the church was packed."

Jacquelyn grimaced at the memories of her wedding which haunted her now like a bitter-sweet page in her life. "Yes, we had a large wedding, but I would never have agreed to marry him if I had known him better."

"I don't know him much outside the church. You both looked like the perfect couple for a while, and maybe I shouldn't be asking this, but I'm curious as to what happened."

His question seemed open, and contained elements of sympathy she usually didn't receive from other members of the church. She looked deep into his dark brown eyes, and tried to decide if she could trust him. Since this was the first time anyone cared about hearing her side of the story, she decided to open up. "I first met Vincent at one of the many activities organized by the church. He appeared to be a nice guy, and everyone at the church loved him."

"I know he's been a member of the church for a long time." Fernando concentrated his attention on her.

"Unfortunately, I never knew his dark side until after we were married. He hid his secrets so well, and he was so slick in the way he pulled me into his sinister side. He started with a bottle of champagne to celebrate, or a bottle of wine to relax."

"I can understand."

"Then he started taking me to one place after another to experience another side of life I never knew existed. After having lived a somewhat sheltered life, I wasn't prepared for the way this lifestyle could dominate me so quickly."

"I've never seen Vincent out in bars, but then again . . . they're not somewhere I ever go either."

"It's a life he's mastered well. He made sure we always went to the far side of town, and to places where he wouldn't be recognized."

"Do you think he went to these places before you started dating?"

"I'm sure he did, but I didn't know it then. Knowing what I know now, I would never have dated him at all. I'm also sure that when he carried me home at night after our dates, he went back out to the other side of town, and who knows what he got into. I know now that he had a history from way back."

"I'm so sorry to hear this, and I would have never guessed at all."

"It's worst than you really want to know. He's also well known at the strip clubs on the south side of town. He often hauled me to them late at night after getting me very drunk. Yes, they can be exciting after a while, and many people there act like friends."

A look of shock spread across Fernando's face. "He has actually taken you to strip clubs?"

"That's a shocker, isn't it? But . . . that's only the beginning. He constantly harassed me into going with him and wanting me to become a part of this life. Of course, he also imposed strict rules about hiding his secrets from his friends at the church." Jacquelyn looked at the ceiling, trying to decide how much more to tell Fernando.

She watched him glance at his watch, obviously wanting his client to show soon. "I never would have known if you hadn't shared this with me."

"Other than booze, I don't think he ventured into drugs, but I'll never know for sure. I know he's heavy into pornography and crazy wild sex."

"Do you think he had an affair while you were married to him?"

"I don't think I would call them affairs, they were more like kinky one-night stands. Like so many women at the church, I tried to hide the truth for a long time, and I did until such a lie became too much for me to handle. This was especially after he kept trying to push me into it further and further." A tear lingered in the corner of her eye while she fought back other memories that were so awful that she would have changed the subject if it weren't for Fernando's eyes that encouraged her to continue. "I know this is all very hard to believe. I now have a restraining order issued against him, but the police do little to stop the continued harassment. He also has many friends, not only from the church, but also from his other life which make my life a living hell."

Fernando motioned to his clients coming down the street. "I'm so sorry. If I can ever help you, I'll be glad to. I want you to know my wife and I are always available to help you."

"Thanks, I appreciate it. You're rare in the church, and I may take you up on it one day. Right now . . . let's make some money." Jacquelyn walked to a large window and looked out. The bright, clear, blue sky over Atlanta illuminated the busy streets, as a swarm of people scurried around. However, it failed to hide one sinister person about half a block away. "Oh my God!" Jacquelyn struggled to maintain her balance.

"What is it?" Fernando rushed over and glanced out the window.

"It's Vincent."

"Are you sure? At that distance he could be anyone."

"I know it's him."

"If you think it is, then we need to call the police." He reached for his phone.

"Yes, that'll be good. There's a warrant out for his arrest now, and I'm surprised they haven't caught him yet." Her attention froze in his direction while the cold and haunting truth sunk in—she might not ever be rid of him.

They watched Vincent push against a wall and rest his back. His stare remained fixed in their direction, while his trademark black clothing made him look all the more sinister.

Before the call could go through, Jacquelyn and Fernando watched their clients walking in the door, but being professional salespeople, they both quickly recovered and greeted the new arrivals. With one last glance over her shoulder Jacquelyn realized that Vincent had disappeared for now, but she would remember to make the call after the meeting.

The presentation soon resulted in a successful sale, with Fernando radiating smiles as he openly thanked Jacquelyn for her help. Jacquelyn, however, couldn't relax as she continued to worry about the proximity of her ex-husband.

After Fernando escorted Jacquelyn to her car which was around the back of the building, the shock set in quickly as she examined her smashed in window. She quickly flipped open her phone and called the police. "My car has been vandalized and I think I know who did it!" Jacquelyn continued to scream into the phone as she scanned the area for signs of Vincent. The inside of the car had her papers scattered all over the back seat. *What the hell is he looking for?*

CHAPTER 3

Jacquelyn checked her suit, and her makeup, but she couldn't force her attitude to change. She knew this might be her last day at work, but she had given it her all over the last five years. Well, more so during the beginning than lately, but still she had generated a lot of profits for the corporation. Many of the current managers and superstar salesman got their start with her. She had hired and trained them.

Maybe it was just as well, since the job wasn't fun anymore like it was when she started. She smiled at a photo on the wall of her office that was taken during one sales contest celebration. Had her life come to this? What happened to the old zest she had for life and friends?

A fire sweltered below her subconscious found its way to explain why? Vincent! With the help of her psychologist she had forced her mind to not concentrate on him so that she could move on, but at times like this she wanted to acknowledge what had caused her problems.

She knew she needed to hurry since Andrew, her boss, had been waiting for her for a while, but she needed this time to clear her mind before she faced him. She knew that the file of sales reports highlighting her career wouldn't be enough to save her. In fact, she wasn't sure she had a chance in hell at convincing Andrew to keep her.

Vincent—damn him. Why did he do this? What made him so evil? Visions of his eyes, a clear liquid gray pierced in close to her from out of nowhere, quickly haunting her again. She closed her eyes. It didn't help. She felt him drawing energy out of her. Not now! She fought back and forced her mind into a dream, a places she loved to visit.

Oh . . . to be able to live in such a dream where all remained perfect and beautiful. She drifted to a world she knew well, a place where the mountain air smelled clean and fresh. With the flowers scattering their intoxicating aromas, which enticed her to breathe deeper with each breath, she slowly enjoyed her energy building inside her, giving her the strength to rid her mind of Vincent.

She eventually opened her eyes to a world she knew she wasn't meant to live in. What happened? Why had life deteriorated into such a hell for her? When she obtained this job her future looked fantastic. She had tons of energy and had always made great decisions.

After she glanced at the clock, she knew she had to go. She tried to clear her head as she forced one foot in front of the other. He had thankfully requested this meeting after the rest of the sales force had left for the day, but she also knew this would make it easier for him to ask her to leave. She could clear out her office without others watching and becoming part of the process.

While seeing Andrew's door open she decided to knock on it anyway and force her best smile. He simply waved his hand to indicate to her that she needed to close the door, another bad sign. "Come on in. I've been waiting for you."

"I'm sorry, I wanted to make sure I located all the material you might want to look at." She walked forward and slid into a seat on the other side of his desk.

"I think you know why I asked for this meeting. I'm sorry, but I don't have much control over it since I've been told to work out a termination package with you. How generous the conditions are depends on you and how much you're willing to cooperate in this."

"I've built this sales force, and you know it."

"I've no problems with what you produced in the past, but we need to look to the future. You used to bring so much energy with you which excited the salespeople here. You *had* a reputation we were proud of."

"My reputation?"

"You've gone from country club darling to the do-drop-in club queen at sleazy bars on the other side of town. Trust me the word gets around."

Jacquelyn started to protest, but forced her mind to remain in control. Her private life shouldn't be part of this discussion, even if the nightlife constituted a part of her life that she detested, but felt powerless in controlling. Vincent had pulled her into that world. He had drained her of all power, all resistance to venture into such places. She never went to those places before she meet him. *Okay, I know I'm screwed up, but who isn't?*

"As you may have heard, we have new problems to consider. Your ex-husband has caused some nasty problems for the company and for me. When he broke in here the other day he had receive permissions from the courts to serve you with papers to recover personal items he says you have of his and that he was supposed to receive after the divorce."

"Such as what?"

"How in the hell should I know?"

"I'll gladly give him whatever he wants that's truly his. He needs to let me know what items he wants. He wants freedom to roam in my personal stuff without me knowing what he wants. I don't think so."

"In a way I can say I don't blame you, but I think you need to do whatever you need to do to get rid of this maniac."

"I think you know I've tried."

"Now, I have problems because of this." He removed some papers from a file and tossed it to Jacquelyn's side of the desk. "I'm now being sued by Vincent."

"Do what?" She glanced at the papers served on him for assault and battery. "He can't win a suit like this. You were just defending yourself, and you had every right to do so."

"You know how the courts are today. The legal fees alone will be astronomical."

"I'm sure the company will back you and cover this."

"They already said they would, but the legal defense will still cost them. The publicity of a trial will also cost the company much more in lost sales. I hope you understand the company officers have little choice if they want to face the shareholders next year and answer questions on this. Several members of the board also think that if you're let go, Vincent might be talked into dropping the charges."

"So what? Vincent has discovered a way to have me fired. Is that what you're telling me?"

"I'm afraid so, but if you say anything about this outside these walls you'll never have any proof. Your termination will be based on your performance, which I hate to remind you is terrible right now."

"So tell me what you're proposing?"

"If you leave quietly, we can offer you a decent severance pay. This should cover you for a while until you find something else."

"In this economy you don't really believe that, do you?"

"The current condition of the economy will be taken into consideration. It's the best I can do."

Jacquelyn hung her head. "I see."

Andrew removed another set of papers and handed them to her. "Take your time and read this. I'm here to discuss any of the terms, but we need to work the details out tonight.

Off the record, I really enjoyed working with you. We spent some great times together earlier."

Jacquelyn smiled at the sign of weakness in his voice. "Do you still keep a bottle of Chivas Regal under your desk?"

Andrew smiled and opened the drawer on his right. "I'm going to miss you." He retrieved two paper cups from behind him. "I hope these will do."

"That's fine." Jacquelyn started to read but stopped. "I really don't have any choice, do I?"

"Not really. The only thing I want to know is what happened to you. I know about Vincent, but there has to be more to the story."

Jacquelyn stretched back into her chair. *Did he really want to become my psychologist now?* "I started working here before I met Vincent. I wish I had known more about him and his secret life."

"I still don't know how he managed to do this to you. You should've left him a long time ago."

"I don't know. It felt like he sucked the life out of me. He made me so dependent on him while isolating me from my friends so that he could get me into drinking and partying. But you know . . . this experience also allowed me to see my old friends in a new light. It has forced me into realizing who they really are. I hate to say it, but my new friends are the only ones supporting me now."

"Really?"

"Oh yes! I remember dreaming my whole life of one day having a knight in shining armor, so to speak, come and rescue me and take me to a far away castle. I feel so deceived by thinking Vincent could be such a knight. Do you ever dream at night?"

"I think all people do, why?"

"My dreams are so very vivid, so real feeling that I feel like I'm materializing in a different time and a different place all together. There have been so many times I wish I could stay inside the dream and never return."

"Interesting. It sounds like you're able to logically think while you dream."

"Exactly. Anyway . . . those so very real dreams have been fading since I met Vincent. I don't know how to say it, but it feels like I'm being attacked in my dreams now, and what was so beautiful before is now turning into nightmares."

"We still plan on paying for the psychologist you're seeing and your insurance for a while. I think you'll see the details in the severance agreement." He paused. "Have you told all this to your psychologist?"

"Oh yes, and I think I'm giving him enough material to write a full paper on how crazy he must think I am. I do appreciate the fact that I can keep using him."

"I should tell you I don't like the idea of being sued by Vincent. Can you believe he filed a suit against me for touching him to stop him from pushing through my office? I never thought the photos of my hand bleeding would be used against me. The photo makes it look like I cut my hand by striking him, but I have witnesses all over the office who'll testify otherwise. With the crazy jurors out there, however, you never know what will happen. I'm sure there'll be a settlement made and the bastard will be paid something."

"This is insane. I thought for sure he would be arrested by now. They also think he trashed my car. When do you think he'll be picked up?"

"According to his attorney, I think he has already managed to get out temporarily. And if not . . . I'm sure he'll be one day soon. I hope they're able to convict him and keep him behind bars for a while at least."

"There's something dark and evil about him. It almost feels like he was sent to earth to destroy me. Does that make sense to you?" *Is there really this evil universe out there trying to get me? Could such be possible and actually be happening to me now?*

"From where I stand, it makes perfect sense."

"Like I said, I also have a warrant out for him on trashing my car. I don't know if they have him arrested on this charge or not, but they acted like they would have trouble convicting him, even after I indentified him near my car minutes before it was broken into. I mean, like what is it with the police here?"

"We have so much crime in Atlanta that I think the police have more than they can handle. It's sad. If they had done a better job in enforcing the law, maybe you would not have been destroyed by him."

"You know, I still remember meeting him and how he made the world appear so exciting. I felt like he was full of passion for life and someone I could share my life with. He wanted to be with me all of the time, and I thought it was because he truly loved me. Now . . . I know it was because he wanted to control my every move. He had manipulated me so subtly that I never saw it coming."

"I wish you had asked for help earlier."

"I wish I had also."

"Have you any idea what you might try to do next? I'm sure you still know many people in Atlanta, right?"

"For right now I've no idea what I might do. I really never thought I'd be looking for a new job. I think I'll take some time off and get my life straight since I need to handle this situation with Vincent, which is something that was supposed to be taken care of when I obtained the divorce.

By the way, I'm still paying an attorney for handling my divorce, which is costing much more than I ever thought it could."

"I assume you didn't get any alimony or support from him."

"In Georgia? You have to be kidding. We had no kids. Vincent never wanted any. Yes he makes a lot more than me, but after fighting him for so long in the courts, I simply wanted to be free of him. I'm surprised he didn't push for me to pay him."

Andrew stopped to pour another drink for both of them. "I know you would like a letter of recommendation, and I hope you understand I have my hands tied on providing you one you might like. However, if you have someone wanting such, please have them call me, and I'll be glad to speak to them off of the record."

"I would appreciate any help you can give me, since I think it's going to be very hard to find anything in this market. You know how bad it is out there."

"So, what are you really planning to do?"

Jacquelyn raised her glass. "I think this is what I'll do for today. I'll worry about the rest of my life in a day or two. Vincent has to be dealt with first."

"My biggest recommendation for you concerns your late night life in the bars."

"I don't think my private life should be an issue with my job, and I think I've a right to have a private life. Since I forced Vincent out of my life, I'm finally able to do things on my own, and to tell the truth, it feels great to have the attention of other men. I love making friends, and I always have. If the only ones giving me the time of day are the ones I run with at night I think I need to appreciate what true friendship is. They're the only ones who ever call me and want me to be part of their life."

"Well . . . the decision is, of course, totally up to you, but I think you'll agree it hurts your performance at work."

"Don't worry since I think I can keep the two separate."

His face reflected the doubts she tried to hide. She knew he told the truth, but felt helpless in changing that part of her life now. At night, she had become addicted to the wild life at bars, the parties which lasted until sometime the next morning, and the feelings of escapism she experienced when she went out.

"I guess we need to take care of business. Let me know if you have questions on the settlement."

Jacquelyn turned to the papers. "Just tell me where to sign." She wanted out of the office as fast as she could pack her belongings. Since her life as the executive for the corporation had come to an end, she could only anticipate the world she would enter later that night. Tonight she would escape back to the world everyone knew her as *Jack*. She would trade in her power suit for jeans and a stretch top, and forget the world of business where many relationships were so fake and contrived. This late night world where no one hid behind false pretense had forced her attitude to be tougher than steel. There, the world was brutal, but honest. Yes, Vincent introduced her to his world, but she was the one who needed to find her way out. The only way to do that was to face it and just hope she knew how to end it. Jacquelyn signed the papers.

"I'm so sorry for this. Please stay in touch with me."

Jacquelyn offered a small smile and walked toward her office without saying a word. The time for talking had ended. Since she needed something to carry her personal items, she dumped out the contents from inside the presentation bag. This would do fine. She added one item after another, trying to decide what she really wanted to take with her. Some would be great, while others would only remind her of times she needed to forget. The packing suddenly reminded her of the time she had grabbed her belongings and ran when she had left Vincent.

Luckily for her then, she had exercised the good sense to rent a truck and transport many files and boxes with it. These few items still remained in a storage building. The packing had been completed fast, and she remembered soliciting the help of her mom and her mom's boyfriend in grabbing what she could. In fact, she couldn't remember all they had taken, since she had never revisited the storage unit. She always hoped to obtain a place later and to be able to use many of the items then. She also knew that the files with old tax returns, as well as some personal files, might be needed if she ever got audited.

Vincent wanted to go through these files, but had insisted on doing so alone. She had no intentions to allow him such access. If he wanted something, he needed to specifically ask for it. She felt glad her attorney supported her in this fight. He wanted something, but she couldn't care less. She wouldn't offer him any help in any way or form. If it caused him problems, so be it. He had caused her enough during the divorce.

After thinking she'd packed all that she could carry, she turned to a wall on one side of her office. This special wall contained photos and small paintings she loved. She would have to take them and would make the extra trip to her car to make sure they wouldn't become lost or destroyed. Each one had spoken to her when she had purchased them. Each one had reminded her of a dream she had that had transported her to a time in history and a beautiful part of the world.

Sometimes she felt like she was visiting her past life. Although she never actually believed in reincarnation, the dreams offered her a much needed relief from her current life. She would love to think she lived such a fantastic life before, but then again, and if so, why did she live in such a hell now? While she didn't understand now, perhaps one day she would. Her psychologist certainly had probed her dreams enough times looking for answers.

While the conflicts in her dreams often confused her, she remembered some beautiful dreams which truly amazed her. Although many of these placed her back in time many years ago, the nightmares, in contrast, covered her current life with Vincent and his continued harassment of her. These nightmares also included a wild orgy type party where men photographed her in the nude, humiliating her.

Her psychologist had told her that many people have nightmares of being nude in public. While he had discussed the many ramifications of these with her, none seemed to answer her questions of why she regressed from beautiful dreams to nightmares.

As Jacquelyn removed one picture after another from the wall, she remembered how the beautiful sunsets or sunrises taken from various parts of the world had offered inspiration to her for years while she worked in her office. She would need these. She wished again for only a way to live in her dreams. *Oh yes, I know many people would love to be able to do that.*

Jacquelyn finished and rested her head on her desk while staring at one small painting of a mountain top sunset she always treasured most. She whispered to the painting as if it could hear her, "Friends may come and go, but what you offer is truly timeless. Somehow, some way, I need to find my way back to you."

The photo appeared to glow as she imagined walking in the mountains with a special person beside her. While she couldn't envision what he looked like, she definitely felt his presence. But . . . that was then, and this was now. She needed to survive in the here and now, and as much as she hated it, she needed the tough character she had created at night to protect her now. On top of the stack of photos she placed a baseball hat. She felt like it was time to let her life as Jack take over.

CHAPTER 4

The smell of heavy smoke mixed with stale beer burned her nostrils as Jack opened the door which brought back memories and the haunting and vivid scars of her past. Scanning the dimly lit bar for trouble, she proceeded to the pool table section and past several tables loaded with half-finished beers and obnoxiously loud drunks. Since her ex-husband loved to hide out in this stink hole, she wanted to make damn sure Vincent wasn't anywhere close tonight. As usual on Friday night in Atlanta, Georgia the Shack was packing in the crowd. With no date or old friends to spend time with, she had returned to the last place she thought she would have ever dreamed of. *What am I doing here? Why do I need this?*

She placed her quarters on the pool table to reserve her place in line before turning to walk over to the bar and past several beer-soaked patrons who silently sized her up. Since she knew some of them to be friends of Vincent, she assumed word would spread back to him soon enough. Yes, in spite of the danger, she wanted him to know she had invaded his turf. She intended to never be intimidated again. He had hauled her into places like this and changed her life by ruining her career with his wicked treacherous lies.

The bartender greeted her with a smile and a gruff voice. "Hello, Jack. What can I get you?" Jimbo's slow moving mannerisms reflected the laid back feeling of the bar as he pushed his jet black hair hanging down his broad shoulders to one side.

"I'll have a rum and Coke." She smiled as she climbed onto a stool and studied her reflection in the mirror behind the bar. It made her wish she had at least combed her shoulder-length hair and applied some make-up on her monotonous face. The streaks of various shades of yellow hair hung limp as she shifted her eyes away, and was embarrassed at what she had become.

At slightly over thirty, however, she knew she still looked much younger than the normal crowd who usually frequented the Shack. She felt indifferent as she endured the intense stares of the regulars, but then again, she didn't come to compete for men with all the bar whores. She realized her petite size made her stand out in this crowd. At five feet tall and weighing only about a hundred and ten pounds, she knew many would think she offered no match for the seasoned bar women and pot-bellied men in the bar.

Memories of all Vincent had put her through resurfaced as she searched the room for more familiar faces. She realized this rough life had taught her to be strong with her old life only a vague memory of happier days. *If only my old friends from the church could see me now. But . . . what the hell, they are the ones who turned their back on me when I needed them most.*

Jimbo walked over as he cleaned the top of the bar. "Vincent has been in several times lately looking for you. I'll let you know if I spot him."

"Thanks. If he shows, call the police. I have a restraining order against him." Her eyes flashed with hate as her mind wandered back to the life she lived with her abusive ex-husband. To fit in now she had to act as tough as the rest of the crowd here.

Jimbo's eyes softened as he leaned forward. Like most professional bartenders, he had learned to be a good listener. "I'm surprised to see you here."

"I just wanted to play a game of pool and relax tonight. It's been a long week." She finished her first drink and had started on the second when her time to play came up. She walked over and selected a partner: a loner she watched play before, and definitely not someone who would be friends with Vincent. He stepped forward, eager to play. His stained teeth and rough beard make it clear to those around that he welcomed any chance to fight. He nodded his head at Jack in appreciation of being picked by her.

Her choice of a partner sent the other guys away from the table while others whispered to each other. These weren't the Bible toting friends Vincent so proudly associated with on Sundays. These were his other friends and a life he dragged her into, changing her forever. She frowned while she remembered her previous Christian goody-goody life with all the two-faced hypocrites who wouldn't give her the time of day now. She remembered parts of her previous life that she loved, but also a part of it she absolutely despised.

The smell of the Shack and the sinister glances of the rough patrons made her wish she had made a different choice for the night, but she had come to make a point and intended to stay until she made it. She wasn't going to be pushed around or intimidated by Vincent any more. This move directly into his domain would make that clear.

Her burly opponent had the break. "You might as well find a seat, sweet pea. I plan on running this table clean." He lit a cigarette and started to play.

"It sounds to me like you're bragging about something else you wish you could finish." The insult reflected off his face as the other men around the table whistled, knowing they might have a fight in the works. Jack knew how to make friends when she needed to, and how to hold her own when she had to. She flashed a smile, grabbing everyone's attention. Her light skin gave her a clean look in stark contrast with the red necks and other social misfits in the bar.

After her opponent missed on the third ball, Jack confronted the table and deposited one ball after another. The overhead light above the table allowed the background to fade into a ghostly darkness as she approached the last ball. She smiled as she knew her skills weren't bad for someone who looked more like the little girl next door than a pool shark.

Jack wrapped her fingers around the pool stick as she watched the bearded bastard move in front of her on the other side of the table. She knew his movements were intended to cause her to lose concentration and miss the ball. She studied the maneuver as he strutted openly and scratched his balls which added to his vulgar demeanor.

As he grinned one time too many, Jack returned the smile and adjusted her fingers to tighten them around the stick and aim for a lower point of impact on the ball. When her opponent moved again, but not precisely where she wanted him to be, she waited and readjusted her angle.

He laughed in a rough country-boy style. "Come on honey. Oh, Jacquelyn, hit the ball."

She hated being called Jacquelyn while she partied out late at night, but attempted to hide the truth from everyone when he hit a nerve. *One day I would love to return to my other life without anyone knowing I was such a bad-ass chick hustling pool.* Finally, he turned around again, and this time his position looked perfect. Jack tightened her grip and drew back. The tip of the stick hit the ball perfectly, slamming its way underneath to send the ball flying off the table and directly into her intended target—his balls.

He screamed in pain, as she flashed a smile at him and thought of how his love life would be put on hold. "You bitch!" he shouted as the pain registered on his face and he attempted to regroup.

Jack moved around the table, swinging her pool stick in the air, allowing the whistling sound to draw attention. She might be small, but she knew how to swing a stick and where to aim. She swung at his head but stopped short. "I'll tell you what. Let me replay the ball and we'll call it even."

She watched the look on his face and recognized the hint of apprehension. She swung the stick again with full intent to use it. He nodded in agreement, but followed it with a sinister laugh. "Just playing with you, honey." She knew the real reason. He had no way of winning and how embarrassing life would be for him to lose to a girl. And . . . if he did win, he would still look like a fool in the eyes of the bar regulars. Having her partner standing behind her flashing an evil sign of approval didn't hurt either.

Her opponent retrieved the ball and handed it to her. "This is not over. Go ahead and play your ball." He turned and staggered to the bar to order another beer.

Jack walked around the table and glanced around. No one questioned her right to replay the ball as she recalled her shot. "Eight ball in the side pocket." She leaned over to concentrate and address the ball without distractions this time.

After she struck the ball perfectly, sending it on its way, a large hand shoved her from the back before she saw the ball drop. She swirled the stick and prepared to strike her asshole opponent, but didn't see him anywhere. Debra, his girlfriend, stood in front of her and not in the least bit intimidated. They both knew the rules of the game: the first one to strike usually wins.

"Hold it right there." A voice boomed across the bar. Jack turned to face Mike, an off-duty cop who moonlighted at the bar to provide security. "Back down now. I don't want any trouble out of either of you two."

As Jack and Debra stared each other down Jack didn't flinch, even though Debra looked almost twice her size. "Don't worry. I'm sure we'll meet again." Debra turned to leave.

"You can count on it." Jack replied before turning her back and looking at the table to see her ball resting safely in the pocket. "Okay guys, who's next?"

As Mike hustled over to the table and escorted Debra and her boyfriend out of the bar, he yelled at Jack in the process. "Don't go anywhere. I want a word with you!"

She flashed a smile. "I'll be right here."

Jack suddenly saw Maria coming in through the front door. As she walked toward her friend, she decided to let someone else take her spot at the table as she handed her stick to her partner. After all, she knew she could dominate the action any time she wanted. Maria was a new friend she had met out on the town. Her platinum hair and big tits always made her a hit with the boys, but just like Jack she acted as tough as nails and didn't take any shit from anyone.

Jack could tell her friend was as drunk as a skunk, which was both good and bad. It was good because she could be a lot of fun when she was drunk, but bad because she would be a handful later.

As Mike escorted Debra and her boyfriend out of the bar, Maria stopped and glanced around when Debra threw her big hip sideways, knocking Maria into a nearby table. Maria's face reflected the surprise and horror of the attack as she fell over the table onto a young couple. Several glasses shattered as they all fell to the floor.

While Jack rushed toward them, Debra only laughed as Mike stepped between them. Others in the bar scurried to get in on the action. As Jack reached to help Maria off the floor, she examined the couple knocked to the floor with Maria. They looked clean-cut, almost preppy, and as if they never belonged in a place like this. The cut to his hand caused by the broken glass had blood spurting all over his starched shirt and his dress trousers. A bar towel landed nearby as Jack applied pressure to the wound. His girlfriend looked scared to death as she held him tightly.

When Jimbo ran from behind the bar, he cussed the crowd around him. She knew the club could receive a nasty lawsuit from this. As he reached for his cell phone and called the police, he glanced at Jack and leaned closer to her. "I think you need to leave and find another place to hang out for a while."

Jack started to argue, but then she glanced at all the blood on her clothes. She quickly agreed that leaving might be a good idea, especially before the police arrive and started asking questions.

She glanced at the young couple again and was stunned by what she saw. A strange glow floated around the young couple as they huddled closer together. Even with all of the tough armor she protected her soul with, Jack felt the flow of love and energy shared between them. She knew her weak spot that was hidden most of the time, but one she clung to desperately was shining brightly in front of her now. She felt these two stranger's shared love engulf her as she leaned nearer to apologize.

They both glanced at her as she stood helpless. The glow around them turned brighter and blinded her. She closed her eyes since she was unable to stand the intensity any longer. "I'm sorry for all of this, and I hope you'll be fine." *Why is this happening to me?*

She never heard a response since Maria was pulling her toward the door. As the crowd pushed in closer, and made it harder to leave, Jack studied the crowd and especially the older women. She knew they have all been in their fair share of fights, which explained the dull feelings reflected on their faces. She realized that one day unless she changed she would be just as hard as these women, these bar whores who she detested so much. The image haunted her as she rushed from the bar.

"Did you see the glow around that couple?" Jack asked as she wanted to know if Maria noticed the lights, or if she was becoming delusional.

"What are you talking about?"

"I'm talking about the glow of light. It felt blinding. You must have seen it."

"I think you've been drinking too much tonight."

"I have not. There was something about them—almost magical. I could feel it." Jack's secret desire for perfect love, the dream she had cherished for most of her life, but destined to disappear time after time, surfaced, and gave her a brief moment of hope.

"Whatever." Maria staggered forward.

They almost reached Jack's car when Debra yelled from the other side of the parking lot. "Anytime you want to finish this, bitch, let me know!" Jack started walking fast in Debra's direction but Mike saw the commotion and walked to the middle of the parking lot to block her path.

Jack suddenly remembered a mud wrestling contest she fought in once and won at a nearby bar "Bring your fat ass over to Molly's tomorrow night and we'll see how tough you are!" *Wow! I can't believe what I'm doing. This is not me. But really . . . who am I now.*

"You got it." Debra shot a finger as her boyfriend pulled her behind him.

CHAPTER 5

Jack twisted to hang up the phone she had placed off the hook a few hours earlier. She couldn't sleep after enduring repeated calls from an unknown caller, but knew it had to be coming from Vincent. The phone rang again minutes later. She placed the receiver next to her ear and listened. "Hi, this is Maria. Are you up?"

"Yeah. I was sleeping late today."

"You wanted me to call you. My back hurts from where that bitch pushed me last night."

"Don't worry about it. She'll get her butt kicked tonight."

"Are you sure about that? She's a lot bigger than you."

"She's fat. In the mud, she'll be slow and awkward."

"I'll be with you to finish the job, just in case."

"Okay, I'll see you tonight. I need to get moving." Jack stood and looked for something to wear. As she glanced at all of her good clothes on the floor, she knew she needed to get her life together. She realized this accentuated one of the many ways Vincent had managed to ruin her life. She thought getting away from him and his influences would make all the difference in the world, but she would love to obtain her revenge first. *No. This is not what I really want. What I really want is to find my life again. I was a well thought of professional once.*

Hours later, Jack heard the knock at the door. "Come on in, Maria." She knew it had to be her friend.

"You sure are a trusting soul. What if I had been a crazy rapist waiting to get in?" Maria said as she walked in smoking a cigarette.

Jack smiled. "I doubt that's ever going to happen, and I think I know how to handle myself."

"Listen, you may be a feisty little bitch and tough, but let's face it, you're still a small girl." Maria pointed to her lean body.

"I can handle myself. You'll see that tonight when I kick Debra's fat ass."

"Are you sure you want to do this. She's as mean as you, and almost twice your size."

"You worry too much. She's nothing but a pig."

Maria raised her dress to show a swimsuit underneath. "Just in case, I want you to know I'm ready to join the party."

Jack flashed a big smile since she knew she could count on her friend to be there. "I knew you would. Let's go."

Maria passed the small dining table and noticed the police report. "What the hell is this?"

"It's Vincent again, what else. He smashed one of my car windows."

"What?"

"The police say I don't have enough proof to put him in jail, but I saw him minutes before it happened."

"Are you sure it was him?"

Jack glanced at her sideways. "One of my salesman, or should I say ex-salesman, Fernando, saw him, but he told the police it was too far for him to know for sure. I think that's why they doubted my story."

"Shit! Did he steal anything out of the car or just trash it?"

"He went through my car looking for something. He still thinks I have something belonging to him, but I simply don't know what."

"What are you going to do now?"

"I talked to my insurance company, and they'll have the damages repaired on Monday. Since my attorney will get involved again, I don't think this will ever end."

"I'm so sorry. Let me know when you want to go after him. I know some bad asses that can come along."

"I may take you up on the offer, but the main problems for me now are the nightmares. They haunt me all night, every night. I hardly sleep."

"You're still having nightmares of him?"

"Yes. I don't think anyone knows how evil he is."

"He has a reputation."

Jack straightened her back. "Tonight I've another ass that needs stomping."

"Are you sure you're ready for this."

"Absolutely!"

***

A huge crowd had packed the entrance to Molly's Bar after word of the big fight had quickly circulated. "What if the boyfriend jumps into this?" Maria asked as they make their way inside.

"I already kicked his butt once, but it'll help if you can watch my back."

"My pleasure. I still have a debt to repay."

Jack scrutinized the bar as they walk in and moved toward the bar to order a drink. The bouncers circulated around the wrestling ring as workers added a new twist for the night. They had filled the shallow pool with jello. Jack smiled. "This'll be even easier than I thought."

Jack glanced around Molly's Bar which was almost tailor made for the night's event. The center of the bar opened two levels high with stairs leading to a balcony on all four corners. The two bars serving drinks were under two sides of the balcony with the entrance on one side, and the band which would play later stuck far back on the other. The owners had expertly designed the bar for the crowds they wanted to attract.

The crew creating the wrestling area worked feverishly as the time for the first match approached. Jack glanced at Maria while the place rocked with loud music and shouting as drunks scurried to find their perfect seats. Her friend smiled back, but Jack knew she was anticipating trouble. At almost six feet tall, she made for one imposing woman, and this time Maria wasn't drunk. Her long, blonde hair shone in the low light as she turned around to scout out the room with Jack. While she didn't mind showing cleavage, especially if it attracted a new man, her attitude made it clear she wanted no competition after she fixed her sights on her target.

Unlike The Shack, this bar catered to a younger crowd with lots of energy. The young guys put down beers as fast as they could and started betting on the girls. Several of the young hunks pointed in their direction and yelled out encouragements.

Jack felt a little amused that her challenger hadn't shown. Maybe she had chickened out. Jack knew she had created a name as a bar brawler over the last six months. It reflected an image forced upon her she now wished she could stop, but she had no idea how to even begin. *Is this going to be the life I'm stuck with, now and forever?*

Finally, the announcer entered the ring and the bar occupants retreated into an eerie silence. "How are you doing tonight?" he yelled into the microphone.

Roars and catcalls immediately erupted from the crowd. "Bring on the girls." The hormones of the men in the audience intensified by the minute as they yelled louder and louder for the girls.

"We have three matches tonight, but one of the contestants hasn't arrived yet." Everyone booed and the chanting began. The word "chicken" circulated as a low cheer, but soon intensified into a crescendo. The hyper frenzy of the audience made Jack smile as she stood to wave at them, just to make sure they all remember she showed as she had promised. Every beer-guzzling red neck in the bar whistled, clapped and yelled as they acknowledge her attitude and spunk.

As Jack turned to take another drink, safe in the knowledge that Debra and her drunken boyfriend have indeed chickened out, she heard the shouting from the entrance, "We're here. We're here."

Jack felt stunned, but it looked like she had received her chance to pay Debra back after all. She replaced her drink on the counter and winked at her friend. "Watch my drink and watch my back."

"You've got it."

When Debra walked over to the ring and dropped her robe, revealing a one-piece swim suit much too tight for the rolls of fat around her stomach, her cleavage rousted the audience on to further shouting. She raised her arms in the air in full appreciation of the outburst.

Jack studied Debra, who must be around five feet ten at least, but Jack knew that Debra's weight, maybe close to one hundred and eighty pounds, was her main problem. Her dark dull brown hair had been cut short and contained hints of gray. With crooked teeth and a large space between the front two, she was no beauty queen.

Her boyfriend walked to the side of the ring with a big smile on his face. He stumbled twice as he found his place, revealing the ridiculous drunk she knew he was. Yes, very comical, but then everyone in the bar joined in on his pursuit of fun.

Jack played it cool, letting Debra wear herself out as she pranced around in the wrestling pool used to accommodate the event. Her fat opponent raised her arms to the crowd, cheering them on, trying to appear absolutely fearless. The prancing caused her to fall in the jello several times. She tried to stand again, only to fall. Jack smiled as she realized that Debra had been drinking heavily as well.

Jack finally walked to the ring and started to take off her dress, which covered the one-piece suit underneath. The audience hollered instantly. "Take it off, take it off." She quickly disrobed to stop the words from bringing back memories. While the one-piece fitted perfectly over her petite body, she knew her breasts looked small, but not completely tiny. She decided to ignore the audience and concentrate on her opponent instead.

The announcer walked to the edge of the ring and motioned for the two wrestlers to come closer. "Okay, girls, I want a clean match. I think you know the rules. I want to see no hair pulling, clawing with the nails, or attempting to remove your opponent's swim suit. The object is to pin your opponent for a count of ten, is that clear?"

Jack growled. "Yes . . . perfectly."

Debra smiled and walked to the other side of the ring as the match referee raised his hands at the audience. "Are you ready?" The bar escalated into a mad house as all of the men and some of the girls fought for a better view. This was why they came, naturally, and they fully intended to have a good time while getting drunk.

Jack knew it was show time, so she stepped forward. When her opponent instantly rushed at her, Jack out-maneuvered her, and Debra went flying into the jello. As the audience hooted and laughed at her attempt, Debra stood with a wicked grin. "Come on honey, you can't hide all night."

She lunged at Jack again and almost placed an arm around her, but Jack twisted and let her fall on her face again. Debra stood much slower this time, laughing at the jello sticking to various parts of her body. "Come on you bitch, let's get it on."

Debra moved slower this time, attempting to corner Jack. She quickly darted in and obtained a temporary hold on her, but lost Jack as she fell again on the slippery jello. This time she appeared to hurt her back in the fall as she slowly stood in obvious pain. Then she slapped her hands together since she didn't like the laughter coming from the audience, and especially the comments about her looking like a pig. When her boyfriend heard the shouts, he stood to defend his girlfriend.

As Debra looked around at the raging crowd, Jack used the advantage of the situation and moved in fast, knocking Debra on her back into the slippery jello. With the jello hanging from her cropped hair making her look pathetic, Debra fell again when she tried to stand.

With all going as Jack planned, she wasn't expecting what happened next. She felt a hand on her back pushing her hard. As she turned to look over her shoulder, she saw the boyfriend shove her toward her opponent. When they met in the center and fell to the floor, Jack luckily moved fast enough to slip away.

As the boyfriend laughed on the far side, Jack walked over in his direction and stopped for a second before kicking some of the jello into his face. "You bitch!" He removed the slimy mixture from his shirt and his red face contorted as he yelled to the crowd. "She's nothing but a chicken shit!"

As he attempted to step into the pool with the two girls, he received a little extra help. Maria stepped behind him and gave him a big shove, causing him to fall over the edge, face first into the pool of jello. The audience screamed louder as they joined in on the developing fight.

When Debra struggled toward her boyfriend, Jack kicked her in the butt, making her fall on her face in front of him. As he scrambled to his feet, he swung at Maria who had come to help, but missed. Maria threw a right and nailed him. When Debra suddenly fell backward in the jello, Jack seized her chance and jumped on top of her opponent, forcing her deep into the jello. Debra tried to throw Jack off, but was unable to do so. The struggle splattered jello all over the place as the spectators hollered and cheered the girls on.

Some of the spectators quickly helped the match referee pull the boyfriend from the ring. As he stood, he yanked away from them to try to find Maria. When he heard his girlfriend going down for the count, he grabbed a nearby empty bottle and turned around toward Maria to swing wildly at her. After he connected with her face and sent pieces of glass everywhere, the cheering stopped when blood splattered across the room.

Maria's yell overtook the rest of the hollers from the bar as the broken bottle cut her face multiple times. Maria lunged at the boyfriend and fell to the floor with him. The spectators stop yelling as the shock settled in and they move in, pulling them apart. As Maria bled more from new cuts, towels quickly appeared to help her.

Jack jumped from the ring and rushed over to Maria where she saw an artery in her neck spurting blood with each heart beat. Several more pushed in close, trying to stop the flow of blood which covered Maria's face. "Hold on, an ambulance is on the way." One voice yelled from behind her.

Jack held the towel tighter, hoping to stop the bleeding. "Back up guys—give us some room here." Panic overtook her nerves as she yelled, "Maria. I'm here and you're going to be okay. Hang in there girl, help's coming." With the final minutes of her friend's life ebbing away forever, Jack yelled again, "What the hell have I done?"

CHAPTER 6

Jack walked into the funeral home and located the waiting room as the nightmare of the last few days replayed in her mind. The large piece of glass that severed a main artery in her neck cost Maria her life. It also might as well have killed Jack. Naturally, she blamed her actions for Maria's death. *Why did I have to prove to everyone I was so damn tough?*

Jack knew the district attorney investigating the case might still be gathering information about the fight and trying to decide if she could be held liable for the death. Only this morning, her attorney told her he might consider offering her clemency for her testimony in the case. Her attorney also thought the boyfriend would more than likely make his own plea to a lesser charge to avoid a lengthy manslaughter charge.

Several of Maria's friends stood around talking about the attack and her death. One of them spotted Jack instantly and walked over to her. Obviously they had been talking about revenge, and how to get away with it. "How are you today?"

"I'm not doing so well. I can't get the images of her dying out of my head." Jack glanced over to the coffin and how they had it covered. Her face had been so badly cut the family had decided it would be best to not let everyone see.

The girl offered Jack a large hug. "Hang in there. We'll get through this somehow."

"I'm not so sure. I should have never gone to that stupid match."

"I'm sure Maria wouldn't blame you for standing up for her, and I'm sure she knows we'll make them pay for this later."

Jack dropped her head and cried. *When will all of it end?* She hated the life she lived now, but how does she stop the merry-go-round? How does she get off? "Why . . . what are you planning?"

"We're planning something, but we have to wait until all of this is over. Jack, I know you want to be part of it."

She heard the emotions in the girl's voice, but wasn't listening too intently. She was the one who caused Maria to go to the bar and fight. She's the one with the attitude. At this moment, Jack's not the one she wanted to be. "I don't know. I don't know any more."

The girl looked surprised at her answer. "I thought you were very good friends?"

"Yes, we knew each other well, but both of us have been victimized before. Very few people knew a different side that we both shared."

"I understand. She was a sweetheart that many people didn't know." As the girl started to cry, Jack reached for a tissue to give to her. "Thank you. It's going to be interesting to see what kind of sentence that jerk who killed her gets."

"Yes, it will be." Jack could only imagine the court proceedings to come.

"Have you heard from the district attorney?"

"I heard from my attorney this morning and it appears they might not be pushing charges against me for any wrong doing. However . . . I understand that he hasn't made a final decision on the asshole who killed her yet."

"That's stupid."

"Yes, one more problem for me to worry about, and now Vincent has all of the ammunition he could ever dream of in coming back after me. I'm now the badass out there, and he's the nice knight trying to rescue me. Can you believe how he gets away with everything?"

"Why, what's he doing now?"

"He has sent word to me by every person he knows who will have contact with me to call him. He knows the restraining order will be ignored right now, and that I have no energy to enforce it. The other charges against him are being denied by his attorney. "

"If I can do anything to help, let me know." This girl had a fighting attitude in her, and Jack could see she needed some way to direct it. On the other hand, Jack wanted no more fighting. She'd had enough.

She walked over to settle in a seat as the girl walked back over to her other friends. Jack lowered her head, thinking of all of the hell in her life. One of her best friends was now dead. Yes . . . Jack's tough, real tough she thought as she questioned her life. It's time to change her life and return to the life she had before. *It's time for me to somehow, someway, to become Jacquelyn again.*

With her tortured thoughts swirling around in her head, she allowed her mind to drift slightly off to sleep while she remained sitting straight up. She realized her mind was working hard to protect her, to direct to her to a private place in her mind where she lived safe and secure.

She felt a warm breeze blowing in across the water, caressing her body and gently massaging her with their its texture. The sound of the waves and the seagulls presented the only interruptions in her peaceful walk. Each step on the sand reminded her of so many before. The endless coastline stretched on and on forever, and like time itself appeared to have no beginning and no end.

A strong hand located her hand, giving it a small squeeze. The fleshy feel of their hands melted together as they walk along in silence while the white sand reflecting the rays of the sun blinded her as she walked.

She recognized each and every part of the beach as she tried to see the guy walking with her. While the sun shined too bright for her to focus on his face, she felt like she knew him very intimately. His sweet and gentle manner relaxed her and made her feel so warm and comfortable. "I love this beach," she whispered loudly several times. She knew the love of her life was there—somewhere—but where?

A gentle touch startled her awake. "Not now," she moaned. *It would be so good for me to live in a dream and escape from this world forever.*

"Are you okay?" Kelly, one of Maria's sisters asked her.

"Yes, I'm fine. I just haven't had much sleep lately."

"I don't think any of us have."

"Life has changed so much over this last year. I don't even recognize myself any more. This tough attitude of mine has to change. I know that my ex-husband's the reason for it, but the divorce was supposed to give me a new start."

"I think you're taking this very hard on yourself. It's not your fault. I'm sure that bastard will get what's coming to him, Jack."

She looked upward with an inner determination leaving no doubt she was serious. "I've used the name Jack for too long. It's time—now—to see if I can find myself. I need to find the old Jacquelyn and start over. Do you understand what I'm saying?"

"Yes, I think I do."

"My old friends at the church have turned their back on me. My career's gone down the tube. The nightmares are ruining my health. I can't take much more."

"I understand."

"The problem is that the only people giving me the time of day are the people who go out to the bars. I know my

life's going to hell, and I'm tired of going home drunk. And
. . . I'm especially tired of Vincent stalking me and
constantly haunting me in my dreams."

"I heard about him breaking into your car."

"I called the police. Little good that did."

"Let me know if there's anything I can do to help."

"Thanks. I need to get away from Vincent. All will be
good if I can simply get him completely out of my life."

CHAPTER 7

It felt good for Jacquelyn to get out of her apartment, even if she was only going to visit her therapist. Since she had been fired, her apartment had become a place of solitude for her, but it also had become a place where she turned in on herself. She had a hard time coping with depression. This therapist she was going to see was like many others she had seen, but the sessions still helped some. Anyway, the company paid for them, at least for now.

After reaching the right floor, she walked down the hall thinking of what she would tell him today. It had been two months since they had finally arrested Vincent. With the help of a top-notch lawyer, he would soon have the charges reduced down to almost nothing, and then it would only be a matter of time until he would be harassing her again in a different form. She knew that. Her money was almost gone, and she decided she had little choice in what to do. She had trouble finding a job paying anything close to what she had made before. In fact, it was hard for her to find any kind of good job. Her old confidence had disappeared, taking her reputation with it.

The therapist's secretary smiled at Jacquelyn as she walked in. "Hello, he'll be with you in a minute. You can go on into his office if you want. He went down the hall for a minute. Can I get you some coffee?"

"Thanks, but I'm fine." With this she entered his office and walked over to the table where they always talked.

While waiting for him, she started to daydream again of walking in the mountains with the fresh air in her lungs, invigorating her. This mountain scene that she knew so well was the only image that created any sense of peace for her to escape to. She always had a man with her to enjoy the setting. Although she never saw his face, she felt very connected to him in the way they walked and just held hands. This simple dream kept her hopes of meeting her true love alive some day.

The doctor abruptly returned. "Hello."

"Hello." She forced herself to smile back at him.

"How have you been since we met last week?"

"I guess about the same since not much has changed. I still don't have a job, and my money's about gone."

"What about your nightmares?"

Squirming around in her seat, she stared at the ceiling, obviously expressing her uncomfortable response. "I'm still having them. It looks like I'll be reliving my sordid past forever."

"Hopefully not. There'll be a day you come to grips with what has happened to you, and you'll have good memories to replace the bad ones. It'll be up to you to work through your past."

"That's much easier said than done. The sentencing for Vincent will be in a few days, and as usual, it appears that he'll get off easy. He has all the members of his church convinced that I'm the one causing all of the problems. They're all a bunch of hypocrites."

"Why do you say that?"

"It's the truth. I used to go there. Tonight they want to meet with me and ask for my help in getting Vincent a lighter sentence. In fact, they've tried before to get me to drop the charges all together. Can you believe that?"

"Well . . . you cannot help but realize that friends do what they can for each other."

While leaning forward and starting to get argumentative, Jacquelyn continued. "It's been almost a year since I went to church there. I've not moved my membership; it's still there. Take one wild guess on how many people out of a church with five thousand members have contacted me to check on me since I quit going?"

"How many friends did you have there?"

"I think it would be easy to say I talked to maybe three or four hundred people there and knew them fairly well."

"And none of them contacted you as you were going through the divorce?"

"I had one call me, one of Vincent's friends who wanted me to take Vincent back. Vincent had a way of manipulating everyone and lying to them. If only they knew the real Vincent. I really didn't want to ruin his name, but he forced me to tell all after he crashed into my old office. He left me with no other choice."

"Have you heard from anyone since the trial?"

"Not directly from the church. I do get some contact from those I run into when I go shopping. People look very uncomfortable around me since he made me out to be this very bad person that I'm not."

"Perhaps you should go back and confront these people and tell them your side."

"I don't think you realize how much people are taken in by him. His family has been in that church for forty years."

"Surely your side of this had to have gotten around to some of the members."

"Oh, yes, but they all think I'm lying. Perhaps it would be good for me to tell you a few facts about this Baptist church. There're some very influential people in it and their reputations are beyond reproach, so to speak. However . . . the truth is much different. Even the preacher can stand in the pulpit and talk about the evils of alcohol. That doesn't keep him from having one nice wine cellar in his house and is why he doesn't return calls after nine at night. It's a time he's supposedly in deep study preparing for his sermons."

"How do you know this to be the truth?"

She watched the shock register on the therapist's face as she whispered, "I've been in his cellar with Vincent."

"I see. I guess there could be worse sins out there than enjoying a little wine."

"Perhaps, but take the music minister. While he loves to prey on little girls in the church, he's apparently so good at teaching that his sordid past is overlooked. Oh . . . he's monitored for sure, but his behavior is well known. Take a look at the bills from the computer service that handles the church's account and you'll see how many times viruses have to be removed that were caused by him going to porno sites."

"I think you're making your point, but surely not the whole church is like this."

"Well, I'd say the divorce rate's over fifty percent. Would you like to guess why?"

"I think I can guess."

"Yes, if you want to have a good old affair—go to the church."

The stories Jacquelyn could tell about events at the church were endless; however, she knew she had other items to discuss. "How much longer will the company pay for you to help me?"

"Not much longer, I'm afraid. Don't worry. I think your insurance will pick up some of the tab for you."

"I wish I could get rid of the bad nightmares and move on with my life. I'm so tired all day, and I don't have any energy at all."

"What is it about the dreams that scare you the most?"

"We've been through this before, and it hasn't changed."

"Well, if it's the most important item to you, let us try one more time and see if we can discover a clue we might be able to use to keep them from coming back again."

She closed her eyes and concentrated on an answer. "Okay."

"Good, I'll try to ask questions along the way, and we'll discuss it and see what we can do to keep them from coming back to bother you. Try to keep your eyes closed and let your mind follow your dreams."

"I'm in a room with no way out, and there are no doors. I'm on a single bed in the center of the room. There are many cameras and lights scattered here and there. Suddenly, I'm naked, and flashes are coming from everywhere. Men are yelling at me. There're so many of them that I cannot understand anyone. The lights are blinding, and I think I must be drunk. It's as if I have no control at all. This goes on and on. I scream, but no one hears me or tries to help me."

"Do you know if this sort of experience ever happened to you in real life?"

"I don't think so. I sure hope no one has photos of me." *I have thought of the possibilities, but no—hell no.*

"I know you said Vincent was very weird and acted crazy at times."

"Yes, my ex-husband is crazy. He wanted to be in control, and I was stupid enough to forgive him and think that he just wanted some excitement. I thought it was harmless the first time he started this crazy mess. If only I knew how far he would go." Jacquelyn held her hands over her eyes.

"You know, I've been thinking that he may have made you pose for friends of his one of the times you blacked out."

"He's a sick man, but I don't think his pride would let him allow other men to see me naked like that. I'm sure I'd have seen photos or heard about it by now if he had. He was more into having weird sex with me. To him, I was only a sex toy he enjoyed playing with."

"Dreams can be a very fascinating discussion. They really can tell us very much. The research into them is extremely interesting. It'll take some time to get to the bottom of this and I wish we had more time. For now, the most important suggestion I can make is to keep writing down your dreams as soon as you wake up each morning. If there's a clue in them you'll spot it one day."

Jacquelyn knew he meant to help, but she needed someone much better at deciphering dreams than he was. "Well, I do appreciate the work you're doing, but I don't think I can afford to keep seeing you for much longer, especially if my old company stops paying the tab. Like I said, I have almost no money and no job."

"What are you planning on doing?"

"I have a meeting with some women from the church tonight. It'll be interesting to see what they have to say. Afterwards, I plan on talking to my mom since I may have to move in with her for a while. I don't want to. She has a boyfriend living with her, but I may have no choice in the matter."

"I see. Let me see what I can do to help cover your bills. I'll call you tomorrow."

"Thanks again." Jacquelyn stood and walked toward the door.

CHAPTER 8

Pulling into the parking lot at the church brought back many memories for Jacquelyn. She remembered many good times in this church and had attended so many functions put on by this "country club in disguise" as she often referred to it. Why she had agreed to this meeting was beyond her, and perhaps curiosity was the best way to explain it. One fact was for sure: she wasn't going to stand for a lot of manipulation and lies tonight. The shorter this meeting lasted, the better she would like it.

After locking her door, she smiled. While she enjoyed her car, it was only a matter of time until she would be losing it. She had very little money left and was behind on her payments.

Since the side door of the church was open, she ventured inside, but she saw no one. As she walked down the hall which ushered back many memories, she heard noises coming from behind the last door that entered into the coffee room where she was suppose to meet with the group who had invited her. When she opened the door, all the conversations in the coffee room quickly ground to a halt— it was very obvious that she had been dominating the topic of conversation. "Hello," she finally said as one woman walked over to her.

"Hello," many women answered. Fake smiles quickly appeared, presenting a comical public relations attempt. These women were so bad it almost made her laugh.

Jacquelyn smiled as she recognized an old friend. "How are you, Linda?"

"I'm fine. It's good to see you again. How have you been?"

"Well I'm still living. Life hasn't been too good lately, but I'll be fine. Thanks for asking." There was a time Jacquelyn remembered loving to be with these women. She remembered being the life of the party on many occasions, but she was also sorry for many of them as they all have their own deep secrets and problems. She knew the previous love she had for them had disappeared more and more, thanks to her ex-husband ruining her life.

"I'm so sorry to hear it. You know you can always call me for anything."

"I think everyone knows I've had a very hard time lately, but you know I've only had maybe two calls since I quit attending. And . . . if I remember right, I'm still a member. At least I must be since I still get mail when the church is having fundraisers." She smiled broadly making her point obvious while waiting for someone to argue with her.

Evidently no one wanted to argue tonight, since they had a reason for asking her to the church. She assumed they needed her help. While looking around the room, Jacquelyn wondered which woman had been picked to confront her.

Linda stepped forward. "I'm sorry you feel like that, but we all assumed you didn't want any contact with us because you felt uneasy with everyone after the divorce."

"Don't worry about it. I'm doing fine on my own. Now, what did you want to see me about tonight?"

"As you know, Vincent has many friends in the church, and we're very worried about him. We've been praying for him and hoping his troubles can be put behind him. Since you left him, he's not been the same."

"So, as I thought, this is all about Vincent."

"No one can believe you left him. Vincent's so highly thought of here in the church, and his family's one of the founding members of this church. You really hurt him."

"I hurt him!" Jacquelyn felt the rush of blood surging through her body.

"You know, sometimes life don't go as smoothly as we all wish, but we're willing to work through problems."

Looking around the room where she was outnumbered by about seven or eight, Jacquelyn decided it was time to drop the gloves and get some resentment off of her chest. "I went here before I met Vincent, and I had some great times. Yes, life's good while you're *in the clique* here." She raised two fingers to dramatize the point. "When you're not, this place is pure hell. The bull shit you shove down the throat of members here is incredible."

The shock on the women's faces grew, but Jacquelyn didn't care. She realized that this was the perfect time to release the anguish she had held in for a long time. After walking over to Barbara, she started. "I'm not surprised you're here, since you're known as the mouth of the church. I'm sure the gossip about me will be flowing all over the church by morning, but before you hit the phone lines tonight perhaps you should tell everyone the truth about your children—you know how they have to go into counseling due to your dominance and religious zeal and how they're not allowed to even have contact with you now."

"I don't know what you're talking about."

"I think you do. If your husband wasn't such a wimp, he would have stood up to you a long time ago and his kids would have led a happy, normal life."

"So, you think my life is so bad . . . ."

"I wouldn't put my kids, if I had any, on drugs to try to control them so that they wouldn't be an embarrassment to me and the church. It's well known that you've started more rumors than even the local news can keep up with."

Without slowing down to give them time to regroup, Jacquelyn continued, "And Martha, before you analyze me for leaving Vincent perhaps you should look at your own marriage."

"My marriage isn't the topic here, but I think it's not bad at all."

"Perhaps you should get out of church early one night and go to some of the places your husband goes to after work. I think you would find it interesting."

"My husband's a good man, and he works at night a lot calling on clients."

"Oh, I've seen him out. He even made a pass at me the other night at Joe's bar."

"You'd love to have someone hit on you, but I don't think her husband would do that." Allison chimed in.

"Really, I think you might like to see this." Jacquelyn opened her purse and handed Martha his card with a note written on it. "And I think he gives this card to many girls there with the standard offer of one hundred dollars. You'll have to ask him why he's offering one hundred dollars."

Allison jumped into the conversation. "It's easy to see why you don't fit in here. You're just jealous of us that have understandings worked out with our husbands so well and support them and stand behind them. It's too bad you couldn't trust in the lord to save your marriage."

"Allison, there's one fact I do know—I don't have to worry about your husband since he's gay. You can deny it if you want, but everyone in here knows it but you. Ask yourself why he never comes home until late at night. If your friends here were honest with you, they would have told you a long time ago, but that would have ruined life in your perfect little world, wouldn't it?"

boy and can do no wrong. Even with all the evidence, they still don't believe me and think I make up lies."

After looking at the glasses, she noticed that he had poured her glass much higher than the other two glasses. It was a small sign, but she knew Shawn would love to get her drunk if he could. She didn't trust him, and felt very uncomfortable around him. If only her mother would listen to her. Perhaps this stay would be good for her and her mother. It might give her time to convince her mother that Shawn was a real jerk and simply using her.

"You know, I'd not be surprised if he doesn't get off with a slap on the wrist. He's always been able to get away with lying."

"Has he been trying to contact you?"

"I'm sure he was behind the women at the church contacting me, and I'm sure he still has friends drive by and check on me. Mom, my money's about gone, and I'm scared of him still coming after me if he gets out. I hate to ask this, but would it be okay if I move back here for a while? I really would appreciate it."

After a quick glance at Shawn, as if she needed his approval, her mom smiled at Jacquelyn. "You know you're always welcome here."

"Thanks." Jacquelyn inhaled a deep breath. She didn't know for sure how this request would be taken. "I brought some of my clothes with me, and I'll make arrangements tomorrow to put the rest of my things in storage. I really appreciate you letting me stay here very much." She walked over to her mom and wrapped her arms around her mother's neck.

"Don't worry about it, honey." Shawn spoke up while maintaining a pleasant look. It was not near enough to quell Jacquelyn's suspicions. While *Honey* is one word she didn't want him calling her, she decided to let it pass for the time being.

Her mom walked around the kitchen island to retrieve another glass before giving her another hug. "It'll be great to have you at home again. Perhaps I'll get a chance to teach you to cook after all. Shawn, please go out to the car and help Jacquelyn with her clothes while I'll check on the guest room, since I may have to move some boxes out of it to make room for her clothes."

"I'll be glad to." He walked to the door and motioned for Jacquelyn to follow him. "It'll be good to have you here."

"It will not be for long, and just until I get a job to get my feet under me again."

As she passed by him on the way out the door, Shawn slightly placed his hand on her waist as if to be friendly and help to lead her. Jacquelyn quickly moved ahead of him. This kind of help she didn't need. She didn't want him to place his hands on her. She expected this was only the beginning of the advances he would be making towards her after her mother turned her head. She knew she would have to address this soon with her Mom, but not tonight.

After walking to her car, she pushed a button on her key ring and the trunk popped open. "I don't have a lot of clothes with me. Thank you for helping me, but like I said, I hope I won't be here for long at all."

"Don't worry about it; we're glad to have you. After all, it's not my house. It's your mother's place."

Jacquelyn felt glad that he at least acted honest about it, but after being together for such a long time, it felt like they were married. She reached over to obtain some clothes out of the back seat and felt him watching her as she leaned over. It felt so creepy for her to think about what she had in store for herself.

The sound of her trunk slamming startled her and a small box fell out of her hand and hit the ground. Several of her clothes dropped out of the box and onto the ground. This includes some of her—most intimate clothing. She quickly recovered them, but not until Shawn saw some of the skimpy panties she wore. With a smirk on his face, he only whispered, "Nice."

The tightness in her stomach returned as she wondered what she could do. For now she had to endure.

CHAPTER 10

The days turned into weeks, and Jacquelyn still couldn't find a job she liked. With her ex-husband in jail for now she did feel safer, but knew his appeals were being heard, and that it was simply a matter of time until he'd be out and looking for her again.

She suddenly noticed the morning sunlight glaring into her room, but she didn't remember leaving the curtains open the night before. The day already felt warm, and she obviously must have kicked off the covers during the night as she laid there totally uncovered. Quickly she pulled her nightshirt down to cover her naked body curled on the bed. Then she noticed her door slightly open as well. "Great! I guess Shawn has gotten his show for the morning already."

It was time to get up and get busy. It felt like every part of her life depressed her, making it harder and harder for her to turn life around. *What happened to the executive, take-charge type of person I was?* She had to get back in the groove.

Jacquelyn walked toward the shower hoping it would bring some clarity to the day. With the house quiet she hoped Shawn had already left for work, but with his work, she really never knew what time he'd pop up.

The shower felt good, making her feel much more alive. After drying and styling her hair she opened the door to go back to her room to dress. As she opened the door, however, she saw Shawn standing there. She quickly pulled her robe tighter around her.

"I see you're up early, today."

"Hello, Shawn. I thought you were gone already."

"Not yet. My first appointment isn't for a while yet." His stare roamed over her in a very obvious fashion, as if to indicate exactly what he had on his mind.

"Excuse me, I have to get dressed and leave." She pushed pass him.

He leaned back as she headed for her room. "I guess you forgot you asked me to take you to get your car this morning."

"Damn, I did forget. I'll be ready in a minute." She rushed to her room. If there was one thing she really hated, it was asking for his help, but she had no choice since her transmission had problems at the shop.

"Take your time, honey, since I'm in no hurry. By the way, your mom has to go out of town this weekend, so it looks like it's going to be just you and me here for the next few days. It'll give us some time to become better acquainted."

"Do what?" She walked back into the hallway where he waited for her to return.

"She received a call from her boss this morning. Some kinds of new line they're introducing in Chicago, and they told her she had to attend. She'll tell you all about it when she gets home tonight." A sly smile curled out of the side of his mouth as if he sealed her fate to a life worse than burning in hell.

What could she say? She'd have to talk to her mom again and soon. She had not been able to convince her mom that this jerk kept making passes at her all the time.

Quickly changing into her clothes, she walked toward the front door. The sooner this was over, the better. She needed her car to be able to go to interviews and not be dependent on Shawn for support.

After arriving at the shop, she located the mechanic who worked on her car. "What do you think?"

With a sour grimace he pointed to her car on the rack. "The transmission's gone. I hate to tell you this, but you'll need a new one."

"You're kidding me. I don't have money for a new transmission right now. What kind of money are we talking about?"

"It's going to be right at three thousand dollars." She felt dizzy. There was no way she could come up with that kind of money.

Shawn walked over and handed the shop owner his credit card. "Put it on my card. We can work it out later."

Jacquelyn didn't like the way he added *we can work it out later*. She knew exactly what he had on his mind. "Wait, I'll have to work out a solution. Can you hold it for a day or two until I find a way to pay you?"

"Sure, but I'm not starting on it until I get paid. That's for sure. Let me know what you want me to do."

"We'll get back with you." Shawn nodded at the mechanic before following Jacquelyn outside.

They said nothing to each other for a long time on the way back until he finally asked, "Why don't you want me to help you with the car?"

"Because I know what you have on your mind."

"For someone who has no job or money, you sure can be a pain. I tell you what, think about it, and you let me know. In fact, we have all weekend to think about it."

"No, stop the car. I want to get out."

"Settle down, we'll be home soon."

Pushing the door open got his attention as he squealed to a quick stop. Jacquelyn stepped out of the car and yelled back at him, "Leave me alone, or I'll call the cops right now!"

After seeing that he had no other choice and how it was only a few blocks from the house, he threw his hands above him, got back in the car, and started driving.

Jacquelyn walked and cried as she strolled through the neighborhood trying to find somewhere she wouldn't be seen. By late in the afternoon she finally found a small hillside with a grassy place for her to sit. While the location looked peaceful and calm, she realized that her life had finally come to where she had nowhere else left to run anymore.

She watched the clouds in the western sky radiating so brightly and beautifully as they formed very distinct shapes. From back in her childhood she remembered how she looked for animals and other images in the clouds. She always had fun enjoying the images appearing in the clouds. While some people could see them, others could not, but it was a fun game to play anyway.

From behind the nearest clouds, a beautiful sunset formed that stretched all the way across the sky. It created such a sight it made her forget for a minute all the bad in her life and contemplate how some facts were always the same—beautiful, no matter what else happened in the world.

Then it started to happen as one cloud in particular changed shape. It formed the most beautiful angel she had ever imagined as it grew brighter and brighter right in front of her. Yes, an angel would be what she really needed right now! After slowly pressing her hands to her face, Jacquelyn whispered softly, but directly at the angel in front of her. "I know I've not always been that good, and I'll admit that I've made many mistakes in my life, but is it too much to ask for happiness? If you are my guardian angel, please help me. Please help me find a way to live without all the problems I have now. I only want the dreams most girls want. It would be so good to laugh and play again, and most importantly, it would be so great to find my soulmate, my one and only true love. I know he's out there somewhere, and I feel like he's looking for me also."

It felt as if the cloud heard her and was actually listening to her as Jacquelyn concentrated hard for an answer. It was no use, she thought, as she realized it would take a true miracle to save her now, but still she examined the clouds and wanted to know what she had to do. Any kind of advice would help her.

As fast as the angel appeared in the clouds, it vanished and different images replaced it. The clouds reconfigured into the image of a mountain range with some clouds folding over on top of others. She even noticed a silver lining cast on them from the setting sun which resembled snow on their tops.

Jacquelyn's daydreams of times in the mountains and her night dreams of moving to the mountains resurfaced in her mind. All became clear to her in that moment. She thought perhaps an angel was showing her the way. With a smile on her face, she addressed the sunset. "Thanks." The sunset slowly vanished, but left her mind engaged with hope.

She stood quickly and walked to her mom's house, where she saw the lights shining through the windows and her mom standing in the doorway. "Where have you been?" she asked.

"I've been walking and trying to clear my head."

"Shawn told me about the car. We can loan you the money if you want us to."

"I cannot ask you to do that. Let me see what I can figure out." There was no use in telling her mom what Shawn said since she'd never believed her before. While they had argued about Shawn many times before, her mom offered a small hug indicating she didn't want to fight tonight. "If it's okay with you, I need to go to bed."

"Okay, but you know I'm leaving for the weekend."

"I cannot believe you're leaving me with—"

"I don't want to hear it. He'll take good care of you, and you know I have no choice in this." Without saying another word, Jacquelyn walked toward her room. She simply wanted to go to sleep.

She started to dream several hours later. It felt like someone or something was pulling her through a number of clouds which constantly grew brighter and brighter, giving her the sense of floating through space. It seemed like time didn't exist at all. The peaceful feeling felt so relaxing.

Then, suddenly, a man dressed in all white appeared in front of her. "Hello, Jacquelyn. How are you? I've been waiting for this moment for a long time."

"I'm fine." She strained to focus on his face. "What do you mean by *waiting for me*?"

"You've been chosen to advance to another level. The desire in you is very strong, but your needs are even greater. I'll help you and lead you to find the one object in life you want most, but it'll be up to you to follow your heart and learn the secrets of love and how to use its power."

"What do you mean I've been chosen to advance to another level?"

"It'll be made clear to you later, but you should know that in large part it's from your past. Also . . . your true love's zest and unrelenting love has compelled the forces of the universe which are more powerful than you can ever imagine. Finally, you're under attack by other forces, dark forces that want to confuse you and hide the light from you. We don't leave our place here often, but when we do, it's with a purpose or a vengeance. However . . . it's best if you can grow on your own, but with some guidance."

This dream felt different for Jacquelyn. It felt so real and like being awake with the full use of her faculties. "That all sounds good, but I've no clue what you're talking about."

"I understand since you've much to learn. Your true love, your soulmate, or whatever term you prefer to use is waiting for you, and I'll do all I can to help both of you. In fact, the entire universe will be helping you. All you have to do is follow all the instructions you receive."

"What instructions?"

"Did you not see the sunset today?"

"Well . . . yes, I did, and it was beautiful."

"And what were you told?"

"I remember seeing mountains after my angel vanished."

"Yes, that's right."

"That would be good, but how am I suppose to go to the mountains?"

"To find your destiny only requires your desire to do so. Your future is totally in your hands, but we'll be here to help you all the way." He smiled softly as he walked back into the clouds.

Jacquelyn woke as the meeting replayed in her mind. She had never had a dream that felt so real. The more she analyzed her dream the more determined she became to leave for the mountains the next day, even if it meant hitchhiking her way there.

CHAPTER 11

After drawing in a deep breath, Jacquelyn stretched her hand into the air as high she could reach, extending her thumb as if a beacon in the sky. There was no more time to think about it and no turning back now. Her new destiny was ahead of her, and she was fully prepared to hitchhike if necessary.

As the panic of the moment settled in, part of her wanted someone to stop quickly and let her get off the side of the road before being seen, while another part of her was actually scared to death. There were some nice people in the world, but she knew only too well there were some very bad animals out there also.

As the cars sped by without stopping, she didn't know if she should be happy or sad. The climb up the hill from her mother's house, which was now about a mile away, had been very tiring. She had what few belongings she could carry with her in a small suitcase. The afternoon was fading quickly, and she knew she didn't want to be out on the side of the interstate after dark for sure. Shawn had stayed home for much of the day and only left a few hours ago, causing her to be so late in leaving. While many people would be getting off work soon, and the real traffic would be coming, she knew that those drivers would only want to make it home for the evening. She really needed someone going all the way to Knoxville. Making a series of these stops would not be very good for her because of the potential danger, and she knew that. She had made her decision however, and in that spirit she lifted her thumb even higher.

She thought about Shawn. *What would he do after he finds me gone? On the other hand, and even worse, what would he do if he spots me on the interstate trying to get away?* Even though Shawn was her mother's boyfriend, she could never understand how blind her mother was. He wasn't a loyal type of guy and had his eye on her from day one. While he tried to hide it from her mom, he watched every move she made all the time. With her mother leaving for the weekend, Jacquelyn knew she had no choice but to leave. She just couldn't be left alone with him.

Another car slowed to look her over, but kept going. It must be someone trying to decide if she was a hooker. The image gave her the chills and was a far cry from the executive life she once enjoyed. She couldn't let herself think of that now. Life had changed, and there was no turning back.

She remembered how she had felt at her mom's place earlier in the day. Shawn was in sales and often went to work late since he had no scheduled time he had to go to work. This morning, when he went to the bathroom to get his morning shower, he had left the door slightly cracked, as if to indicate it was open. She noticed it as she went down the hall and could tell that he was in the shower from the sound of the water running. *Did he really think I would join him? Is he that stupid or plain dumb?* In a way she thought he might be harmless, but she knew if given the opportunity, he would act on it. With her mother gone for the weekend and knowing how he liked to drink, she was too afraid to chance it.

As another car sped by with no signs of slowing down, she started wondering if she was in the right place to hitch a ride. However, she was on the ramp entering the interstate which headed north out of Atlanta. Perhaps she needed to go on a little further and actually stand on the side of the interstate. With no other options, she strolled in that direction.

As she almost made the interstate, she heard a truck slowing down to stop. With her heart racing, she felt glad someone was stopping, but still had an intense fear. She had no idea what would happen next.

The large four wheel drive type truck with an extended cab stopped and backed up. At least it was a newer model and maybe had someone with a little class in it stopping to check on her. *What do I do now?* She had never hitchhiked before. Her heart started pounding. She considered turning and running, but change her mind as the truck finally backed to where she stood. She watched the driver slowly roll the window down.

She yelled so she could be heard over the noise of the interstate. "Hello, how are you?"

A man in his forties sat in the passenger seat. "I'm fine."

She looked him over quickly, still trying to decide what to do. Finally, she continued, "I'm trying to get to Knoxville and hoping for a ride."

She watched a big smile on the man's face grow as he informed her he was going to Chattanooga and would be glad to help her get that far if she wanted a lift. That would be part of the way, and she felt sure she could get another ride from there. Hopefully, he would drop her off somewhere she could get a ride easier than from the side of the interstate. Besides, it would be better than waiting for Shawn to come looking for her and finding her here.

"Thanks," she replied as she waited for him to get out and let her in the back door. It was a high step. She pulled up and shifted into the seat before she gave her faith much more consideration. In a flash of an eye, he closed the door behind her and returned to the front seat before slamming his door closed.

The smell of the truck's strong odor burned her nose. It smelled like a mechanic's truck with the scent of oil mixed with the smell of beer. As she looked around the compartment trying to comprehend her surroundings, she studied the driver of the truck who was staring back at her while she settled in.

The driver of the truck had a big smile on his face and looked to be about the same age as the other man. He watched her positioning her stuff in the other part of the cab as she turned around to face him.

"My name is Barry, and his name is Mark." The driver shifted gears and drove onto the interstate. "We're glad to help you. I've been stuck on the side of the highway myself before, and I know what it's like trying to get a ride. Are you having problems with your car?"

She thought it might be easier to lie. "Yes. My husband is in Knoxville getting it fixed now."

Looking around the cab, she realized the truck was almost new and perhaps expensive. Anyway, it felt better than standing on the side of the road. While her suitcase took up a lot of room and made it hard for her to fully stretch, she finally took a deep breath of air, knowing she was on her way now.

It felt so crazy and hard for her to imagine that she was actually leaving town and heading for the Smoky Mountains. This first part of the trip would take her toward Knoxville. Then she could move on from there. It felt like destiny was calling her as the dream she had the night before kept repeating in her mind. This was a dream like no other she could remember before since it felt so real and clear to her. She had talked to a guy who gave her advice and who really must have her interest at heart.

He had dressed in all white clothing and stood in a solid white room with all white furnishings. His blond hair and radiant smile make him look so trusting, so caring. As he told her in the dream, in order to find what she really wanted, she had to follow her dreams. If true love was what she was after, then she'd have to fulfill her destiny. If she thought the Smoky Mountains was the most romantic place on the planet, then that was where she needed to live.

While she had met someone she decided to call the Dream Master for the first time, she still had no idea who or what he represented, but she knew he certainly had made an impression on her. She had to admit it was a very interesting dream and unlike any she had ever experienced before. It had haunted her long after she woke up the next morning and had dominated her thoughts all day.

After her memories slowly faded, she was startled by Mark peering over the top of his seat. He appeared to be totally analyzing every part of her. As the stare intensified, it set off alarms. While she was thirty, she knew she looked like she might be in her early twenties, and with her small size making her look very vulnerable. However, she knew *Jack* could handle the situation and these two would have a rude awakening if they tried anything. Her experience in handling jerks like this while out in the bars made her strong and much tougher than they would expect from someone so small.

But really, what am I doing in this truck? She could only hope for the best. If the guy would quit staring at her, she would feel much better. It felt like men only have sex on their minds. Since she knew there were some good guys out there, she only wanted to find what every girl wanted—true love. While she had some friends who have found their soulmates, she wasn't so lucky since she always found everything else.

As Mark continued to study her, she shifted around in her seat, enduring the intensifying stares of a man she knew was mentally undressing her as his eyes moved around her body. She now wished she had buttoned her blouse higher as he kept staring, but since she barely filled out a B-cup, she knew there wasn't too much there to excite anyone. However, with a firm stomach she felt like she had definitely stayed in good shape for her age.

Her blue jeans fit tight—too much so right now, and they hung lower than she wished at the moment also. Since her crotch appeared to be where he concentrated his attention the most, she shifted again to one side and pulled her purse over her lap as if to hide slightly from his stare. She started to question her motives more and more.

Barry finally broke the silence. "What kind of car problem are you having?"

"Transmission needs to be fixed."

"I see. That kind of problem can be expensive."

The afternoon light slowly disappeared as they traveled north on the interstate. With any luck, the entire trip would be over soon. She still couldn't believe that she was acting like a little runaway kid.

"We're going on to Chattanooga, and you're welcome to come on with us," Mark shouted over the top of the seat. His voice remained calm but carried a very serious undertone. Yeah, like really, the one thing she didn't want to happen was spending the night with two beer drinking men in Chattanooga.

"Thanks, but I need to make my way on to Knoxville as soon as I can get there."

The conversation ended again as they drove on. That suited her fine since the less talking she did, the less chance she had of getting in trouble. With the approaching darkness concerning her now, she worried about what she would do after they let her out of the truck?

She suddenly noticed the sunset in the distance to the west. It wasn't very impressive, but still reminded her of the previous day when she had seen the beautiful cloud looking like an angel. She even felt as if the angel had talked to her as she remembered asking questions of why life is as it is and why she had no one special. She wanted to know why the men in her life haven't been what she needed or wanted. She even questioned if this idea called "true love" existed at all. However, she felt a comfort in the sunset she had not felt in a long time. She also prayed like she never prayed before. While praying in earnest and as deeply as possible, she knew she needed help. She needed a guardian angel more than ever.

"Give me another beer, Mark," Barry ordered.

"We don't have any more. That was the last one."

"Damn, I need one." With that he whipped to the far right lane and up to the service station at the top of an incline. After pulling up to the station, he looked around. "And what kind would you like, sweetie?"

"Don't worry about me. I don't drink." Getting drunk with these two was definitely not what she wanted to do.

With a quick grunt, he opened the door and went to the store to make his purchase. Mark turned around again as his grin intensified. "I guess it's good that we stopped to pick you up. It's getting dark, and it will be cold soon."

"Yes, thank you for your help."

Barry soon returned, jumped in his seat, and started the motor.

"What did you get?"

"Just some beer."

"And nothing for our lady friend here. I thought your mommy taught you better."

"How much do you think it'll cost to get that transmission fixed?" Mark suddenly asked.

"I'm not sure, but not too much I hope."

"Maybe we could help a little. I don't have a lot on me, but a little."

"I couldn't ask you or let you do that," she replied.

"Now give Mark a few minutes of your time back there in the back seat, and I'm sure he can come up with at least a hundred."

"Just what kind of woman do you think I am?" She knew somehow this would happen. Staying calm and in control was going to be hard as she prepared herself to kick some butt.

"Calm down. We were just asking is all."

"Perhaps you should let me out."

"In the middle of nowhere? That wouldn't be too smart. We'll be at a truck stop in a few minutes. If that's what you want, you can get a ride from there."

She breathed a little easier, but her heart still raced. The inside of the truck became quiet again, but she could see the men making motions to each other as a road sign she saw announced a truck stop ahead. She felt so nervous by now her hands started sweating. Just a few more minutes and she would be away from them. She had to be more careful next time.

After easing off the interstate, the truck proceeded to the truck stop, but then Barry pulled the truck to the very back corner of the lot and stopped. The quiet darkness felt like a big blanket shutting out everything but the pounding of her heart.

Both men turned to look over their seats at her. She knew it was too late to yell and she was all alone, but not helpless. She needed her guardian angel or the man from her dream the night before. She tried to think of what she could do. She knew she had to act fast or these two men would be trying to rape her. She closed her eyes as the fear escalated and yelled out into the depth of her mind looking for help. "Please help me. I need you now!" She opened her eyes as she shifted into Jack, her tough character mode. Her foot moved back ready to kick right at the first face she saw and her claws arched ready to spring into action.

Suddenly, blinding lights from a truck in front of them startled everyone. The lights radiated from the dust kicked up by the big truck with the energized dust expanding in every direction. Then, she saw the outline of a man walking from this new truck until he stood between the two trucks. The two men squinted and tried hard to see what was going on.

Jacquelyn unexpectedly saw a glow on the door handle beside her, a kind of a radiating pulse shining strong enough to be noticed. She immediately grabbed the handle and pulled hard to open the door. While moving quickly while she had the chance, she grabbed her suitcase and jumped from the truck and ran past the man in the new truck. As she passed him, she smelled the most interesting cologne she had ever smelled on a man. It was so overpowering that even in a moment like this she couldn't help but notice it. Her eyes, however, quickly locked onto the store ahead of her that also glowed with the same weird light she had seen on the door handle.

After rushing into the truck stop, she wanted to yell, but all appeared so calm inside. She hurried thru the shop as she glanced back over her shoulder to see the truck driven by Barry and Mark speeding out of the stop. Strangely enough, the other truck was nowhere to be seen. The whole situation felt very weird since there was no way a truck could disappear that fast. After moving closer to the window, she looked up and down the lot.

The stranger and his truck had also vanished.

CHAPTER 12

Shaken by the ordeal of the night, Jacquelyn rested at a small table in the grill and ordered a sandwich and fries with a lot of coffee. She had no intention of repeating the same mistakes again with men as she remembered her past few years. After being married to her abusive ex-husband, she kept telling herself she'd never allow herself to be treated like that again. Because of men like her ex-husband, her own mother's boyfriend, and now these two men, she had suffered and lost everything. Because of Vincent, the great job that she had was gone forever. He had harassed her to the bitter end, and even now, long after the divorce, he never stopped. It didn't matter what court orders she obtained, she knew he would always haunt her. Even in jail he had managed to reach out, and she knew it was only a matter of time before he would be released.

It felt amazing how busy this place stayed. People from all walks of life kept coming in to either pay for gas or order a bite to eat, and believe it or not, the food wasn't that bad. A little girl of about five years old eventually wandered over to Jacquelyn's table and stopped in front of her. "Hello," Jacquelyn said as she winked at her.

"Hello," the little girl replied.

"What's your name?"

"Kristi." She twisted her curls in her fingers.

About that time her dad walked over and lifted her off the floor. "I see you're making friends again."

"She's a real cutie." Jacquelyn smiled and gave her another wink.

"Thank you. She's my princess, and she's dying to see the mountains."

Jacquelyn smiled as she heard those words. Her heart filled with excitement just thinking of the place where she also wanted to go. "That's great. I know she'll love it. That's where I was heading until I had car trouble."

"I'm so sorry to hear that." He offered her a compassionate smile. "How long is it going to take to get it fixed? Are they working on it here?"

"No, it's back in Atlanta being worked on. I have to get to Gatlinburg, and I'm trying now to figure out some way to get there. The ride I had is gone."

His wife walked over and joined them to listen to the story as Jacquelyn finished. "Wow, I'd hate to be in your shoes. Is there anyone we can call for you?"

"I wish there was, but don't worry. I'll think of something."

"We don't have a lot of room, but you're welcome to ride with us if you want." The dad glanced over to his wife, who gave an approving nod.

Beaming with acceptance, she could not have been more thankful. "My name's Jacquelyn."

"Hi, this is my wife Carol, and I'm Rob."

"Thank you so very much for this." She retrieved her suitcase as she prepared to go with them. Her luck had changed. As they walk out to the van, she noticed them holding hands and smiling at each other. It provided a frozen moment of the life she wished for. He appeared to be a kind and loving husband who loved kids. She felt very happy for his wife and knew it was possible to find her soulmate out there, she just needed to keep looking and hoping she had the luck this woman did.

After pulling out of the truck stop, she glanced one more time around to see if the two men were anywhere, and felt relieved to see that they weren't. She also started thinking about the mysterious truck that had appeared, and the man who walked forward. In a way he was her hero, and he never knew it.

The van was dark in the back where she stretched out, and most of all quiet. Her attention returned to her situation and the previous day when she watched the sunset. It looked so beautiful and so different from images she had ever seen before. It was more like a command for her to look and enjoy all the mystifying wonders of the world. She sensed the world wanting to tell her what she needed to know. Almost like a psychologist, she felt like her angel in that cloud wanted to help her and give her advice. It was also a lot cheaper than the therapist she had seen over the last year.

The magical look of the sunset shifted the whole time she had watched it. Almost like there were angels at play in the display of colors. When the light faded, it was almost like the sunset itself announced that it would be back to help later.

Jacquelyn knew she must have fallen asleep for a little while because when she opened her eyes she saw the entrance to the Pigeon Forge area. Like most tourist traps, lights flashed everywhere hoping to lure in the traffic.

Rob noticed her awake. "Where do you want us to take you?"

She didn't have a place, and she didn't want them to know it. "Leave me at the conference center. I can get a ride from there."

"Are you sure? We'll be glad to take you anywhere you need to go."

"I'm not sure where my friends live, but I know I can get in touch with them shortly. You've been so kind to me already—really."

Not wanting to press any further, Rob remained quiet and drove on toward Gatlinburg, where they soon entered the main street to the conference center. After pulling off the road, Rob reached over and gave his wife a small kiss before he walked around the car to let Jacquelyn out and help her with her suitcase.

"Thanks, your family has been great to me. More important, it's great to see how two people can be so good for each other. You have a wonderful family, and I hope you have a great vacation here."

"Thank you for saying that, and I hope everything works out for you also." With that he walked around, entered his car, and drove off.

Jacquelyn breathed in deep as she realized she had made it. *Now what should I do*? While looking around the entrance to the conference center, she felt happy to be there, but was also scared since she had nowhere to stay. After lifting her suitcase, she headed toward the center of town looking for anyplace that might be of help to her. Perhaps she'd stay up all night and drink coffee. In the morning she'd have to look for a job and try to decide what she needed to do after that.

While walking down the street she remembered Gatlinburg as a family town and without the wild single scene or crazy bars. In fact, it had always been a place where many couples traveled to get married, or after getting married came there for their honeymoon. Jacquelyn's dreams of the fantastic scenery and one of the most romantic places on the planet came alive as reality hit her that she was actually standing there.

When she saw a small coffee shop that looked interesting, she went inside. It felt cozy enough and was not very busy as she studied several couples and one family with two kids. The adults drank coffee as the children enjoyed assorted candies and sweets.

"Can I help you?" a young girl asked as she walked toward Jacquelyn.

"Yes, a cup of coffee would be great! And by the way, how late do you stay open?"

"We close at twelve, which is about an hour from now." She smiled and walked off.

Great, Jacquelyn thought, trying to decide on her next move. With almost no money, she had to think of a solution. She studied the couples in the shop who all gazed into their partners' eyes and enjoyed their time together with no distractions from anyone. It appeared as if they were floating in time and totally locked into each other's soul. This was exactly what she wanted. Now if only she could find her own love one day.

As she finished her cup of coffee, the workers started cleaning the floors. She had to leave. She closed her eyes for a minute and reflected on her dream from the night before. That dream had made her decide to make this trip, and she still couldn't believe she would make such a wild journey like this just because of a dream she had. Anyway, she was here now and needed help. She remembered talking to a man in her dream and being told to follow her heart, her dream, and then she would find true love. Thinking about it, she began to wonder what true love was.

She knew it wouldn't be too long until daylight, and she had an idea. The sunrises here could be incredible, and there had to be several good locations to see one very close to town. She closed her eyes again and sent a small prayer into the darkness. If she could have this one small blessing, she knew her day would be good.

With that she walked out of the coffee shop and started hiking toward the visitor center at the entrance to the national park. When she had visited the mountains earlier, she had made many trips to the center before and remembered some of the trails around it.

On the way out of town, she noticed one small bar still open. There used to be no bars open in Gatlinburg. At least it provided somewhere she could go to think about what to do next. After carrying her suitcase through the front door, she found her way to the bar where she dropped her load. She studied a small crowd milling around inside, an obvious mixture of locals and tourists.

A tall, lanky bartender worked his way over to where she waited for him. His black pants and shirt were obviously company-issued and not in keeping with the rest of his appearance. The long, black hair he combed straight back over the top of his head as well as his long sideburns presented an interesting imitation of Elvis. With a flirty type smile, he walked closer. "What can I get you?"

Thinking it might be good to relax and not to worry for a while, she decided she would stay for a few minutes anyway. "What kind of wine do you have?"

"We have many kinds of beers, but only one red and one white wine."

"I see. Then, let it be red."

After looking around, she should have known this from the layout of the bar. The bar reflected a cozy and quaint atmosphere. The people appeared relatively quiet and like they wanted to simply chill out for the night and listen to the music playing. In fact, at the bar itself, she was the only one sitting there. All of the rest of the customers sat at tables with friends or family.

After a few minutes, the bartender wandered over with an empty glass and a bottle of wine. He placed the glass on the counter in front of Jacquelyn and started to pour. "Are you here by yourself, or is someone joining you in a minute?" He waited for her response as he intensified his stare.

"It's just me tonight." After saying so, she wished she hadn't. All she needed was someone else hitting on her.

"I see. That'll be six dollars." He corked the bottle.

Reaching for her purse, she handed him the money for the drink. At this rate, she would not be able to stay at the bar for very long, since she needed to make her remaining cash last as long as she could.

Over the next hour or so, she had several guys come over and ask to buy her a drink, but she wasn't in the mood to socialize and only wanted to think of what to do after this place closed. Since it wouldn't be too long until the sun came up, she decided she would walk to the visitor center to wait until morning. While it looked dark outside, she decided she could make it.

Once outside the bar, she kept walking and looking for signs telling her where to go. She remembered trips to the park and the visitor center on the road ahead of her when she was younger, and if nothing else she could stop there. It'd be a good place to wait until morning. She soon noticed a glow in the darkness ahead of her, a kind of a strange glow which was not very bright, but still visible. As she walked closer to the light, she noticed a path to the left and to who knows where. It glowed enough to allow her to see a trail. She started to turn the other way when a voice behind her shattered the silence.

"How are you? It's going to be a great sunrise today, don't you think?"

"Yes, I guess," she replied, trying to regain her nerves after he startled her. Nevertheless, in a flash, he walked by her and headed up the mountain in front of her. She would have to hurry to keep him in sight. Why she suddenly wanted to follow him, she didn't know—maybe because he had a friendly voice. Anyway, he was at least human, and the only one on the way up the mountain.

She started to yell out for him to wait up, but she knew he had already walked out of range. Her suitcase weighed too much for her to carry and make good time. Then she smelled the air, and there it was again: the same smell she noticed on the stranger at the truck stop. There was no doubt about it.

After another hour of hard climbing, she reached a summit and a large clearing with an overhang. She studied a slight glow above the horizon indicating where the sun would be coming up. While still early, this had to be a great place to see the sunrise. Feeling exhausted, she dropped to the ground to rest. She then slowly drifted off to sleep for a few minutes as she waited for the sun to appear.

Even in those few moments of sleep, she began to dream. She felt transported to a place that was so warm, secure, pure, and innocent all at the same time. The glowing white surroundings encased her. After looking around the room, she suddenly recognized the man she had talked to in her previous dream. He appeared familiar, perhaps as if an old friend. As she approached him, he pulled out a chair for her.

With a smile as pure as gold, the blond-haired man spoke in words deep but smooth. "It's good to see you."

"It's good to see you also." As the white glowing room increased its effect on Jacquelyn, it made her feel like she was floating effortlessly inside a cloud. Her head remained clear enough, however, to want some answers—answers to questions she could only ask a good friend. "I had a very bad day."

"Why is that?" he responded.

"I was almost assaulted, and who knows, I could have been killed today."

With a quiet smile, he asked her a question she had a hard time believing. "Is that what you were expecting or anticipating yesterday?"

"No! Why would I want or expect that to happen to me?"

"Concentrate on your thoughts when you stood on the side of the road, and then tell me exactly what was on your mind."

"Well, to be honest, I felt scared to death about being there. In addition, I knew there was a possibility of being picked up by someone bad. I was trying to be careful, but I had no choice. I know I didn't dress properly after I got on the road, but I haven't been able to think clearly lately. It was kind of as if I was hoping for a guardian angel to help me."

"So, you were concentrating on a bad situation that could happen to you?"

"Yes, I was thinking of the various possibilities that could happen to me."

"The power of prayer and anticipation is very strong. Your thoughts are the forces that direct you to the dimension that sets your life in motion. It's our dreams, wishes, and hopes that lead us to our destiny."

"You mean the thoughts I have actually make events come true? I don't know. That's kind of hard to believe."

"What about the ride you received for the second part of your journey? How did it go?"

"It was very good, and I could have not asked for a better family."

"When you were eating and drinking coffee at the truck stop, what were your expectations there?"

"I was scared and knew I had to find a safer ride. I concentrated on looking for a good family to ride with."

"So, you knew you would find them, and you anticipated it and prayed about it."

"Yes. Okay, I see where you're going now. Are you saying that my thoughts of finding a good ride actually led me to that family?"

"You have much to learn about the power of your prayers and your expectations. You must learn to analyze your inner thoughts, including your dreams and the hopes and wishes you have. When you know what you want, it's easy to have all the forces of the universe helping you accomplish them."

"I think I know what I want."

"Yes, and what is it then?"

"I think it's the one dream almost everyone wants: I want to find what I call true love."

After smiling at her with a kind heart, the blond-haired man asked, "Can you tell me exactly what you mean by true love?" Pondering the question for a minute, she knew the answer wasn't simple, but one she assumed all people understood without explanation.

After sitting quietly waiting for an answer, he finally added, "You know, this is a question mankind has been asking forever with many different answers and decisions being given by those considered to be wise and intelligent. To find the answer to this question, it would be good to know what different philosophies, religions, and wise people have discovered. I wish you good luck in finding an answer to this question." With that he began to glow very brightly until he disappeared.

To her amazement, as he vanished, she woke from her dream, with the sun appearing slightly above the horizon to shine brightly in her face.

CHAPTER 13

The sunrise exploded across the sky with various pink and orange colors swirling around clouds which radiated energy full of expectations of fantastic events to come. The rush of colors and the explosive nature of the sunrise looked beautiful, and it felt more incredible than she could find words to describe.

The more she studied the sunrise, the more beautiful it became. It was as if all her dreams she could describe or hope for were in that display of beauty. Inside she felt a high she had never known before as a flow of energy and passion lifted her off the ground and made her float as if she was actually drifting among the clouds. Her mind felt clearer than she could have ever imagined. It felt like a high she knew many people only experienced once in a lifetime.

In the cool of the morning, she felt a gentle breeze blowing and heard a slight rustling of the leaves. Then she thought she could hear a faint whisper coming from the sunrise. In fact, at one point, she could swear she heard voices talking. There was no way she could make out what they were saying, but at the same time it felt nice to know angels were trying to communicate with her.

In the clouds, she noticed more images forming. They looked like angels moving around, changing shapes, trying to organize. Feelings like she had never known before kept building inside her. She knew without a doubt there were angels in these clouds, and they wanted to communicate with her, but after trying as hard as she could, she wasn't able to understand what they were saying. The more she studied the clouds the more she appreciated the beauty of the morning and the energy flowing from the sunrise. She felt happy with the realization that someone or something out there wanted to talk to her.

As the area around her started to become lighter, she finally recognized the valleys below her and the mist rising out of the streams and lower hills. She watched a new world springing to life to replace the one which had been asleep the night before.

The rocks she rested on were part of a large ridge of many rocks jutting out and standing ready to absorb the morning rays. Magically coming to life with every second, the energy of the sunrise melted the night before and gave new life to a world waiting for the angels of the morning to awaken it.

On her right, she suddenly noticed someone about ten or fifteen yards away who was sitting still, but stretching out his arms and absorbing all the sunlight and energy around him. Startled, but not scared, she watched as the glow of the energy made him radiate more and more intensely. Who was this person? What was he doing here? Jacquelyn knew she had climbed way up in the mountains and not somewhere she would expect to see someone else.

After the colors of the sunrise started to fade with the light of the new sun establishing a brand new day, it was then that the man rose, bowed to the sun, and started to look around. With a big smile on his face, he glanced at Jacquelyn and waved at her. She didn't know if she should wave back or not, but decided it was best to be friendly and returned a small hello with her hand as well.

Climbing over the rocks of the overhang, he slowly worked his way to her. His facial features indicated that he must be in his early sixties, but the clothes he wore could be best described as leftovers of the peace generation thirty or forty years ago, since he looked like a flower child that never grew up. He wore his long brown hair in a ponytail behind him, and he had wrapped a bandana around his head. His hand painted tee shirt had scenes of nature, and his blue jeans sported holes in the knees. Even though the weather was chilly, he wasn't wearing any shoes. It had also been many months since he shaved, or even had his beard trimmed. Yet, rather than looking like a wild man, there was something about his manner that made him appear very well educated and cultured.

"Hello." He smiled as he approached her and removed his deep-blue, small-rimmed sunglasses.

"Hello," she answered back to him. "I didn't know there was anyone else up here."

"There are many trails in these mountains, with many spots to watch both the sunrise and the sunset. You never know which one will be the best, because the clouds look different every day. We're slightly inside the national forest right now, and that's why there're no homes here."

"I think I noticed some cabins somewhere back along the trail on the way in here this morning."

"Yes, there're some, but they're the last ones before you get into the National Park. You have to be careful not to trespass on private land, which makes the owners very unhappy with you."

"You seemed so at peace watching the sunrise this morning. It was almost like you were in a trance. I couldn't help but notice you."

"It's awesome up here. This is one of my favorite places and where I can get in touch with my angel of the sunrise. It's interesting what information she brings me in the mornings."

This sounded amazing for Jacquelyn. "Angels—you say you noticed angels in the clouds?"

"Yes," he replied, looking straight at her. "Didn't you hear them?"

It was such an honest and open question, Jacquelyn was taken aback and tried hard to think about how she should answer his question. She closed her eyes for a second to concentrate. "You know something. It's hard to describe, but I heard something that almost sounded like voices, but I couldn't understand them."

After smiling, he looked at her with tender eyes. "That makes perfect sense to me, and it will to you in time." He then turned away to open a backpack he had with him. "It appears your angels are trying to talk to you, but your energy level's too low for you to hear them."

Oh yeah, right, she skeptically thought to herself, but he acted so sure in what he was saying that it made her want to ask more questions. "It was a very beautiful sunrise."

"Yes, it was." Without looking around he unrolled a yoga mat between them.

"What do you mean my energy level's too low?" she asked him, but continued talking before he could answer. "I'll have to say I feel like I'm on a mountaintop, and I have all kind of feelings in me this morning that are incredible."

"Your angel sent you her energy this morning as she tried to help you, but you'll need to learn to create your own." He retrieved several items, including some food he had with him, out of his backpack and placed them on the mat. She suddenly realized how hungry she was as he prepared his spread. He had raw vegetables like cucumbers, carrots, and broccoli, and also some fruits like oranges, plums, and apples. She then watched him retrieve some eggs from a container made to keep them safe. She also noticed how he kept all his food in pouches, like those used by pizza delivery boys to keep food warm.

After he placed the food in front of them, he smiled as if he was preparing to give her a lesson. "To increase your energy, you need to consume foods that give you energy. In food that's alive, there's a life force, and in foods that are dead there exist only elements that need to be returned to the earth, which is why we have bacteria and other agents." After using his hands to illustrate his point, he finished opening his container of eggs. "I think the old saying that you are what you eat really does make sense."

Opening a new pouch, he removed some nuts and handed her several different kinds that were still in their shell. "These are raw nuts. If you plant them, they will grow and make big trees or bushes. When you consume them, think of it as being a very large life force that entered into your system. If you had eaten roasted nuts, you would have entered a dead seed into your system. You would have only invited yourself to self-destruct. Does any of this make sense to you?"

Since she wasn't sure how to respond to his comments, she decided to be as honest as possible, but tried not to say too much. "I'm sure a good diet's always important. Some of my friends are vegetarians."

After smiling, he continued, "It's much more than that. Take this vegetable here. If it can be planted back in the ground and continue to grow, it would have a life force in it. I'm sure even those that will not grow still have the vitamins and nutrients in them that scientists rave about, but they don't have the life force in them any longer. Also, take the fruits, and you'll see another miracle that God has for us. Around these seeds is a precious food that helps the seeds to stay alive and to grow. It's an item that our bodies also recognize and can utilize."

"I can see that you have studied this in depth."

"I've studied the energy in foods all my life. Only recently has mankind finally started to realize that we're more than material beings and that we're truly energy vibrating in the form of matter. I know this is very hard to comprehend, but its information for you to start to think about."

While his ideas were very interesting and she didn't mind this man talking, her interest was more on eating the food he had with him. As she started enjoying the food she continued to listen while she noticed that she did become more alert. In fact, she felt the energy in the food bringing back the mountaintop experience she had earlier when she watched the sun rising and the angels in the clouds.

After she finished the last of the food, she watched him carefully lift the container of eggs from the pad. She didn't see any kind of pan to cook them in and thought to herself that he must have hardboiled them before he hiked up here. "I thought real vegetarians didn't eat eggs."

Looking at her with a curious smile, he opened the egg container and removed the first egg. And with the skill of a surgeon he opened a small knife and created a hole in the top and on the bottom of the egg. Lifting the egg in to the air, he sucked the egg out of the shell with a very content look on his face.

"You eat raw eggs?" This was something she wasn't expecting. "I'm not sure I can do that." She concentrated on her own stomach and what it must be like to eat an egg raw.

"These are from my own hens and very fresh. In fact, they were laid yesterday. Also, I keep them warm."

"I think I'll pass on these," she whispered.

"The reason I eat these is along the same lines of what I explained. What's important to remember is consuming the life force in the egg you eat. There's an animal in the egg. It hasn't grown yet, but by eating it you absorb the life energy in it as well. It's the same reason animals in the wild will not eat prey after it has turned cold. They'll only eat warm meat."

"Wow that's interesting! But . . . just the same, I'll stay with cooked eggs."

Reaching one last time in his bag, he removed a container that appeared to have a liquid in it. "This is raw milk from one of my cows. It's pure, and good for sustaining life also."

"Thanks, I can use a drink. How does it taste?"

"I'm sure you'll like it. However, it's still warm also." After drinking the milk, he picked up the remains of the food and placed them back inside his backpack, looking satisfied with the explanations he had given. With an exquisite eye and true tenderness, he glanced at Jacquelyn. "Now that you have more energy, is it okay if I ask you a question?"

"Sure." While wondering what it was, she stared at her new friend.

"What is it you have come to the mountaintop in search of?"

"I'm looking for true love, and I guess to understand exactly what true love really is."

"I see . . . come back tomorrow, and when your energy's higher. I think we'll be able to have an interesting conversation on love. I'm late today, but I'll make more time tomorrow." He rose and smiled one last time before he turned and hiked down a path.

CHAPTER 14

After looking around her, she surveyed the mountains and the valleys one more time, treasuring the beauty around her. She felt sure there was no place on earth like it. She enjoyed being here at this moment, and in her heart she knew she had made a good decision.

With little left to do, she hiked back down the mountain, making her way over several ridges. She was amazed at how she had ever found her way there the night before. If it hadn't been for the flash of light in front of her which led her, she knew she would have never made it. It did feel strange that she didn't see the man who walked in front of her on the ridge. Perhaps he continued on to an even more beautiful site to see the sunrise.

As she walked around many trails leading back into the mountains, she could see why the old man had told her there were many places to see the sunrises and sunsets. She studied several small cabins scattered along the path in front of her which remained halfway hidden from view. Upon seeing them, she realized that she must have left the national park boundaries.

She saw a small trail break off to her left, which appeared to be a shortcut of some kind. While thinking seriously about taking it, she remembered the words about trespassing on private property and decided it wasn't good to get in trouble, especially on her first day in the mountains. The small, farm-like property beyond the trail intrigued her however. It looked like a place where someone lived who cared for it. Yes, it would be better to go around the long way, she decided.

After she reached the road to Gatlinburg, she walked around with the other tourists into town. Since it was still early, she watched the shop and restaurant owners preparing their places for the morning onslaught of tourists. The restaurants were naturally swinging into full operation since eating breakfast out was a big event in this tourist town.

A young man carried tables out to the front of a restaurant as she walked by. He flashed a big smile at her as if he thought she was waiting in line to get in to eat. "We'll be open shortly."

"That's fine." She smiled, not knowing what to say. "When do you open?"

"Give me fifteen minutes."

"It sounds like you need some more help here."

"Oh yes . . . I had two girls quit a couple of days ago and haven't had time to replace them. We stay very busy this time of year."

While she knew she had never even considered waiting on tables, she realized she needed to make some money for food and lodging until she figured out what to do next. Without thinking about it she asked, "Then you're looking for someone quickly I assume?"

"Well . . . yes, I am. Do you know of someone interested in working?"

"I actually arrived in town yesterday, and I need to work to make some money."

"Have you ever worked in a restaurant before?"

"No, is it that hard to learn?"

"It can be pretty fast paced here, but the tips can be good if you work hard for the tourists and cater to them." For the first time, she watched him take a look at her closely and smile. "Are you planning on moving here permanently? Do you have family here?"

She assumed he was wondering if she was an attractive enough girl to keep his clients happy. She hoped she retained some of her young innocent girl look she used to be so proud of. "No, I don't have any family here. It's just me and a wild passion to live here."

"Look . . . I can't start you today, but I'll give you an application and let you start tomorrow when I have another girl here that can train you. You won't make much in tips until you're out of training, but the minimum wage I pay you will give you some money until you get to where you can work your own tables."

"That sounds good to me."

She followed him into the restaurant and watched several people hurrying around and getting tables set up. While this could be an interesting place to work, she thought, as she tried to imagine the different types of customers coming in to eat, it was work she knew she had never done before, and a far cry from the executive work she was used to doing.

"Hello," a cook said as he smiled and walked by her. In the air, she could already smell the aromas coming from the kitchen. The smell of bacon cooking was intoxicating, since she was still hungry.

"Here we go, this is the application form you'll need to fill out and bring back to me tomorrow morning." After he closed the drawer in a manner to indicate he was busy, she turned and walked out the door.

Once back on the street, she felt a rush of relief in finding a temporary job so fast, and as she reflected on her meeting with the stranger on the mountainside, she realized that her energy level was, in fact, very good. She considered that perhaps her energy did have a lot to do with her being directed to this place. It was amazing how events could work out so well. The world around her started glowing beautifully as the morning passed. She sensed a fresh clean smell in the air, and everyone looked busy and happy up and down the street.

A young couple eventually approached Jacquelyn and handed her a camera while she was resting on a main street bench. "Can you take a photo of us?"

"Sure." While reaching for the camera as she stood, she motioned for them to move closer to each other before she snapped the photo.

"Thank you," the guy said as he retrieved the camera.

"You make a great couple."

"It's our honeymoon, and we want all the photos we can take to remember it by." He turned to give his new wife a sweet but quick kiss.

"Well, you couldn't have picked a better place than Gatlinburg to come to. It's a very romantic place to visit." In fact, it was exactly what she was looking for in life. She wanted a pure love that made everyone happy and would say to the world that they were one—one that proclaimed to all that they had found their soul mate and their one and only true love.

Jacquelyn stayed on the bench for a long time, and from her vantage point, she studied many couples who walked by. While both the young and the old had the look of love in them, it was more obvious in some more than in others. Sadly, in a few cases, she could tell there was nothing there, and that they were only going through the motions of having a good time.

In studying everyone, she started to see images she had never seen before, as an intense glow of colors shifted around some of the couples. This bright glow of colors surrounded those she thought were very much in love with each other. They started with variations of reds and slowly moved to dark blues. Around those with no real love, the colors weren't there, or maybe only around one person.

After making the rounds to all the shops by lunchtime, she couldn't ignore her hunger any longer and decided to order some food inside a grill. She went inside and started to look over the menu. "What's good here?" she asked the girl who came to the counter.

"It depends on what you like, I guess."

Looking like she was in no hurry, Jacquelyn studied the menu and finally decided on an Italian sausage hotdog. After she paid for it, she ventured out to the street to eat it. It tasted good, and she enjoyed it immensely as she continued to watch people walking up and down the street. As she ate, she noticed the colors around the couples fading until she could no longer visualize them.

Since it would be time to watch a sunset in a few hours, she wanted to hurry and find a good spot. She also needed to think about where to spend the night since the little sleep she received the night before wasn't near enough to keep her going for much longer.

The hike up the mountains revealed many different paths and trails, and since she had time to explore some of these side paths, she soon noticed that, to her amazement, many of the cabins were vacant. She ventured close to one in particular, which appeared to be not only abandoned, but isolated, private, and very small, which might be why it was still vacant. Being nosey and after looking around to make sure that no one could see her, she walked around to the back of the cabin. Since she felt safe enough to walk up on the back porch, she saw a large table, but not much else.

If nothing else, she could sleep on the back porch under the table where she would at least not get wet if it rained. After walking over to the door, she twisted the handle, just to see. The doorknob turned with ease. Someone had forgotten to lock it.

After she walked inside, she quickly studied the furnishings. Yes, this could be attractive to a lot of couples. She even thought about how nice it would be to rent something like this place with her true love, if he could ever be found that is. One fact was for sure: the cabin was vacant for now, but how long would it be so? Without hesitation, she quickly walked to several windows and opened the locks on them before she sprinted to the back door and pulled it shut while making sure it remained unlocked also.

Within seconds she reentered the trail, but glanced over her shoulder at the cabin one more time. If she stayed there she would have to be careful. The prospects of her being arrested for trespassing scared her, as she could only imagine the scene now in her mind of a sheriff placing her in handcuffs and carrying her off to jail.

When she saw another couple walking on the path in front of her, she quickly guessed they probably were also recently married. They had that look about them, and of course, an intense glow shinning all around them. After flashing a big smile as she came close to passing them, the guy handed a small digital camera to her and smiled broadly. "Would you mind taking a photo of us?"

"Sure, I'd be glad to." She considered checking into becoming a photographer here. It could be good money, and there certainly was a big demand for pictures.

Taking the photo was interesting and fun as she watched the two of them kiss and hold each other. "Where are you two from?"

"We're from Florida," the woman answered with her husband nodding in agreement. "What about you?"

"I'm from Atlanta." The happiness of the couple started to make her feel better, as she realized that she must be receiving that good energy from them. She wondered if it was wrong, since she felt like it was stealing from them, or something like that.

"We've recently married, and we heard so very much about this place that we had to come here and see it for ourselves. Call it a late honeymoon. It's beautiful here, and we love it." The woman studied Jacquelyn before continuing, "Are you married?"

The question felt like a knife in Jacquelyn's heart as it made her think of her situation and the fact she had never found her true love, but it was an honest question. She glanced down to concentrate before she glanced up and answered, "I was once, but it didn't work out."

"I'm sorry," the woman replied. "Are you walking up to see the sunset this evening?"

"Yes, I've heard there are many places to see the sunset from these hills."

"As long as you stay on the western side of the ridge, I'm sure you'll find many places," the man added. "You're welcome to walk with us if you want."

"Thanks. That would be great, but when we get to the top I'll leave you two love birds alone."

As she hiked along the trail, the terrible memories of her previous marriage flashed across her mind. While it had started great, as most marriages do, it had grown worse and worse, and to the point where it became unbearable all of the time. Yet, she remembered her wedding and how happy she had been. The excitement of the wedding was overpowering in every respect. The gifts they had received from everyone and the attention made her feel so good, but the passion she assumed her husband had for her soon left her feeling ill, as she learned he was more of a sex maniac that just couldn't be satisfied. It didn't matter what she did or agreed to, he always wanted more, and it was all about him, while her own needs went unmet all the time. There were other problems too, such as disagreements about religion, money, and friends.

Later, he had been unable to accept getting a divorce and had made her life terrible from the moment she had suggested it. He always wanted her to return more and more items to him, and it was as if he was hunting for something.

Another item that worried Jacquelyn was that Vincent made money from some unknown sources. While she felt glad to be rid of him, the divorce had been very costly, and had thus ruined her career and her life. Moving in with her mom, at the age of thirty was very hard for her. After her dad died many years ago, her mom had always moved from one boyfriend to another, but she was never able to find the right guy.

With all the problems she had experienced with men, it was surprising, even to her, that she still had hopes of finding true love. Maybe it was all the old romance movies, songs, or romance novels she had read that kept her hopeful. She knew there had to be someone out there for her—there had to be!

After reaching the top of a ridge, she studied several rocks jutting out the edge and providing a great view of the western sky. "It was nice to walk with you two." After waving, she studied the glow around them as they waved back at her.

After she found a comfortable rock, she settled in and studied the mountains around her while time moved slowly on. The clouds scattered all across the horizon were beautiful. As she felt very tired and worried about the days to come and what would happen to her, she reflected on Atlanta and wondered what her mom's boyfriend was doing, and if her mom even knew she was gone. In addition, she wondered if her ex-husband had found out. She didn't want any of them to know where she had moved. While she wanted to put her past behind her, she worried that her mom or her mom's boyfriend might find her if they looked hard enough. She'd have to worry more about it later she decided. She was just too tired at the moment.

The sunset began with its amazing beauty as its colors filled her heart with joy. Since only the hands of God could make an image this beautiful, she looked deeper into the center of the sunset, hoping to discover answers to her problems.

Then she noticed something she had come to expect. In the clouds she saw angels moving around, forming for a second and then suddenly vanishing. While concentrating on the images, she felt drawn through space and away from the mountaintop. As the world around her became a slow moving blur, she felt very light and as if she were walking on the clouds themselves.

As she reached out, wanting to see more clearly, she felt the clouds surrounding her, but she also realized that the angels couldn't see or hear her. She knew without a doubt, however, that they were trying to reach her. She felt like exploding and yelling, "I'm here!"

Thoughts of the morning conversation with the stranger entered her mind suddenly. Perhaps he was right and her energy level wasn't high enough. While she still had doubts about what she had heard, she decided she would concentrate and see if there was any way she could ask for their help. Her efforts to communicate with the angels felt very invigorating, but soon started to drain her.

"Please," she started. "I'm not sure if you're real, or if I really have an angel to watch over me. All I know is that I need help. My life isn't good, but it was angels in the sky like you who forced me to consider this crazy trip. I'm here now looking for a love that I've not yet experienced, but I still believe exists. There's so much I can offer, and somehow, someway, I know that I'll find my true love. Please help me."

Like a slow blowing breeze, she felt a wave of worry and anxieties vanish, leaving her rested and calm. However, she didn't feel energy coming into her as she had that morning. Instead, almost the opposite occurred, as she felt like she was losing energy. The sunset faded and appeared to pull life from all corners of the world into a big abyss, sucking all of mankind and the world into the darkness.

She felt all alone again as the cooling breeze turned colder, alerting her to the oncoming darkness, and the fact that she needed to hurry down the mountain. While smiling as she reached in her purse, she pulled out a small flashlight she had purchased in town earlier. With the skies turning darker she didn't want to be in the shadowy woods at night again.

Becoming more and more tired as she walked, she searched for the side trail to the cabin she had found open earlier. "It'll only be one night," she whispered as she diverted from the trail and in that direction. She saw no lights on anywhere, but with the use of the flashlight she found her way to the rear of the cabin where she immediately entered it. She slowly walked to the bedroom and climbed on the bed carefully, wanting to be sure that she didn't leave any signs of having been there.

Sleep came very quickly for her, and she started to dream. She heard her ex-husband talking on the phone loudly and shouting demands as he often did while she had been married to him. The image of him made her shudder with a fear she had become so accustomed to. "I'll find her!" He cussed and slammed the phone onto its receiver, followed by his fist slamming the table in front of him.

"That bitch, that bitch, that bitch!" He turned, as his haunting grey eyes quickly penetrated her deepest fears.

She was no match for him. She knew that he had always had his way with her earlier, until she finally had enough and moved out in the middle of the day with only what she could carry with her. The ensuing restraining orders never stopped him, since he always found ways to be just outside the law where he always harassed her and made life miserable. She felt like a slave to him, and it appeared that she would be this way forever.

Would he find me here? Surely he'd give up after finding out she had moved away. In her dream she ran and ran until she could run no more. "Please, just leave me alone!" Jacquelyn screamed into the night, until the sounds of her own squeals woke her. Startled, she looked around, not sure where she was. Then, she remembered, but she still quivered as she curled into a tight ball.

Minutes later she ventured to the bathroom and found a cloth which she ran under the water. Since she felt soaking wet with perspiration and hadn't had a full bath since she left her mother's house, she decided a sponge bath would be great as she undressed. Hopefully, the owner would never miss one little washcloth. Being what she considered a nice looking girl at one time, she always kept, well until recently, a good appearance and tried to take good care of her body. Yes, that was until she had problems with Vincent. Her looks had been important to her as she remembered being teased about looking like a high school teenager many times.

After finishing with her quick bath, she crawled back into the bed, but didn't drift off to sleep for a while. This latest dream had her thinking of many possibilities. *Why am I still having nightmares*? *Would they ever go away*? She hated the way Vincent had humiliated her so many times, but she knew she had been responsible to some extent. While she remembered how, in the beginning, it had been fun to play little sex games with him, she never would have dreamed that he would try to turn her into his own sex slave.

She remembered one night in particular, one where Vincent bought her a special gift she had been wanting. The watch looked beautiful, and it was one she had admired for many weeks. In addition, he had made reservations at an expensive restaurant for no reason at all, she thought, except to make her happy. They spent a lot of time there, and they even drank two bottles of champagne. He had gotten her very drunk.

When they returned home, his other side came out. He bought her some nice lingerie, very skimpy, but still expensive and sexy. It was then that he brought out all of the sex toys that he wanted to use on her. She remembered attempting to resist, but she had become very drunk. In the fight that followed, he had kept saying that he would get even with her if she caused problems. The part that made her so mad was that he wanted to photograph her in the nude. It wasn't just nude shots that he wanted, but they were very crude shots of her involved in very explicit acts. The memory of all of this made her shudder and whimper loudly. This was a nightmare she had to free herself from one day soon.

While attempting to calm herself, she relaxed as she enjoyed the cool refreshing night air. She could hear some wildlife in the mountains and thought it might be an owl and some other creature of the night she couldn't identify. The peaceful setting relaxed her for a while and allowed her to drift off to sleep again. She slept for a while until the next dream disturbed her.

Her mom and Shawn were talking in her mother's kitchen. "Why would she leave like that?" her mother asked.

"I love my daughter, and I know she's under a lot of pressure and not doing very well, but I really needed to stay at this meeting." She paused to rub her eyes. "Have the police been able to tell you anything?"

She could see him lying to her mother. He was such an asshole. Why her mother couldn't see it was beyond her. "Don't worry, I'll find her. There're not too many places she can go, and with no money she'll have to call soon."

Jacquelyn could see him going through the clothing and other items she had left there as he looked for clues he could use to find her. Memories of the looks he always gave her made her feel sick. He always tried to sneak a look in her room, or if she ever bent over, he was always watching her intently—not to mention the hugs, which were always too tight and too personal. Yes, he was a total jerk.

Jacquelyn woke again to face the darkness, but she was unable to do anything about it. She had been vulnerable for a long time, and she knew one day she would have to get accustomed to it. It would take some time.

Gradually, she started to float in space, a kind of drifting with her mind as she noticed a slow but steady change to the room. An eerie white glow crept into the room replacing the deep darkness. Even the bed, carpet, and walls started glowing with this pure, white, iridescent radiance. She felt more comfort than she had for a long time. Where was she?

Then, she noticed him, the blond-haired man with the perfect smile that she had met the night before, standing on the other side of the bed. "Do I know you?"

"About as well as you want to," he responded. "You've had a very busy day, and an even more eventful night." His smooth and calming voice made Jacquelyn wonder how he knew so much about her.

"Yes, I had a very long day and nightmares all night, but how did you know?"

"You're a very special woman and need my help, especially if you want to really find the item you so very much want. Finding true love is a very noble goal."

"Yes, that's the one goal that's most important to me, but how can you help me?"

"I'll be your teacher, and you've very much to learn. Controlling your thoughts and your expectations are some of the first items we'll have to work on. Your energy level is also very low, and you will need to increase it, but I think most of all . . . you let your dreams control you instead of you controlling them."

"How do you know that?"

"This is what I do. I'm the one who can offer a link between the physical world and the spiritual world. One day soon, mankind will advance to this level and they will be able to move between the two worlds as easily as I do. Let me ask you some questions, and you'll discover the answers on your own. Is that okay with you?"

"Sure." She concentrated on the most amazing dream she had ever had. It felt almost like dreaming and almost like being awake. In fact, it was hard for her to not believe she wasn't totally awake. She assumed that this man was actually in the room with her.

"When you awoke this morning, you saw a sunrise. Do you remember how you felt watching it?"

"It looked very beautiful." Thinking back to that moment, she even remembered the high she received at that time.

"And was there anything special about the sunrise you noticed?"

"I think you must know about the angels I saw in the clouds. They're amazing! I think I could almost hear them singing. They made me feel good, energized, and eager to

He smiled at her, and she could tell that he was glad she asked questions and was trying to understand. Then he continued asking her about her day. "Did . . . this good feeling last all day?"

Thinking about it, she remembered how she felt exhausted in the afternoon. "After lunch, I didn't feel as good, and many of my problems I'm facing resurfaced."

"What did you have for lunch?"

Nodding her head, she gave a brief smile "An Italian sausage type hotdog." She grinned, knowing what he would think of that.

"The meat was from a dead animal that consumes very bad forces that were also dead. That meat was in a piece of bread that has been baked, which destroys all of the life in it. I'm sure that you haven't considered the life force in your food before now, but perhaps its importance will begin to make sense to you as you learn." After pausing for a minute to study her reaction, he continued, "Your energy's low because of what you ate, and that's unfortunate."

Slowly but surely his message started sinking in. She had to admit it was worth thinking about.

"You said you had problems you're worried about. Your worrying is what we'll have to work on later—much later. It's best to not cause your own undoing. Let us talk about your sunset. How did you enjoy it?"

"It was beautiful, also. I think one of the reasons I wanted to come here is because of the sunsets. For some reason, I think I'll find my true love here. It's interesting since I think I saw angels again in the clouds. They're much different than the angels I saw in the morning."

"They also wanted to communicate with you, but they were unable to hear you. Again . . . it's the same problem. Your energy's simply not high enough. There are four steps to increasing and using your energy. You're learning about the first one. It's up to you to decide how fast you learn."

"When the sun was fading, I felt like all my remaining energy was being drawn out of me. I so wanted to ask for help."

"Yes, it was with a pure heart you asked for help, and the angels are trying to help you. You'll see them in many forms and shapes. Sometimes, you'll only see them as a glow, but always remember that they want to help you."

"I still don't understand why."

"I know, but just remember to control your thoughts and keep your energy up. It is only then that you'll not have dreams controlling your life like you did tonight."

"I had very bad dreams."

"Since your dreams provide you with insight into your future, you need to remember to control your thoughts, and then you can control your dreams. This way you'll make progress in your quest and eventually find what you're searching for."

The prospects of Vincent hunting for her the rest of her life felt very scary for her. Surely, that wouldn't happen. Since she felt petrified that it might, she asked, "Is there anything I can do to change the dreams I received tonight?"

"Since you have much life ahead of you, you need to rest and concentrate on learning. You will have many teachers who will help you in time. I know you want answers, but you must master one step at a time. You'll learn in the proper order. As I said, you have been chosen to advance to the next level, and the entire universe wants to help you." With those words, he stood and walked into a blinding light of whiteness before the room gently shifted into darkness again.

CHAPTER 15

With her eyes open she wondered: Was this a dream or was it real? She really didn't know and she felt too tired to try to figure it out as she drifted off in a deep sleep to rest for several hours. When she began to wake later, she was fully aware that it wouldn't be long until the sunrise so she hurried to get ready.

After moving around in the very dim light, she gathered her stuff together and walked for the door where she stopped to think. Since her suitcase felt heavy and she planned to come back this way from the top of the mountain, she threw her suitcase in a closet and walked out the back door. It would be safe there for a little while.

While hiking up the mountain, she knew she only had an hour to get back to the cliff, where she had been the morning before. As the hills and valleys started to come alive, she quickly passed the last cabin and starting up the mountain. From somewhere she smelled breakfast cooking and knew that it must be from farmer John's cabin, as she named the owner of the cabin situated on her right.

Exhausted and huffing, she struggled to the spot she wanted to watch the sunrise. After looking around she saw no one, but being alone was okay with her since she liked the peace and quiet of the sunrise she started to enjoy more and more. She looked forward to seeing the colors and the excitement of the explosion of new life and energy that would emerge from behind the distant mountain range.

Clouds suddenly floated in a new pattern with colors she hadn't seen before. She realized it wouldn't matter how many sunrises she had seen in her lifetime since they're all different and must be a true gift from God. The images of the night before and her dreams ran wildly through her head and became too much for her to comprehend. For right now, however, she only let herself think of the beauty that unfolded in front of her.

The light of the new day grew as she soon noticed the man from the day before above her. Almost embarrassed at not seeing him upon arriving, she started to move to another spot since there were many spots to choose from.

"You're fine." A smooth voice from behind her broke the silence. "It's remarkable how the light's shining this morning, and it'll not last long."

Looking back at him with a quick smile, she decided to do exactly that. "Have you been here long?"

"No, not long. Here, this is for you." A small bag landed next to her, which contained a mixture of fresh raw vegetables and a small milk container.

"Thanks. I'm hungry, and this is very nice of you. How did you know I would show back up here today?"

"I knew."

The sunrise evolved as she stared hard into it to study the early morning rays making their way across the horizon. Suddenly and almost without notice, she found the images she recognized instantly. Her angel in the sunrise appeared. As her angel smiled and looked directly at her, Jacquelyn felt thrilled at seeing her angel again. Today, she saw no hazy window images like the day before. It felt as if she had a crystal clear picture.

She studied harder and did her best to concentrate on the image standing so peacefully in front of her. As the angel eventually lifted her arms and waved at the scenery around her, Jacquelyn could almost hear her angel's words. While not audible, Jacquelyn knew the angel told her to look around and enjoy.

As Jacquelyn did as requested, the amount of joy the sunrise brought to her soul made her feel human again. She now knew that she had someone who would look after her. It was as if she suddenly had a reason to feel secure and safe in her future. She knew exactly what her angel was telling her. There was beauty everywhere, and Jacquelyn needed to see, feel and enjoy that splendid slice of life. After turning back to thank her angel, however, she noticed that the angel had disappeared, and that the sunrise had now given way to a whole new day, offering many possibilities and opportunities.

She kept reaching into the bag she had been given to munch on the fresh vegetables and fruits. She then found a small jar she removed from the bag, which appeared to have a jam of some kind inside. "What is this?" She asked as she turned around and stood to talk to the man behind her.

"A surprise for you that I think you might like."

Opening it up, she sniffed an aroma she wasn't used to and frowned. "What is it?"

His chuckles shattered the morning quietness. "It's from my own private stock and something I harvested from my own fish."

"What?"

"It's caviar, and I think it's very good. I hope you'll like it as well."

"Wow, caviar's not what I expected, and I'm not sure I've ever tasted any before. What does it taste like?"

"Well, there's only one way to find out. Take the small spoon and try it." He then opened his own jar and spooned some onto a large slice of a cucumber.

With a little apprehension she followed suit. The crisp clean taste of the cucumber with the salty taste of the caviar provided a very unusual combination—one she knew she would never forget. "Not too bad."

"Good, caviar is fish eggs and has a lot of living energy in them. You get the energy of the young unborn fish directly into your system. And . . . I thought you might like this better than the chicken eggs."

"I think I can do better without the thoughts of eating eggs again, but I understand what you're telling me."

"In all of life the energy we absorb keeps us living and growing. We can choose to live forever and consume good food, or we can die early by consuming bad food. It's a simple choice."

While smiling at him, she still had reservations in all that he said. She, however, did start to think about it. "Are you a teacher?"

"Why do you ask?"

"You appear to be extremely intelligent, and last night I received a dream where I would meet many teachers to help me to learn."

"That's very interesting. Yes, I was a professor in California for many years. I taught philosophy."

"I kind of thought so. Perhaps you can help me with a question I've been asked to answer. In my dreams and my life I have a yearning that I've been searching for and I desire very much. It's something I call *true love*. As a professor of philosophy, let me ask you: How would you define true love?"

After smiling broadly, he studied her for several moments. "I think love's an object that men have tried to define for as long as they've been on this planet. Would you like the one-minute version, or do you have the rest of your life to listen?"

"I want to know your opinion."

"Perhaps it would be easier for me to answer a question with several questions. First, is true love simply a special person, or, on the other hand, is it a feeling, an emotion, or perhaps a state of being that you're in when you're with someone special?"

"Well . . . like yes, I think it's the special person, someone that I think you can call a soulmate."

"So, you think love's just the luck of running into the right person then?" His eyes remained very intense and yearning for an honest answer.

"While I think people who fall in love will have many common interests and be made for each other, I think you're telling me that you think I'm missing the point here."

"It's a consideration for you to think about and to discover as you learn the four steps in your quest to find true love. The ability to give love and to receive love can be much more difficult than you can imagine. When you meet the special person you speak of you might not ever know that he was that special person . . . unless you have mastered this ability. You'll be like ships passing in the harbor, never knowing what might have been. It will also be easy to pick the wrong person."

"What are these four steps that you're talking about?"

"That's knowledge you'll learn in due time, but you haven't even mastered the first one yet. You have a very pure heart, but you also have much to learn in controlling your thoughts and your emotions. If you don't learn properly, the power that you'll receive might be very detrimental for you. Since the energy will bring events to you quickly and strongly, it's possible to get events that you really don't want. I was raised in a period of time where mankind was expanding at a very rapid pace, and my generation has been called everything from flower children to free love hippies. We placed no importance on other's opinions and always wanted to experiment on our own and find our own way."

"I have heard about people from California like you mentioned, but my understanding is that most of it was just a lot of craziness."

"If I can leave you one nugget of wisdom for your quest, it would be this: Love's never demanding. Our free love way of living might be strange to many, but to those like me it's important. If I have a love and she's happy, she'll stay. If I'm happy, I'll stay. If either one isn't happy, either is free to leave. We don't believe in marriage and the other commitments society pushes on people."

"I'm not so sure I agree with everything that you're saying. If there's true love, then you want it to last and you want to commit your life to your soulmate. With no commitment, there's no security or comfort. True love to me means forever."

"Then let me ask you one question. How do you do that without being demanding?"

"It's not demanding if it's given freely and naturally. You don't love because you're forced to. You love only because you want to." The energy Jacquelyn felt and her command of the subject was astonishing as she started to listen to her own words. It was as if she was suddenly becoming the teacher.

"I think you're well on your way to finding your answers. You'll learn much and become stronger each day, but be sure to remember to eat well and think of it this way. Even in the wild, animals eat live food and from it gather the energy they need to survive. You see the energy in a mother defending her young. You also see the energy when a male stays with a female and defends her in the wild. The same reasoning's true of us, if we only learn to maintain proper energy and life force within us as well."

"I'll admit that eating properly is very important. Thanks for the food and the conversation. It's late and I have to get to work in town, or I won't be able to even afford vegetables."

"Good luck to you." He smiled as she walked away.

While walking down the trail, she moved quickly and noticed many of the events happening around her as the forest came alive from the night before. Her mind focused on the many problems facing her including her new job and looking for a place to stay. She also had to retrieve her bag before someone entered the cabin and discovered it since getting caught was one experience she didn't want to happen. The prospect of it sent a wave of fear through her again as she walked even faster down the mountain and right past Farmer John's place. While she heard some sounds coming from his place like perhaps someone was chopping wood, she kept moving along the path, hoping she wouldn't be seen.

After looking around the side path to the cabin where she had stayed, she saw no one and quickly walked to the back door and slipped in. Her bag was where she had left it. Feeling tired, she decided to lie down for a brief minute before leaving again. That brief minute turned into a short nap.

Much later, images around her offered only a dull daze as someone shook her. Jacquelyn wasn't ready to wake yet. This couldn't be another bad dream she was having. When she felt another shake, she realized that she wasn't dreaming. Reality set in as she attempted to rise on her elbows.

"Who are you?" A strange man grabbed her arm and forced her to sit still. "What are you doing here?"

"Damn!" she yelled before she screamed. She had been caught red-handed. Her heart raced. How could she explain her presence in the cabin?

"How did you get in here?" he demanded.

"The back door was open. I didn't mean any harm. I didn't hurt anything."

"Are you here by yourself?"

"Yes, it's only me. I can explain."

"I'm sure you'll have plenty of time to do that."

"What do you mean?"

"Breaking and entering, stealing, trespassing are all criminal offenses here."

"I didn't steal anything. There's no one here, and I only wanted to stay for a few minutes. I truly meant no harm."

"If we had someone coming to stay here, you would have scared them to death. My job's to look after my client's properties and make sure people like you don't destroy them."

"I'm really sorry." She started to cry.

"I am too," he replied, pulling a cell phone out of his pocket.

"What, wait, what are you doing?" She studied him as he flipped open his cell phone.

"I think it's best if I simply call the police and let them handle this."

"No, please. I'm really sorry. I'll leave, and you'll never see me again, I promise."

"You're not going anywhere until the police get here."

"Isn't there anything I can do to stop you from calling the police? It will destroy me."

"I guess you should've considered it before you broke in here."

She cried openly now as she faced her worst fear. She was going to jail, and possibly back to Atlanta to her mom and the same hell she left. "Please, let me do something."

"These cabins rent for $150 per night. If you can pay for it, I think it will be fine."

"I don't have that much. I start a job today and I could perhaps pay you very soon."

He smiled. She knew that he knew she didn't have any money. If she did, she wouldn't be here trespassing as a vagrant. "I wish I could help you, but part of my job's protecting the property of my clients."

With all hope vanishing, she thought hard about what to do. There seemed like no way out of the situation. "There has to be some way we can work this out." Her plea conveyed her desperate situation and how vulnerable she was.

Listening to her, he lowered the phone and glanced at her. "You're a very pretty girl, and I hate this for you."

They were both quiet for a moment, and she studied him as if for the first time. He looked slightly older then her and carried a professional appearance. While he wasn't fat, he was slightly overweight, and not an outdoor type guy. His hair looked dark, full, and well trimmed, and he was neatly shaved. Having all of the trademarks of being a nice guy, she wondered why he was being so mean to her. "Please."

"I don't need to get in trouble myself. I'm just doing my job."

Noticing a small weakness in him, she glanced at the ceiling and decided to do what she had never done before. "Please, let me know what I can do. I don't want to go to jail."

She could see the wheels turning in his head. Tempted, but not sure what to do, he continued to examine her. She at least thought she was young and attractive enough to tempt him into giving her a break. He surely had heard of situations like this happening before, but perhaps he never had the deal presented to him.

"I hate to turn you in," he finally muttered slightly loud enough to be heard.

"Then don't. Just let me leave; no one will know." Desperate, she added, "Please, I've never done this before. I'm willing to do anything to not go to jail." To dramatize her point, she softly added, "Anything." As the word left her mouth, she still couldn't believe she said that.

He lowered the phone again and scratched his chin. "You know, you could get me into trouble that way, too."

"No one will know, and I'm certainly not going to tell anyone. I don't want to go to jail."

"What are you actually talking about?" he asked.

"It doesn't appear that I've much choice. I'm at your mercy, am I not?"

"You're asking a lot of me and will put my job at risk, you know?" Looking over at her and apparently thinking that he might get away with having some free sex, he continued, "This will have to be between me and you, and you cannot come back in here again. Is that understood?"

"Yes." While not sure what she had obligated herself for, she did know, however, there was no turning back now.

He walked over to the bedroom door, shut it and smiled as he walked over to the windows to make sure they were locked. The moment stressed the nerves for both of them.

She has been used as a sex toy before. It was as if she knew what was expected of her. The sooner she did what he wanted the better. While she was mad at him for taking advantage of her, she was also glad to not have to worry about going to jail.

She watched him coming closer. He stopped directly in front of where she was sitting on the edge of the bed. With his loose fitting jeans, she can tell that he already was excited with a hard-on. Reaching for his belt, she unbuckled it. With little effort, she opened it, and went to work on the snap and the zipper. He had on boxer shorts. With little effort, she was able to get his dick out of the opening in his boxers.

He placed his hand on the top of her head, massaging it softly. "I'd like for you to take your top off first."

She started to object, but changed her mind and lifted her top over her head. She glanced at him and saw him indicating the bra was next. She reached behind her to undo the snap. It fell down to her waist revealing her breasts.

"They look nice. Not too big or too small." He reached over and touched one of them and used his fingers to pinch it.

As she looked up, she noticed his eyes watching her closely and content on the way the events were going. Her hand softly touched him as she started to stroke him with a smooth rhythm. Increasing the tempo, she hoped she could get out of there before she changed her mind and stopped. A hand job would definitely be much better than sucking on a strange man's dick, but she knew he would be demanding it soon. He pushed closer to her with an excited thrust, and she felt she has no choice but to let her mouth take in his dick.

Honk, honk, honk, the sound of a horn from the front of the cabin suddenly shatters the silence. Someone was in front of the cabin.

"Oh shit!" he yelled as he ran to the window. "I think the owner's here."

CHAPTER 16

While the agent hurried to the front of the house, Jacquelyn grabbed her clothes, suitcase, and purse before she ran out the back door. She found no trail or path behind the cabin, but just open forest for her to run blindly into, which immediately turned into a steep downhill slope. It didn't matter where she was going, as long as it was away from the cabin and as far as she could get away from them.

Stopping once to catch her breath, she surveyed her surroundings, but she could only see an endless forest, and a never ending downhill terrain. With her heart pounding, she glanced directly above her and uttered the words, "Thank you." Her angel was out there somewhere, and saving her from an episode than she knew she would regret later. If only her angel could help her a little more. She wasn't out of trouble yet.

She faintly heard the sound of water cascading down in front of her and knew that following a creek bed would be much easier than running straight through the forest. Moreover, if it led her to a main stream she could find her way back to town.

Two hours later, Jacquelyn was indeed back in town and walking to her new job. She needed this new job, now more than ever. It was so important that she started to worry about it. What would she do if the job didn't work out?

After arriving at the restaurant, she rushed in and hunted for the manager. He was nowhere to be found. Deciding to have a seat, she waited for him for some time, and still no one knew what time he would show up. When finally someone told her that he had gone to the bank, she relaxed and studied the employees as they worked, and kept an eye on her as well.

He soon walked in and started issuing orders, making the place shift into high gear promptly. Jacquelyn waited for a few minutes to give him time to take care of business before approaching him. "Hello." She edged over closer to him.

"Hi," he responded as he turned to her with a serious face. "I didn't have any way to call you, but I had some girls who worked here before come by and want jobs yesterday. They have experience, and I can really use that now. I'm sorry."

Her heart sank to the bottom of her stomach and she felt sick. "I need this job."

"I know. What can I say? At the hotel across the street you might find some work. The manager there's looking for someone I think."

"Thanks." With nothing else to do but leave, she walked out the door. She told herself she knew this job wouldn't work out and wondered why her angel had let her down. This job was important. Then, like a deep voice inside her head talking directly to her she heard words she had not heard in a long time. "When a door shuts, it's for a reason, and other doors can now open."

A feeling of peace settled upon her that felt warm and cozy. Perhaps it was for the best she acknowledged as she walked across the street. She also started thinking of what the Dream Master had told her about the importance of expectations. *Did my fear of losing the job cause this to happen*? The idea started to play havoc with her mind, but nevertheless, and with no other obvious option, she walked towards the door of the hotel office as she whispered. "I need to think positive, and I need to imagine myself getting this job."

After brushing her hair and putting on a big smile, she went inside to see the manager standing behind the counter in front of her. "Hello, my name's Jacquelyn." She walked as close as she could to the counter. "I understand you might have a job opening here."

After looking back at her, he returned a small smile. "We have a small hotel here . . . not a lot of openings."

"I see, but the manager at the restaurant across the street said you needed someone."

"The only person I need is a maid to do some work in the mornings. It's only five or six hours a day, but it is seven days a week."

"Since I have no money or place to stay, this is good for me right now." She knew she couldn't work there long, but it was at least some income.

"I see. If we have any rooms unrented, you can use one at no charge, and . . . if all of them are rented, you can use the cot in the laundry room." His face looked compassionate but stern at the same time.

"I'll take it. When can I get started?"

He smiled. "Okay, let me call my wife in here. She can show you what you need to do and get you going. One other thought: I've a feeling that you'll not stay long, since most employees who take this job don't. Therefore, if you don't mind, I'll pay you in cash under the table. That'll help in keeping my unemployment taxes and paper work down. Is that okay with you?"

"Yes, and like I said, since I have no money, the quicker I can make some the better."

His wife promptly walked in and Jacquelyn started to learn her duties. The time went fast, and she left in the early afternoon to roam around the town some more. It would be late in the evening before she would know if she had a room or not for the night. Of course, she at least had the cot. In addition, she now had somewhere to leave her bag, and she wouldn't have to carry it with her all day.

By walking along the main streets of Gatlinburg, she had much to see. Signs used to attract the visitors flashed outside all the shops. Even in the middle of the day, she noticed many people walking around and shopping. Many small shops had been set up as sales offices for timeshares or condos, and they drew in the tourists by offering specials on the many shows available in nearby Pigeon Forge. After going into many of the tourist traps, she noticed how many of them sold the same items, and that most of them were made in China. And then there were the candy shops. Everyone apparently wanted to take home sweets. Taffy machines set up in the front of the candy shops demonstrated how they made it fresh daily.

After stopping at one counter where they sold fudge, a young guy offered Jacquelyn a small amount of a dark chocolate on a stick. "Try this one. I think you'll like it. If not, let me know which one you'd like to try. All samples are free."

"Thanks, it does look good."

"It is. Let me know which one you'd like next." He turned to look for the next target coming down the street while she decided. The chocolate-flavored fudge tasted very good, but Jacquelyn knew she needed to watch her money and indulge herself later after she earned some more.

She soon passed in front of a small jewelry shop and noticed a guy who she assumed was the owner. He was in his late thirties and wore very nice clothes, indicating that his shop must be very successful. As soon as he saw her looking in his direction, he flashed a large smile. It was one of those million dollar smiles, with big white teeth and dark chocolate-brown eyes radiating such seductive warmth she felt her heart melting immediately.

Jacquelyn raised her hand to give a quick wave and smiled back at him. *Wow, he looked good!* While she wanted to go in and talk to him, she quickly decided not to because she hadn't changed clothes in days, and her hair was such a mess. Since now wasn't a good time to meet him, she decided to keep walking, but . . . she would definitely remember this shop.

When it started getting late, she decided to hunt for another place to see the next sunset. With so many hilltops around, she decided to head in a direction directly above the center of town toward the mountains. After roaming for an hour and a half she finally found a location she could reach before the sunset faded.

She ran into many people along the way and all of them were looking for a special place to watch the sunset. The place she selected looked quiet, very nice, and open, which allowed her to have a great view. After all that had happened to her that day, she looked forward to the sunset.

As if floating on air, a woman with a small bag walked to the edge of the cliff and stood there surveying the area. After smiling at Jacquelyn, she dropped her bag beside her. The woman looked Asian, and was very fluid in every move she made. "How are you? This looks like the best place here."

"I'm fine," Jacquelyn replied. "Yes, I think we'll enjoy a very good sunset from here."

From the bottom of the bag, the Asian woman retrieved a large candleholder containing a candle with many wicks emerging from it, before she pulled out a glass container to place around the candle. After carefully lighting all of the wicks, the woman placed the candle on a rock beside her. She then opened a large bottle of water and poured it into the container. "There. Very soon, we'll have hot water for tea." She glanced around while maintaining her air of mystery. "Would you like to share some tea with me?"

Tea did sound good to Jacquelyn. After surviving all day on the fresh vegetables and fruit given to her that morning, she was very hungry and thirsty. "Have you been here before?" Jacquelyn finally asked.

"No, this is my first time here, but I think I'll return here again tomorrow."

"My name's Jacquelyn. What's your name?"

"I'm Kayo. It's good to meet you, and thank you for sharing this space with me."

"You're welcome. You know I couldn't help but notice how graceful you are."

After she closed her eyes for a second, Kayo reached back into her bag, retrieved two mats, and handed one to Jacquelyn. "I've studied movements since I started walking. Have you ever tried yoga before?"

"No I haven't, but I've heard about it, and I've seen a little about it on TV. Is that how you became so graceful?"

"I think I can safely say that yoga has been a major part of my life. If you're interested, there's much you can learn about being graceful both outside the body and inside. If you wish, I can show you how to get started. How much you advance will depend on you and your wants."

Jacquelyn accepted the mat and unrolled it beside Kayo. Feeling self-conscious but willing, she waited on Kayo to show her what to do. "I had some friends that were into yoga at one time, but I never joined them."

"Let us relax and enjoy the beauty of the light as it delights our souls." Kayo pointed toward the horizon as she waited for Jacquelyn onto step on her mat. Kayo was barefoot, and her posture looked so straight and graceful.

Jacquelyn tried as best she could to follow Kayo's lead. Noticing she still had her shoes on, she stepped off the mat and removed them, acknowledging that it must be the proper way to exercise. Jacquelyn felt slightly embarrassed. "Please let me know if I do anything else wrong."

After smiling at Jacquelyn, Kayo turned toward the sunset. "First, we'll relax the head. Rotate your head in a big circle. You must feel the tension going out of your body." For the next thirty minutes, Kayo went through various basic movements, and took time to explain her actions as she shifted from one to another.

Jacquelyn felt much better as she followed Kayo's instructions. Life was going to be good. Yes, life was indeed looking up. Jacquelyn watched Kayo's movements, trying hard to memorize them. "You're very good."

"The movements come with practice, and it's the best way to learn how to build your energy field."

Due to the words of the Dream Master, Jacquelyn studied her with a new curiosity. "You must be a teacher also."

She simply smiled in response to the question. "Yes, I can see you've eaten well all day today. Your energy isn't bad. The first level of energy is from materials that vibrate with life energy in them, a knowledge I think you're learning."

"I'm slowly getting the picture."

"Good, how energy flows will become easier and easier for you to understand. The next level of energy is from the universe around you. It's in the beauty of this sunset, the sounds of music, the smell of a flower, and many of the other simple pleasures that exist all around you."

"So, I'm to draw energy from the world around me?"

"No, that's an assumption many people make. The truth's a little different, and it's a little harder to explain. I think I can best demonstrate it this way." She reached into the side of her bag and found two crystal teacups. They looked both simple yet elegant. After handing one of them to Jacquelyn, she kept the other and remained quiet for a minute to give Jacquelyn time to clear her mind.

"They're beautiful," Jacquelyn said as she studied the designs etched into the side of them.

"Yes they are. I want you to listen to what happens to the cup after you tap it with your fingernail." With a quick snap of her finger, Kayo's fingernail struck the side of the crystal cup, making it ring as it vibrated.

"That has a beautiful tone to it." Jacquelyn smiled as she listened.

"Furthermore, just as the cup vibrates and is beautiful, all the forces in the universe vibrate in their own way. Now, let's try one more time. This time after I tap the cup, I want you to hold your cup close to mine."

"Okay."

After Kayo taped her cup and it started to ring loudly, she swiftly brought the two glasses closer to each other. Jacquelyn almost dropped her cup when they became within inches of each other, and her cup started to vibrate and sound the same as Kayo's cup. "It's a simple principal known in science. The frequency of the first cup is picked up by the second cup when the two frequencies are close to identical."

Since this was very interesting, she would have to remember what she learned, and tell someone else about it later since it would be impressive knowledge to pass on. "Wow," she finally uttered, not knowing the exact word to say.

"Now, I want you to look at the beauty of the surroundings around you again. Think of them as one of the cups that was ringing, and you as the second cup you have in your hand."

Why not give it a try, Jacquelyn thought, as she looked toward the mountain ranges, where the sunset started building colors which radiated beautifully across the sky. With the cool breeze carrying hints of the fresh clean forest aromas, and the sound of a stream below them playing a melody surpassing any symphony she could remember, it would be hard to imagine this place as being anything other than beautiful.

Kayo spoke softly, as if not to disturb the tranquility. "Now, I want you to concentrate on all the objects around you, but think of them as energy that's vibrating in its own special way. When you feel them vibrating, let me know." After making this request, she left Jacquelyn alone and closed her eyes to concentrate on her own.

Jacquelyn looked at the newly forming sunset, trying more and more to see it as an energy form, but it was too beautiful. She did feel happy inside and revitalized, but as far as vibrating—she wasn't sure exactly what that would feel like, so she simply stood there and acted as if she was concentrating.

Kayo opened her eyes and glanced at Jacquelyn. "It's not easy, I know." Kayo slowly rotated her head and stared at one side of the sunset to the other. Amazingly, the whole sky came alive with exploding colors of red and orange. The previous days were not close to as vivid as this sunset kept getting brighter and richer in color.

"Oh . . . my god!" Jacquelyn exclaimed in total astonishment as she forced herself to breathe. She saw a glow next to her that was also becoming increasingly brighter. With this distracting her attention, she turned to see where it came from. It was Kayo. While she had a strange red orb of light surrounding her, Jacquelyn couldn't help but question if it was really Kayo, or was it the reflection of the red sunset. All Jacquelyn really knew for sure was that it was awesome.

After returning her attention to the sunset, another surprise was waiting patiently for her—her angel. While standing still and studying her angel, Jacquelyn thought she saw the angel smiling. Since in the red sunset it appeared as if the angel had a red party dress on, Jacquelyn wanted to ask if they were going to a party. In fact, there were so many questions she could have asked at this time, but with all that was happening to her today, she only managed to say, "Thanks."

While holding onto images of her angel for as long as she could, Jacquelyn watched the last of the rays disappear. Only then, did her thoughts return to her new friend, but Kayo had totally disappeared. The only objects left were the two crystal teacups, filled with a great smelling tea.

CHAPTER 17

After finishing her tea, Jacquelyn suddenly noticed Kayo beside her again. "Where did you go?"

"I've been here beside you, but you couldn't see me. Some levels of energy vibrate much too intensely for you to see unless you possess the same range of energy. I see you like the tea."

"Yes, it's very good. I noticed you glowing as the sunset became so very intense tonight. It's unlike any experience I've ever had before."

"I have a thought for you to think about until tomorrow. Every day the sunset's much the same. Someone will think it's beautiful, and someone else will hardly even notice it. Do you think the spirits of the sunset, so to speak, offer different colors to different people?"

"I don't know."

"I see. Well . . . here's another question to consider: Could it be that different people are like different tea cups? Some are in tune with each other, and others are not. In other words, if you want to receive the energy around you, you have to be in tune with it. The rays of light from the sun casting colors across the sky aren't the items that are beautiful. What's beautiful is your ability to recognize it. You have a lot to learn on your second step, and even on the first one, you have just started. Concentrate and learn; it's the only way."

"I've enjoyed talking to you tonight, but I need to get to the hotel to see if I have a place to stay or not."

"I understand. Remember to have good dreams tonight."

With nothing else to say, Jacquelyn nodded, and hiked down the mountain with her flashlight in her hand. It would be so nice to have a bed to sleep in tonight. That vision kept her moving faster and faster toward downtown Gatlinburg.

Within no time at all, she entered the hotel and walked toward the desk. Since no one was there, she decided to ring the small bell and wait. Within a minute he appeared behind a side door. "Hi, I'm back."

"Hello, I see." With most of the keys still on the wall behind him, and with only a few cars in the lot, she assumed that they must have many vacant rooms. "My wife thinks you can be a hard worker and likes you. Take this room tonight. Remember to clean it early in the morning and have it ready by ten."

"Thank you." She accepted the key and hurried for the room. On the way she almost forgot about her bag and turned around to go to the laundry room. It was exactly where she had left it. Excitement began to overtake her, since she was going to get a real bath and some good sleep tonight.

All the rooms looked alike, and this one wasn't an exception. She sat on the bed and bounced a time or two before turning on the TV and flipping channels. Since nothing was interesting for her, exploring the bathroom became her next big thrill, even if it looked small and presented nothing fancy. With a quick turn of the handles the water came shooting out of the shower head. The steam from the rush of water indicated that it was hot.

Stripping off all her clothes and jumping in the shower felt invigorating. Wow, she never knew how good a shower could feel until she hadn't had one for a while. After searching around the bathroom, she found a package of shampoo and started working on her hair, which was oily and needed washing badly. Finding a bar of soap, the next item was to get rid of all the grime and sweat she had accumulated in her walks up and down the mountain. She knew she had to take good care of herself, or her young and fresh looks wouldn't last much longer. She thought back to her days as an executive where she enjoyed the attention she had received, and hoped one day to have the ability to pamper her body again. One day, she thought, yes one day.

After drying off, she opened her suitcase to see what kind of clothes she had with her. There wasn't very much. Deciding on a dress pair of jeans, a pullover, and a few more items, she started to pull together the first of some working outfits. To get a better job, she knew, however, that she would have to have some new clothes. Lucky for her, there was a large discount mall not far from the hotel. She would have to visit it as soon as she had some extra money.

With the evening still early, she decided to walk down the streets of Gatlinburg for a few minutes and watch the tourist trade still milling around. After finding her way to the center of town, she managed to find a seat on the street where she could watch people. With so many couples walking about, she had no doubt many of them had traveled there to celebrate their honeymoons. It felt exciting to watch for a while since they all appeared to be so happy, but as she kept watching, the realization of how she didn't have anyone started to bother her. She suddenly felt all alone in Gatlinburg.

She stood and walked down the street some more. As the smell of fresh pizza floated out of a shop she passed, it hit her like a sledgehammer. Vegetables and fruits were good, but give her a pizza any time. She was almost through the door when she noticed him. The guy from the jewelry shop was in a chair at the counter eating. Later, not now, she thought as she turned to leave.

She had walked almost a block before her heart slowed down. Why was this guy having such an effect on her? Yes, he looked hot, but perhaps it wasn't meant to be. There were so many parts of her life she needed to get straight first, and she knew it. After making the rounds up and down the street, she headed back toward the hotel while thinking of all the problems in her life, the energy from earlier dissipating with each step.

Back in her room, she crawled on the bed, still concentrating on all the wrongs in her life. Why me, she thought. After slipping off her clothes, she pulled the covers back and snuggled inside. With her dreams from the last several nights occupying her thoughts, she wondered if tonight would be any different. The more she concentrated on it, the harder it was for her to go to sleep. She felt so tired, but still had a hard time drifting off to sleep.

Within a few hours of twisting and turning, she finally managed to sleep, only to find herself in a room with her mother and Shawn. "Why did you do this?" her mother asked. "Is this the way you repay me for all I did for you?"

"I had to leave," Jacquelyn started screaming back and crying deeply. "You don't understand. I had to go." From the corner of her eye, she could see Shawn watching her. Almost like daring her to say a word. It was as if he knew her mother would believe his story first. He hadn't done anything wrong that she could prove. Her mother was so blind for not being able to see him for what he was.

Jacquelyn had to get out of there. She pushed the door open and rushed out. She ran and ran until she was totally out of breath, and her heart felt like it would explode any minute. Gasping loudly, she sat up in the bed, but even then, she was still breathing hard. She knew that she had just had another nightmare, and wondered if the nightmares would ever stop. Since it had become such a part of her life she had to get a handle on it; she had to, no matter what.

While sitting up straighter, she started to think about the images of the angels in the clouds which had produced such a calm feeling. Could such an event be true? Was there really such a creation as a guardian angel? The question kept going through her head and made it impossible for her to go to sleep, yet her weary body made it hard to stay awake. She finally drifted into a world somewhere in between.

Suddenly the walls started to glow a soft, pure white and the air became fresh and clean. Her body relaxed as the tension in her body dissipated, and it was as if she was receiving a very good massage. She even noticed the texture of the sheets changing to a pure silk-like material. She couldn't tell if she was dreaming, or if what she was experiencing was, in fact, real. She simply could not understand.

While looking around trying to understand what was going on, she noticed him walking into the room. It appeared almost as if this guy with the blond hair and the fantastic smile walked through vapor and out of nothing. "How are you?"

"I'm very tired." Jacquelyn heard her voice sounding weaker than normal. He appeared to be real, but at the same time he looked too perfect in all his details. Everyone has some faults here and there.

"It's good to see that you're learning about the various energy levels, but you still have so much to learn. To be honest, the whole universe is here to help you."

"Really? I was almost arrested this morning for trespassing."

"Yes, but you learned to call on your angel that's there for you and always comes when you're in danger. Sometimes, at the energy level you are at now, only when you have a lot of fear or deep emotions in you, do you have the ability to communicate with the angels, as you call them. Your power of expectation is stronger than you think also. Your expectation of being caught has a lot to do with it coming true. You'll need to control your negative thoughts."

"That's much easier said than done. With bad things always happening, how am I supposed to think of anything else?"

"It's a skill you'll learn. Just like you'll eventually learn to control your dreams rather than have them control you. You've much to learn tomorrow as well. For the rest of the night, simply sleep. Think of only resting, concentrating and watching the sunrise and the sunset. All will be good with you the rest of the night."

CHAPTER 18

A blasting horn from a car going down the street woke her. What time was it? A quick glance at her watch indicated it was almost five in the morning. While it would feel so good to go back to sleep, she felt the top of the mountain compelling her to see another sunrise. After Jacquelyn quickly cleaned the room and had it ready for new occupants, she stashed her suitcase again in the laundry room before she headed out.

While the air felt cool, she saw almost no traffic on the street. Before heading up the mountain, she stopped at the local quick mart and purchased a few items. What she ended up with was fresh fruits and a bottle of water. She smiled, realizing the lessons were getting through to her.

Climbing the mountains got easier and easier for her, and she soon reached the top of a ridge facing eastward. While she enjoyed the delicious taste of the apple as she walked along the pathway, she knew that this day was going to be excellent.

When the light started to glow, casting low hues across the sky, she looked around her but she saw no one else as an isolated lonely feeling crept over her. There had always been someone in the mornings to talk to and learn from. She concentrated on the knowledge she had learned and tried to make sense of all of the events going on in her life.

As the sun started to make its appearance, the colors were all there, but in a solid glow with no defined texture or interesting designs to consider. Perhaps the meaning was simple—today would be a normal day. She walked back to town admiring the beauty of nature around her as she hiked.

The work proceeded without incident, and soon she had cleaned all the rooms. Walking into the office, the manager gave her a big smile. "What do you think so far?"

"Not too bad."

"Here, let me give you this. I've a feeling that you're broke, and this money might help some." With that, he opened the cash drawer and pulled out one hundred dollars in small bills. "This is a small advance until the end of the week when I will pay you. I hope it helps some."

"Thanks, I'm . . . kind of low on money, and this will definitely help." While a hundred dollars was a lot to her at this moment, she remembered when a hundred was only pocket change to be spent any way she wanted.

After walking out of the hotel, she wandered the streets and went in and out of shops just looking around. She would soon take a trolley to Pigeon Forge and see if she could perhaps find a better job. She had all afternoon, and it would be good to do some exploring. The fruits she had purchased that morning were almost gone, and a good solid meal would be great.

Going from shop to shop, she didn't notice which shop she had entered until she realized that she was standing in the middle of a jewelry shop. The quality of pieces in this shop looked very good. The layout of the store appeared very professional, and offered an appearance of containing very expensive items, the kind of places she remembered going to in the past. However, she mused, that was out of the question for now.

Looking up above the counter, her eyes met his. *Oh my gosh.* She wasn't ready to meet him yet. It was the same man she saw the day before when she walked by the store.

"Can I help you, miss?" His deep masculine voice also projected a smooth professional image.

"No, I'm . . . I'm just looking." She searched for words to say. "You have very nice jewelry in here. I'm very much impressed with the quality."

"Thanks. I try to carry some nice items." His manner remained patient and kind, and he didn't make her feel uneasy at all.

"When I get some money, I'll have to come back and look more seriously." Sometimes truth was the best policy. She felt drawn to him, but still couldn't decide exactly why. Maybe it was his fantastic smile, or the way he appeared so open. In any case, he charmed her in a very interesting way, and not like any previous guy ever had.

"I hope to see you again soon, then. My name's Tadd, by the way."

"That's a good name. I'm Jacquelyn and it's nice to meet you." Wanting to continue the conversation, but also not knowing what else to say, she turned slowly toward the door and started walking.

Before she could reach the door he was in front of her holding it open. "I do hope you come by again before you go home."

"I'm moving here and I'm sure you'll see me again."

"Wow, that's good news." His words made Jacquelyn smile as she walked out the door and offered him a small wave as she walked down the street.

She had met someone, finally, and the feeling felt great. Now, with a little luck, she would be on the trolley and heading for Pigeon Forge in a few minutes. Getting a better job was important to her.

After a few hours of walking on the side of the road in Pigeon Forge, she had stopped in several places, asked for applications, and talked to several people, but didn't find any promising job prospects. She knew she had just started, and it would only be a matter of time before she would find a better job to help her get established again. She could then look for a real job like the one she had been fired from. Above it all, she still considered the future to look bright and promising.

With little time left, she caught a trolley and headed toward Gatlinburg. Then, she saw a man on the street, walking and looking in all directions. She knew in an instant that it was her mom's boyfriend. *How did he find me here so quickly*? Her heart felt like it was sinking as she panicked, and sank down in the seat. Was her mom here also?

She didn't know what would happen when she saw him again, since he was known to have a temper, and he could be very violent like her ex-husband. Oh yes, she could hear it from her Mom now as to how he was only there to try to find her and bring her back home. Why could her mom not see the evil inside Shawn and how he always tried to touch her, not to mention the comments he made to her. To Jacquelyn, he was the perfect example of just another sexual predator out to get her.

The panic of the moment kept her mind scrambling for answers as she tried to figure out what it was about him that made him so determined to have her. While she had questions about Shawn that just didn't add up, the trolley quickly picked up speed, and she began to inhale and breathe regularly again. *What am I to do now*? One fact was for sure; she couldn't go back to Pigeon Forge, or venture on the streets for a while.

As soon as she reached Gatlinburg, she hiked straight up the mountain, since she wanted to get somewhere she could remain hidden for a while. The walk felt good for her as she enjoyed the peaceful and calming sounds of the forest. After finding a place on the ridge, she glanced around and saw no one which made her feel lonely again, but secure in a funny way. The sky contained many heavy clouds and became cloudier as she watched. Maybe it would rain tonight. She saw no angels or beautiful sunset, and of course, no teachers to help her continue her lessons. All she had were her memories about what had happened during the day. While she had met a great guy, Tadd, whom she had thought about all day as she walked around, she had also seen Shawn looking for her, a problem which scared the hell out of her.

After realizing there would be no colors in the sky tonight, she left and hiked back to town with the thought of getting wet not very comforting. While she hoped to be safe inside the hotel soon, she quickly studied the look on the manager's face as she walked in the entrance to the motel. "We only have two rooms left, and it's still early yet. It'll be a while before I can tell you where you can sleep tonight." With a concerning look, he pointed to the key rack.

"I understand." She smiled as she prepared to turn and walk out. "I'll be back later."

"Okay."

That was great, but since she really didn't want to be on the streets tonight, she had to think of somewhere to hide for a while. While constantly on the lookout, she went from store to store as they started to close. After walking by a pizza bar, she smelled the aroma, and it was all she could do to avoid going in. She felt hungry as she told herself she would be okay.

Within a few feet of the door, she heard a voice yelling from behind her. "Jacquelyn, wait up."

Her heart felt like it would explode. She had been found. She felt too tired to run and turned around. "Oh shit."

As she watched Tadd suddenly stop, she knew her facial expressions must have given away her fears as he looked up at her with a questioning look. "Sorry, I didn't mean to scare you."

"No, you're fine. I imagined for a minute that you were someone else." She replaced her scowl with a forced smile, reflecting a little bit of her embarrassment and hoping that he wouldn't ask too many questions.

"I . . . see." He acted confused. "Are you with someone else tonight?"

"No, it's a long story." She breathed deeply. "It's good to see you."

"I'm eating some pizza. Would you like to join me? It's my one bad habit, and one I do too often. I guess everyone has their faults."

"I don't know, I . . . ."

"Come on, it's really pretty good, and I have much more than I need."

While trying to decide if she should play hard to get or go ahead and join him, she realized she didn't have many options right then. "Okay, but only for a little while."

Once inside the restaurant he quickly moved another chair to the bar where he was eating. "This one is Italian sausage and cheese. If you don't like it, I can order you a different kind."

"Don't be silly . . . this pizza looks great. This is an interesting place." In reality it wasn't much of a place, just a hole in the wall that was located very strategically along the sidewalk to catch the tourist trade.

"I would offer you a beer, but this is Gatlinburg and many of the places don't have a license to sell alcoholic beverages. It keeps the family tourists coming and the wild party goers out of town."

"Yes, I know about this place. It's okay. Coke will be fine."

"So, tell me about you." His smile intensified as he leaned closer, and acted as if he truly wanted to hear what she was going to say.

"Well . . . I don't know where to start." Besides, that was the truth, since she has no idea what she should tell him about herself. She had just met him. "Tell me about you first."

"Okay, that's fair, I guess. I run a jewelry shop, as you already know. My father started it and turned it over to me before he died. I'm thirty-nine years old and have never married. My family traveled most of my early life, and I was kind of an army brat. When my father returned to the mountains here, I stayed with my mother and attended school in India. After living with my mom for a while, I came back home to Gatlinburg to see the mountains, and I fell in love with them. My father was ill, and he wanted me to take over at the jewelry shop he had started here. That was eight years ago, and I'm still here and plan on staying for a very long time." His story sounded like music to Jacquelyn's ears, and it felt as if she was hearing herself talk about the mountains.

While she could feel the common interest between them growing, he caught his breath and indicated that it was her turn. "Well, I'm thirty and divorced. I've always loved the mountains, and I decided if I'm ever going to make a move, this would be the perfect time." That wasn't too much and not too little—perfect.

"It's a great place to live and perhaps the most beautiful place on earth." She watched his face glow as he talked.

"You said that you came back home. Did you live here before then?"

"My father was born here on the Cherokee reservation and I'm one-half Cherokee. My father died a few years ago.

I'm so glad we had some time to spend together, and do some things like build the cabin I live in now."

"Interesting, I think I can see that in your dark hair."

"Yes, so let me ask you a question."

"Sure."

"What kind of work do you do? Do you have a job here yet?"

Her head suddenly hung low since she hated to answer his question. Rather than admit she was cleaning rooms she decided to sidestep his question. "Not yet, I'm looking."

"I see. What kind of work did you do before?"

"I was a sales manager in the telecommunications business."

"Well . . . I'm sure a good job will turn up for you here. There're many businesses around."

"I think so too."

When the place started shutting down and management turned off several of the lights, they hurried to finish the last of the pizza as he mentioned, "My place is only a few blocks from here, and I do have some wine there if you're interested in telling me more about you."

"I'm not sure." She wanted to go. It was hard to believe that he was asking her to his place. "I need to get going."

"I really am a nice guy, and I can take you home whenever you're ready."

His smile became so intoxicating she felt helpless in refusing his invitation any further. "Okay, but only for a minute."

CHAPTER 19

As they walked out the door and headed up the hill toward a line of condos overlooking the city she realized that must be where he lived. She felt him slip his hand under her arm tenderly and very naturally as he helped her across the street. His extremely good manners made her feel very comfortable with him.

They walked by several condos and kept hiking up the mountain, making many turns and twists along the way. It opened onto a part of the mountains she hadn't seen, but she knew it wasn't too far from where she went to see the sunrises every morning and the sunsets every evening. He reached over and squeezed her hand. "We're almost there."

"Good." She felt her hand in his and had almost forgotten how good holding hands could actually feel.

She eventually saw an outline of a building or cabin of some kind with a few outdoor lights on down a long driveway. Looking harder, she managed to make out some of the details of what looked like a log cabin, but a good sized one.

"This is it." He pointed toward the cabin.

"It looks great. Do you live here all alone?"

"Yes, someday I'll meet that special person, but who knows when." He walked toward the door, pulled out his keys, and opened the lock. After the door opened, he waited for her to go inside first.

The splendor of the amber color wood glowed brightly, adding to the warmth of the room. For a bachelor, he was a very good housekeeper. "This is very nice," she said as she continued to study the decorations around her.

"Thanks, I built most of it myself. Would you like to have a full tour?"

"This is so awesome, and I know you're proud of it." She glanced around again. "Sure, I'd love to look around some."

"Help yourself. I think you'll like the wine cellar over there. You can pick any one you want." He pointed to a small door exiting to the side of the dining room.

"Wine cellar, you must be joking. Let me see what you have." Her voice heightened as she started to laugh. This was getting to be fun. The door opened with ease, and the room shocked her at what she saw. The large cellar must have contained a thousand bottles of wine all neatly arranged in the wine pegs holding each one. She knew a little about wine, like many people, but learning more was going to be interesting.

While she strolled up and down the cellar and studied the labels of so many choices, a totally black bottle with a gold seal quickly caught her attention. After removing it from the rack, she noticed that it was a pinot noir from California. This would do, she thought, as she walked toward the kitchen.

Tadd smiled as he accepted the bottle. "Let's see what you like. Yes, that's a good choice with lots of flavors and very smooth. I think we'll enjoy this bottle very much."

Jacquelyn felt happy she made a good choice. Well, at least he made her think that she had anyway. "Wow, you have a lot of wine in there."

"It's a hobby of mine. There're not many places to buy wine here, and I've found that a bottle of wine makes an excellent present for some of my clients."

"Okay, I'm impressed."

After taking her hand, he led her around the rest of the house. "Let me show my piece of heaven, and then you can tell me what you think."

In the great room the ceiling reached about twenty feet tall, and the walls were constructed with logs that looked very beautiful as they glowed under the lights shining on them. The fireplace stretched all of the way to the ceiling. "The rocks making up the fireplace were all collected close to here, and I had an old friend of mine help me build it. I would say we had over ten bottles of wine while we were building it." A deep chuckle emerged from deep within him as he obviously concentrated on the memory. She could also see that he felt very proud of his work. Moreover, he should be since he did a fantastic job.

"You did this yourself? If so, wow! You did a very good job." She also noticed how the furniture in the room looked extremely well coordinated, creating a rustic but comfortable setting. The style stayed very much in keeping with the settings of the Smoky Mountains.

Looking toward an adjoining room, Jacquelyn saw an office she could tell he used very much. Tadd walked into the office in front of her. "This is where I do my real work." Perhaps this was his excuse for not keeping it as neat as the rest of the house.

He then showed her two guest bedrooms, which he had decorated in much the same manner as the great room. As he approached the last door at the end of a hallway, he stopped, and hesitated, as he bit his lower lip. "This is my bedroom. I think you'll find it a little different."

Not sure exactly what to expect, she slowly opened the door. It did look very different. In contrast to the rustic feeling in the rest of the house, this room presented more of a modern style, completed in an all-white design. Jacquelyn, without giving him her verbal opinion, acknowledged it looked different.

"Yes, I wanted my bedroom to be a place where I could relax and escape the look in the rest of the house. Call me an old romantic, but I hoped one day I would be glad I did it this way." It became obvious that he was waiting for her to say how she felt, and that he was hoping for approval.

"It's very beautiful, but it has to be hard to keep clean."

"Well, I only go there to sleep and rest. It doesn't get very dirty. The clean, white setting can be very peaceful."

Off to the side she saw the large master bath constructed of very intricate looking Italian marble. It had an old-fashioned French tub with clawed feet, as well as a super large shower. The beveled mirrors looked unique, and an expensive white coral lighting fixture finished off the decor, making the room extremely beautiful.

"I know you're proud of your work, and you should be."

With her approval, Tadd looked happy. He held her hand again, pulling her out of the room and toward the kitchen. "Let me see about opening that bottle of wine now."

"That sounds good to me."

It became very clear he did well for himself. After removing the cork, he reached above his head and retrieved two wine glasses. "You know the weather is nice. Would you like to go outside, or would you rather stay in here to listen to some music?"

While thinking about the choices, she glanced around at the amazing interior and decided it would be great to stay right here. "What kind of music do you like?" she asked as she looked around to see where he kept his music collection, but saw no indication as to where it might be.

As he watched her looking around he smiled and pulled a computer keyboard out from under the desk in the kitchen.

"I have all my music on my computer. What kind do you like?"

"All different kinds of music are interesting to me." Since she wanted to hear what he liked before she continued, she smiled at him and waited for a response.

"This is one of my favorites." He entered several keystrokes and the music came alive from around the room. It sounded soft and smooth, and obviously a song she felt sure she had heard before, but at the same time, she would never be able to name the tune.

"That sounds good." The incredible sensitive sound system brought delicate sounds to life without being overpowering. "You have very good taste in music."

"Thanks, but feel free to select any music you want to listen to." With a broad smile and a steady hand, he poured the shimmering, dark red wine into two glasses. He picked up her glass and handed it to her.

"What should we drink to?" she asked as she held her glass and waited for him to pick up his.

While leaning over, obviously in deep concentration, he stared at her as he examined her face. It was as if he truly looked at her for the first time. "I guess . . . we could drink to friendship or to happiness, but that would be like many other toasts out there." Slowly, he kept studying her, almost as if he tried to memorize her entire face one inch at a time.

"I agree that a first toast should be different." The stares she was receiving from Tadd intrigued her. What was going on behind his piercing eyes that grew darker with each glance? "What are you looking at?" she finally managed to ask with a small giggle in her voice that she could no longer suppress.

"Sorry, I'm just noticing your features. You're extremely cute."

She managed to keep her laugh soft and sweet. "You know most guys say that after they've had a lot of wine, not before."

"I very often say exactly what's on my mind. Okay, now back to the toast, perhaps we should toast to—"

"To true love!" She offered almost without thinking. "I've been through a very bad divorce, and I know many people think they know what love is. I thought I did at one time also, but I was so wrong. Yet . . . I still believe in it."

After touching his glass to hers with a soft ring, they completed the toast. When the wine glasses produced this distinct sound, she remembered what she learned on the mountain about two tea cups and smiled at the memory. He raised his glass to his lips and sampled a small sip. She liked his big lips and chiseled chin giving him a very masculine look. His face was also very smooth. She remembered reading how many native Indians never had to shave.

"Tell me more about you. What kind of sports do you like to do?" Jacquelyn quickly found herself wanting to know more about Tadd. He was becoming very intriguing.

"Have a seat, and I'll tell you my life story." He offered a big smile. "It should only take about fifteen minutes or so." He held onto his *million dollar smile* as he walked around the room.

For the next hour, they talk about events that had happened to them during their lives. The openness and frankness felt kind of strange to her, and the wine soon disappeared. "Let me have your glass. I think I have another drink you'll enjoy even more." With that he walked to the other side of the room and picked up a pair of brandy glasses and a canister she assumed contained brandy.

Setting it on the coffee table in front of them, he walked back over, retrieved two more glasses, and walked to the kitchen. He slowly allowed the tap water to get hot and almost filled the two glasses with the hot water. These he placed on the table in front of her. After taking the top off of the brandy canister, he poured two drinks, tilted the glasses slightly on their side, and placed them on top of the glasses with the hot water in them.

"I think you'll like this. This is a way to warm the brandy and make it more aromatic." He moved over to the couch and settled in next to her before he placed his arm on the back of the couch behind her.

She sensed his arm on top of her shoulder, where it felt so good to have the presence of a man around her. She didn't realize how much she had missed the physical touching she had gotten used to when she was married before, and of course, that was back when she was first married. "It's good to have a night like this. I'm really enjoying your company," she told him as she turned to look at him.

The pleasure of those words returned a pleasant smile from Tadd. After retrieving the brandy glasses, he carefully handed her one and then lifted his own as he slowly enclosed the glass with his hands to keep it warm while she followed suit. At the same time, both leaned over to smell the brandy with its very intoxicating aroma. Tadd lifted his glass in the air. "I think we should toast again to the quest for true love and the happiness it brings."

Their glasses touched and then they both enjoyed a sip of the brandy. It tasted very strong, burning, but good at the same time. Jacquelyn closed her eyes for a moment to relax. She knew the brandy would get to her fast, especially after the wine, but at this moment she didn't care.

As she stretched her head backwards she could sense Tadd studying her as she rested against the back of the couch. With her throat arched and vulnerable she glanced down at Tadd, who she assumed was considering kissing her softly at that moment. She watched him studying the details of her face and hoped he liked what he saw. Being a petite girl, she knew she had a small head, high cheekbones, hopefully a cute nose, and lips that were neither too big nor too small. At that moment, they had to feel moist and fragrant with the smell of the expensive brandy on them.

Tadd leaned over and kissed the top of her forehead. She didn't even move, but remained still and quiet since she felt very comfortable. Tadd asked as he continued to study her neck and collar bones. "How is the brandy?"

"Very good, thank you," she whispered as she breathed in his scent and closed her eyes before she had another sip. When she opened them again his eyes pressed inches away, gazing fully into her own. It felt as if a moment of time had frozen, and the two of them had become totally focused only on each other. With a slight smile, Jacquelyn leaned back into the couch to become even more comfortable. Even with her eyes closed, she felt Tadd looking over at her intently and how his own heart rate was increasing quickly. She could imagine her breasts, still somewhat soft yet firm, under her blouse catching his attention. She always hoped her waist would stay so small, especially with the small amount of exercise she did to stay in such shape.

He raised his glass to have another sip and she watched him glancing upward as if in deep concentration. Jacquelyn raised her glass as well. She kept hoping he liked what he saw in her. Jacquelyn certainly liked the way he looked and smelled. Really, in fact, she liked everything about him so far.

Wanting to get more comfortable, Jacquelyn slipped one shoe to the floor. "Here let me help you." Tadd offered as he helped her remove the other one. With a curious glance Jacquelyn allowed him to lift her foot on his lap where he started to massage the bottom.

"Wow! That feels good." Jacquelyn's feet hurt from all of the hiking she had been doing. She wasn't in as good a shape as she needed to be.

"Just relax. Here, let me help you lean back a little bit."

Jacquelyn settled in with her back on the couch and her head resting on a pillow at the end as her body melted into the soft and very comfortable couch pillows. While massaging her feet, Tadd kept studying her. Even her feet were dainty. Without apparently thinking, Tadd moved his hand up her leg to massage the calf muscles. It felt good and she stretched, enjoying the treatment. "Thank you," she whispered.

Even with her eyes closed, she noticed the light being turned out. The brandy had slowly drained her resistance, and she knew it, but . . . for the moment, she really didn't care as she felt Tadd sliding in beside her on the couch.

She appreciated the light kisses on her hair and then on her forehead. With the strong presence of him next to her arousing her, she knew she should put an end to this, but she had no will power right now to resist. She thought it would be good to cuddle for a few minutes, but then she knew she would have to leave. After all, she had just met Tadd.

A soft finger inched under her chin, lifting it slightly. His lips slowly touch her lips with soft kisses. Once, twice, three times, and the kisses became stronger each time, until they rested fully on her mouth. Jacquelyn felt the warmth and tenderness of each kiss. His tongue pressed against her lips and licked them softly at first. With a passion building inside her, she felt his relentless teasing as his tongue wickedly started exploring every part of her lips.

With a second of hesitation, she felt him again pressing his tongue at her, and she opened her mouth and allowed him inside. Venturing inside, he explored every part of her mouth as his lips pressed hard against her lips. Her heart raced as she touched his tongue with her own.

After moving his lips from her, he reached over to kiss her neck before he uttered a small groan. She could only reply by saying, "You're a good kisser."

His hand slipped around her back and pulled her closer to him. With his presence feeling better and better by the minute, the full pressure of him next to her felt very powerful. When his hand slipped lower and soon rested on her rear, alarms went off in her head. He had moved too fast. "No, please don't."

While his hand moved back up her torso, he managed to work his hand under her blouse in the back and now touched her bare skin. This wasn't as bad, so she didn't say a word. It was then, that she noticed that her own hand was rubbing his chest, as his muscular body played havoc with her emotions.

His mouth returned to her lips again, and he became much more passionate than even the time before. His hand moved up under her blouse and now was firmly in place over her bra and feeling of her nipples through it. She grabbed his hand slightly as if to say no, but didn't pull hard. What was she doing?

In a second, she felt fully conscious of what he had on his mind, and in another, she felt like she was dreaming. Partly because of the wine and partly due to the fact that she wanted to be loved, she felt confused and not sure which way she planned to act from moment to moment. She felt him release her breast and move his hand down. Good, she thought as her breathing returned to normal for a second until she noticed his hand kept moving lower.

"Please!" She managed to mutter as she followed it with a groan. His hand found the top of her pants, and he worked several fingers under the waist band. Her heart almost exploded, but she knew she needed to stop him. She prepared to scream for him to stop when he managed to reach all of the way down and advance to her pubic hair line where he started to explore around with his fingers. Was it too late to stop now? She liked him, and he liked her. She couldn't get her head to clear.

Removing his hand, he slowly placed it under her chin again and arched her neck back to kiss her deeply again. Part of her felt relieved he had removed his hand, and part of her wished he would play with her more.

Taking her hand to his lips, he kissed it like a gallant knight. Then, slowly, he lowered her hand to his waist. "I'm not going to make you do anything you don't want to do, okay?"

"Okay," she managed to whisper as she felt him slowly move her hand lower until it rested on top of his penis. It felt very hard and large. She tensed at first in touching it, but he didn't pressure her any further. It was as if he wanted her to know that he was excited, as if she couldn't guess that already.

Letting her hand go, he cupped her face and again enjoyed the pleasures of her mouth. His lips felt firm and persuasive as he worked the magic of his tongue repeatedly on her. He pulled her closer to him again and began to suck on the side of her neck, just enough to build up the sensation of devouring her again. After his hand slipped down and went under her bra this time, his cupping and massaging immediately excited her nipples. She knew she wasn't exceedingly large, but she hoped a perfect shape and in good proportion to the rest of her body.

"You feel so good," he whispered in a soft whisper. His fingers gently played with her nipples, as they grew harder. Then, he moved his tongue down to her breasts, and she felt his wild tongue playing havoc with them.

"Oh my God," she whispered as she started to enjoy him more and more. It was definitely too late to turn back now. While trying to make a decision to make love with him or not, she reached over and wrapped her fingers around the bulging penis in his pants. It felt good to her, and she heard him moan instantly as she massaged it.

His hand went down to her pants again, and he unsnapped the top button and pulled the zipper down in seconds. She had on a small set of panties with almost no material to them at all. Without any hesitation, his hand found its way down through her hair line again, as he quickly ventured lower. As he massaged her clitoris, she started to moan even louder. His finger entered her and opened her up as she breathed harder and harder. She became very wet.

"We have to stop." She managed to force herself to say with her mind and body torn in two different directions. How could anything feeling so good be wrong? Having sex with someone she just met was an experience she had never had before. She didn't consider herself a one-night stand or a free piece of ass.

"Don't worry. I'll be gentle. I promise." The words sounded very tender and sincere, but still Jacquelyn fought the urge as hard as she could.

"I have to stop. I mean it. You do feel so very good, but this is too soon." Grabbing his hand, she pulled it up and out of her pants. At first he resisted, but then gave in, realizing she was serious. *Yes, I know I'm confused with my own emotions and desires, and this has to be driving this guy crazy also.*

She knew his hormones were in overdrive. In addition, like her, he had a lot to drink, with the brandy having its effect on him as well. She could tell he was trying to think of what to do next. While noticing the moment of weakness in him, she sat up quickly and moved over to the edge of the couch where she snapped and zipped her pants in a flash. "I'm sorry if I disappointed you tonight."

Sitting up, he glanced at her. "Don't worry about it. We both had a lot to drink." He leaned over slowly and kissed the top of her head. After finding her hand, he raised it to his lips and kissed it one more time.

"I really need to be going. It's late." The prospects of walking back down the mountain weren't very appealing to her, but she knew she had to.

"It's too late to go anywhere, you can stay here. Boy scouts honor . . . I'll not bother you, and I'll let you sleep. I have an extra bed as you know."

"Are you sure I can trust you?" She glanced at him with foggy eyes and really wanted to believe him if she could.

"Yes, let me show you to the room." After standing up, he reached over and squeezed her hand. She managed to stagger as they made it to the bedroom. He pulled back the sheets and made her lie down. Falling back in the bed was the last memory she had as she drifted off to sleep.

CHAPTER 20

In a deep sleep Jacquelyn started dreaming the kind of dreams she had been enduring for a long time. While the current problems in her life were not like the hopes she had for herself in the future, the details in her dreams appeared so real and it was why they frightened her.

This dream started out good as she sat in her office, where she reflected on the accomplishments she had achieved. Obtaining an office in the executive section of a telemarketing company at the age of only thirty had been remarkable and the result of a lot of dedicated work on her part.

While she worked there, her phone rang. She answered, "Hello, this is Jacquelyn."

"Hello, bitch." She heard her ex-husband on the other end of the line. "I called you all night. You can't keep ignoring me."

"Vincent, you have to leave me alone. I'm working, and I have a lot to do." She disconnected the phone and started shaking. Would it ever end?

The phone rang again. Her nerves made her shake, as she let it ring again, and again. Finally, she picked up her phone as he shouted into it, "Don't hang up on me again, do you hear me? You have property belonging to me, and I want it!" She hung up again.

The dream went on and on, and every time she tried to make the phone go away, it kept ringing. People from all around her office watched and whispered comments about her until she finally ran out of the office. She had nowhere specific to go to, but just ran and ran. When she stopped, she could hear a phone ringing somewhere near her. It might have been a payphone, a phone on the wall, or on a counter somewhere, but she always heard a phone continuing to ring.

When she thought the ringing had stopped, she could see Vincent in the crowd somewhere. He was always there and always stalking her. He would be there one minute and gone the next. She couldn't get away from him. There was just no way. She felt herself running again and again.

Suddenly she saw her mother's house in the distance and she quickly ran inside. Surely this could be a safe harbor. Like a blessing from above the phone didn't ring there. She collapsed on the sofa, crying relentlessly. Life's not supposed to be like this.

However, when one nightmare ended a new one began. She remembered being back in her mother's house, and trying to hide. As she shifted in her bed, she felt eyes staring at her from somewhere. It was her mother's boyfriend. "Shawn, what are you doing here?"

"I'm just here to be a friend." His grin contained wicked sinister implications.

"Where's my mom?"

"She's still working. It's just you and me here, honey." He stared at her again, adding another creepy smile before darting his eyes around to study her body. "We need to get to know each other better, honey."

"I don't think so."

"You know if you don't start acting right, I can make life very hard for you here." Thinking he had convinced her, he tried to put his arm around her, but she bolted away from him.

"Stay away from me, or I'll tell my mom."

"Tell her. It's your word against mine. You know I've been watching you walk around here for a while in your skimpy little nightgowns. Sooner or later you'll come around."

"I would rather die first. You're a real jerk," she yelled, but got nowhere with him. Shawn kept staring at her as the thoughts of running and hiding crossed her mind again. After making it to a door she opened it and entered another room where the light blinded her. With no other options, she rushed into the light as the door shut behind her.

Her breathing slowly returned to normal, and the feelings of panic disappeared. She felt as if she had walked onto a cloud where all she could see was white. She enjoyed the soft comfort of the space around her. With her surroundings looking so pure white, she recognized it as a place where she had been several times lately.

As her mind cleared while she glanced around, she saw the blond-haired man she had seen before smiling at her. "I knew I would see you here."

"I'm always here. This is where I live."

"But where is this place?"

"This place is nowhere and everywhere. It's totally up to you to decide where it is."

"Am I in a dream?"

"Partially, that's correct."

"Okay, then am I awake and thinking about my dream?"

"That's also partially true. I'm the gateway between the life of the physical and the life of the spiritual."

"I'm confused."

"In your physical form, all you can sense is what is physically there in front of you. You can see it, feel it, hear it, and smell it, but that's all, and it has to be in the one dimension that you're in."

"Okay."

Smiling at her, he continued, "In your dreams, you can float around to all dimensions, both in the past and the future, and sense your surroundings by a pure energy exchange with all other energy sources. You can create and destroy whatever you want. This world's much more powerful than the physical world, and to a large degree controls it."

"This is too hard to comprehend. What exactly are you trying to tell me?"

"You have a need to love and be loved that's very strong. While the process of deciding which person to help advance is a hard one, you have been chosen to learn."

"Chosen?"

"When you first looked upon a sunset and placed your prayer for a way to find true love, you demonstrated the desire to move into a world that makes that possible. I'm here to help you to do that. And . . . to tell the truth we have followed you for many previous lives."

"Kind of like a guardian angel."

"I'm not an angel, but only the one that can help you understand your dreams and how to use them in your world."

"So, I think you must be like a Dream Master then."

"I think that name will do as good as any right now. There are enlightened ones here that you call angels, and they would love to help you, but you need to get your energy up much higher to be able to communicate with them and receive their help. There are four steps in the process. First you must take care of your physical body by eating properly and giving it the energy that it needs. And . . . we're not talking about physical energy, but a life energy that comes from absorbing the life in the food you eat."

"Yes, I think I understand that a little."

"Then . . . you need to get in touch with the universe around you. This force brings beauty to the world. To resonate with this energy, you'll become one with it and know that material objects aren't beautiful on their own, but beautiful because you perceive them as beautiful."

"Again, I understand a little."

The smile faded as a stern look pressed closer to her. "You'll have to study these two steps and become very observant. These steps are only the first two steps you need to accomplish. The third step will require much from you as you learn to create your own energy. In the process, you will also need to learn how to control your dreams as well."

"Control my dreams? You can't control dreams—that's impossible!"

"You can have your dreams control you, or you can control your dreams. It's a simple choice really. In either case, your dreams will control your life. As I said, your dreams in this world are much more powerful than the physical limitations you have while you're awake. As in tonight's dream, you fled Atlanta, but the fears you experienced there are still controlling your life here. Moreover . . . if you don't control it, it'll become your reality here as well."

"I hate these nightmares. I'll do whatever it takes to make them go away."

"It's up to you to control them. And . . . to do that, you must learn how to build up the energy within you. You'll need to get your rest as the entire universe really wants you to be successful and wants to give you what your heart desires."

That was the last memory she had as all turned dark and quiet. She slept a long time before she woke. As she became alert she heard noises from outside the house bringing in the new morning. After slowly opening her eyes, she glanced around to see a room she had never been in before. Then, it all came back to her, as she remembered the wine and the brandy.

"What a night." Gathering up the covers around her, she leaned forward, rested on her elbows, but saw no one—not from the nightmares, or from the strange dream with the Dream Master. She thought how she would sure have a lot to tell her therapist if she ever got to see one again.

Removing the covers, she glanced down; her blouse and pants were gone. What did she do last night? Thinking hard, she couldn't remember. Also, where was Tadd? Spotting her clothes at the end of the bed, she quickly climbed into them and began to walk around as all remained quiet in the house.

After opening the door, she walked toward Tadd's bedroom where the door stood open and she could see Tadd sleeping in his bed. Jacquelyn hurried to the other bedroom and looked for whatever else she might have brought with her as she heard the alarm clock in Tadd's room going off. With a move of pure nerves, she hurried to the back of the bedroom and waited. After the clock stopped beeping, she heard some movement in Tadd's room until she finally heard the sound of the shower running.

Good, this would be her chance to get out of there. After leaving the bedroom toward the kitchen door she stopped when a phone began to ring. "Not now."

The phone rang several times before the answering machine picked up. Since Tadd didn't hear it, luck appeared to be on her side at last. Then she heard the message being left by the caller. "Hey, this is Shannon . . . . I just called to thank you for the beautiful bracelet. I guess I just missed you. If I don't hear from you today, I'll come by and see you tonight. Bye."

Rolling her eyes, she opened the door and started running down the mountain toward the center of town. How could she have been so stupid?

CHAPTER 21

She realized that it was much later than she had originally thought as she made her way down the mountain as memories of the night before drifted through her mind. He had acted nice and polite and was someone who she thought might be good for her. She reflected on the many mistakes in her life, and much like the one she had nearly made again last. She didn't have time to make any more like it.

After walking into the hotel lobby, she saw the manager already at work. He looked up to see her coming in. "How are you? I didn't see you return last night."

"I didn't come back last night. I . . . found somewhere to stay."

"That's good. We were full, but many of the guests are leaving today so we should have many rooms open tonight. We should also be able to finish early today."

"That'll be good since I've some errands I'd like to do later." With those words, she walked toward the laundry room to get ready for work.

After she finished her work, she walked toward downtown where she wanted to get away for a while. As she studied the tram descending down from the top of Ski Mountain, the tram shifted to a soft white unmistakable radiance she had seen before. By looking around at others watching the tram, Jacquelyn could tell no one else noticed it but her. The glow looked both pure and beautiful, and one she could not deny seeing before. She hurried in the direction of the tram center and once there she obtained her ticket in time to get on the tram as it worked its way back up the mountain. The view looked awesome from up so high.

"The mountains are beautiful, aren't they?" Even without turning around, Jacquelyn recognized the voice as her yoga master, the Japanese woman she met on the mountain side earlier.

"Yes, it's beautiful," Jacquelyn replied as she turned around to see Kayo gracefully standing by a window. "For some reason, I thought I was summoned to get on this ride. Did you see the glow around it?"

While smiling at her in a calm and soothing manner, Kayo continued, "You still have much to learn." Her gaze ventured outside the window again. "When you see the mountains, what is it you feel?"

"I think the same feelings many people have. It's as if it's larger than life itself, and that makes me happy. Something draws me to them."

"That's good. I want to show you something after we get to the top, but there's some more walking that we'll need to do first. Have you eaten today?"

"No, I haven't had time to eat yet."

"I didn't think so. You don't have many good colors around you. Here, I think you'll find some food in this bag you might like."

Jacquelyn opened the bag and saw a full variety of fresh raw vegetables and fruits. "Thanks. I think I'm starting to like eating this type of food." Being broke, she also appreciated a free meal. After looking away from the food and toward Kayo, she had to ask some more questions. "You said my color's not good. What did you mean? Do I look sick to you?"

"Well, not sick, but it's also not full of good energy either. We'll see if we can change that in a few minutes."

The tram made its way to the top, where Jacquelyn and Kayo exited and walked toward a small trail. The walk was easy, but had many twists and turns as it climbed even higher up the mountain. Around one turn, Jacquelyn saw many flowers growing along the path. Kayo stopped and leaned over to observe one. "Take a closer look and tell me what you think."

Jacquelyn kneeled to obtain a closer look. "It's a beautiful flower."

"Yes, I think it can be said that it's beautiful. Now look at it again, and this time I really want you to concentrate on it deeply and pay full attention to all the unique and beautiful details of this one specific flower."

As Jacquelyn did as she was told, she noticed that every petal looked perfect and without any defects. The bright and vivid colors glowed and even the smell was fresh, clean, and fragrant. "Yes, it's very beautiful. I think it's one of god's gifts to us."

"Do you remember the two teacups we used the other day?"

"Yes, I do remember them. Why do you ask?"

"I now want you to do this for me. Think of the small flower as a teacup and think of yourself as a teacup. The energy in this small flower's much more powerful than I think you understand. When you see the beauty in this flower, I want you to also be aware of the feelings in you. The beauty around you is like the love in you. The more beauty you perceive, the more love energy you'll have. In addition, you'll see that the more love you have in you, the more beautiful objects are around you."

Jacquelyn started concentrating on the flower in front of her again, and how beautiful it looked and made her feel inside. She began thinking of love in a pure state with no demands or hidden agendas. The flower became even more beautiful as she studied it while she also felt a warm fuzzy feeling growing inside her.

After taking her hand and pulling her up, Kayo then pointed to all of the flowers around her. "All of these are the same, but we have concentrated on only this one."

"Yes, there're many here."

"I have a question for you to think about as we walk. Does the flower have beauty in it that makes you happy and full of love, or is it the love in you which makes the flower beautiful? In other words, which teacup causes the other one to vibrate in harmony?"

The question intrigued her. In the forest above Ski Mountain the scenery looked beautiful. As she surveyed the area, she examined all of them in a new light as they appeared no longer as simple trees and objects, but points of inspiration which made her think of the beauty around her and a love deep within her for all of the stimulation around her.

Every time she stopped to look at a new object, the feeling of love in her grew stronger. It became a feeling stronger than the one she remembered having on the mountaintop while watching the sunrises and sunsets. The love felt like a warm burning rush of passion and energy which gave strength and vitality, making her so at peace with all around her.

As she took in what she learned, she remembered the time she met Kayo. Her thoughts returned to how much more beautiful the sunrise became after Kayo concentrated on it. Feeling perplexed, she turned to Kayo. "Can I ask you a question?"

"Sure, what is it you want to know?"

"The other day at the sunrise, I noticed you were in deep concentration when the sunrise exploded with colors like I've never seen before. Why was that?"

With a very broad smile, Kayo explained. "I was in deep appreciation of the sunrise and returning my love to it. In doing so, the sunrise passes that love on to someone else that's looking at it. Perhaps that's why so many people love to watch them. You'll learn much more about this in your fourth step, but for now, learn to be one with nature and how to vibrate with it."

Jacquelyn had so many questions. As she turned around to ask another one before returning to the ski area, she discovered that Kayo had disappeared. Just as if she had vanished in the wind, Kayo was nowhere to be seen.

Happy nonetheless, she hiked back toward the tram where she saw him. Tadd was walking toward the tram. After ducking behind some other people, she waited and watched him as he walked along. He was constantly looking around and she had no doubt he was looking for someone, and Jacquelyn knew for sure it must be her.

She had mixed feelings, since she knew in a way she could grow to like him, but she didn't want to get hurt again. How could she have been so stupid and get off to such a bad start with him? Moreover, if he lied about a girlfriend, she had no place for him at all.

She waited until she felt sure Tadd had gone and had enough time to leave the tram station below also. She had to stop thinking about him because of so many other problems she needed to take care of now.

After making it through the station, she walked down the street and noticed a sign with a shimmering white light illuminating it. It glowed much like she had seen several times the last few days. Taking this as a sign, she stopped, pulled the flyer down and studied it. It was for a tai chi class being offered for free. Learning tai chi could be very interesting.

She felt hungry and started to stop in a small restaurant when she had second thoughts. She wanted to stick to a healthy diet, but the food smelled so good that she decided that it wouldn't hurt to eat one meal there. She entered the restaurant and found a seat.

"Would you like some coffee?" A small perky acing girl quickly stood in front of her wanting to take her order.

"Yes please, coffee sounds good to me."

"Would you like to see a menu?"

"All I want is a cheeseburger and some fries."

"No problem, I'll get it going for you. It'll only be a few minutes." With this she placed a cup in front of her and poured some coffee. "If there's anything else I can do for you, please let me know."

While waiting for her to get the order, Jacquelyn reached into her pocket and retrieved the bulletin on the tai chi meeting she had placed there. She had heard of this ancient Chinese form of exercise, but didn't know much about it. The meeting was to be held at the visitor center down the road. Jacquelyn would have to see if she could make it. It was being held late in the afternoon the next day, which should be a good time for her to attend.

"Here you go, I hope you like it." The small girl with the ponytail smiled as she placed the plate in front of her. "Do you need some more coffee?"

"Yes, please. It's very good and exactly what I needed." After receiving food Jacquelyn recognized, she devoured the cheeseburger and fries in minutes. Living on vegetables was good, but it didn't take care of the craving that she had for the foods she was accustomed to eating.

As she finished her last bite, she glanced over her shoulder and noticed someone peeping in the window of the restaurant. At first, it was curiosity that attracted her attention, but then a deep fear started to set in. Could it be someone looking for her? Not willing to chance it, she ducked back in her seat and turned her head from the window. She didn't get a good look, and at first she thought that it might be Tadd still looking for her.

Taking a deep breath, she lowered her head and rushed for the restroom. She started shaking and didn't want to confront him now. Before she reached the turn heading down the hall, she glanced over her shoulder. The face she saw coming through the front door sent a new wave terror surging through her body—it belonged to the man she used to be married to. It appeared Vincent did get out of jail as she feared, and now he was coming after her again. But how did he know she had fled here?

CHAPTER 22

It felt like forever as she waited in the restroom. She wasn't sure if Vincent had seen her or not, but she wanted to make sure he left before she came out. *What is he doing here? How did he know where I am?*

After taking a full breath of air, she slowly opened the door and peeked around it. No one was in sight. Walking slightly out of the bathroom, she could see her table was vacant and her dishes had been cleared.

"There you are. I thought you'd skipped out on me." The waitress rushed to her.

"No, I have a stomach ache. How much do I owe you?"

"One minute, and I'll get your bill."

As she walked off Jacquelyn had a little more time to survey the area. She saw no sign of her ex-husband anywhere. When she received the bill, she paid it quickly and eased out into the street. *Now, what do I do?*

It became obvious she couldn't stay downtown long, so she walked out of town toward the mountains and the ridges she had come to know well the last few days. As she hiked the trail, she realized that she wasn't too far from where Tadd lived.

As she approached the ridge, she noticed a person on the edge of the ledge in a perfect pose, and glancing over the scenery. She knew in an instant it was Kayo as she hurried over to her. "Hi, I lost you a while ago. Where did you go?"

"I had other chores to do, and I could tell you had tasks to attend to on your own. When I left you a while ago your color looked good, and now it's bad again."

Almost ashamed of her day, she admitted to her last meal. "I had a cheeseburger today."

"I can tell, but I know there's much more to it than that."

"I spotted Vincent, my ex-husband who is here looking for me. The thought of him being in Gatlinburg is like a nightmare."

"Sometimes your dreams come from past events, and sometimes they tell the future. It all depends on how you control your dreams."

"How does one control a dream?"

"It's much easier than you think. The power of prayer and anticipation originate from your thoughts. The universe is here to give you what you want. If you think of bad events, you get bad events. If you have good thoughts, that's what you get. If you think you'll have nightmares, you will, but if you think that you'll have beautiful dreams and the freedom to explore the universe, you'll have that instead."

Not feeling like she received a straight answer, she decided to change the subject. "How did you learn to be so graceful?"

Kayo Smiled at Jacquelyn with an elegant look that represented more than style, almost like a statement of fact. "I've studied yoga since I began walking. It's a discipline that you have to learn and study. You can either have your body control you, or you can control your body."

"I wish I could be as poised as you are."

After reaching into her bag, she removed the two yoga mats. "The basics are not hard, but to get good at yoga you'll have to practice for a long time. The main thing to remember is that you're doing what you can, and your practice is about you and no one else."

Kayo directed Jacquelyn through the various poses she needed to know. The bending and stretching quickly became hard for her, even though she thought she had stayed in fairly good shape. Holding the poses required much more strength than she had ever realized before. While she knew yoga would be good strength training for her, she also found out standing on one leg was a lot harder than she could have imagined.

An hour later, she could do no more and with slow poses to relax her muscles, she soon felt much better. The whole time she followed the instructions, the one item Kayo insisted on is that she focus the most on breathing. Almost every other sentence from Kayo stressed the importance of breathing. "Inhale through your nose, now exhale through your mouth."

She knew the session was almost over as Kayo told her to start tightening up every muscle. From her toes all of the way to her chin, she squeezed every muscle as hard as she could for a long time, as instructed, before letting it all go. As she did, she felt a rush of relief, producing an incredible awakening. "That feels good. I really feel the difference in my muscles."

"To be in tune with nature and the whole universe, you must also have your mind and body in shape. If you really want to find your dream, you have to be ready for it when you find it. You'll see what I mean when you work on the fourth step. Enjoy the sunset. I have to go for now." She packed the yoga mats and hiked down the trail, leaving her all alone.

Realizing the sun would set shortly, she decided to stay and watch it, since she had so many thoughts going around in her head now. Both Shawn and Vincent were in town looking for her, and now there was this local guy also looking for her as well. Perhaps it would be better if she left town and found somewhere else to live.

While noticing the sun setting, her thoughts of leaving, however, quickly vanished. The sunsets from this point were always so beautiful with new sets of colors and patterns emerging each time. She could never resist watching the colors ignite across the sky in burst of pinks and reds.

The ideas she had heard earlier from Kayo echoed back in her head as she looked deeply into the sunset. "You are beautiful," she whispered as she filled her heart with inspiration. She felt herself glowing with an extremely warm sensation as the sunset turned richer and more colorful. She decided that if this was what being in harmony with the universe felt like, she loved it.

Without even trying to find her, Jacquelyn's angel or enlightened one as her Dream Master implied, appeared in front of her. The angel covered much of the sky and looked at her patiently, waiting for her to speak. The angel's presence looked that obvious today.

Jacquelyn spoke to her angel as she leaned forward. "I've made many mistakes in my life, I'll admit. I hope there's only some way I can make up for them and get people from my past to leave me alone so that I can start my life over again, but perhaps it's too much to ask. Maybe I don't deserve it. I still believe in love, and to be specific, I still believe in true love and I know that special person's out there for me somewhere. If you can help me, I would greatly appreciate it." She wasn't sure anyone would hear the words, but it made her feel better to whisper them.

She watched her angel in the clouds slowly disappear, almost as if in a whisper, as the sun retreated behind the mountains. While her heart remained happy and light, she knew that it would be dark soon, and she needed to get off of the mountain. She hoped she had a place to sleep tonight.

While walking down the mountain, she realized she knew its paths by heart now, especially the wide trail. The shortcut she always avoided. She noticed some movement today in the field behind Farmer John's house. It would be interesting to one day sneak down and take a closer look at it, but she didn't know all the trails and this one had to be close to the ridge where Tadd lived. She would hate to get lost and end up at his place.

After walking into the hotel lobby, she saw the manager. With a big smile on his face, he turned around and tossed her a key. "We have many rooms open tonight. How have you been today?"

"I've been fine, and just doing a lot of walking. I really appreciate the use of a room tonight."

"No problem. We're glad to have you helping us out."

She retrieved her suitcase and hurried for her room, knowing that a good shower would be perfect right now. As soon as she entered the door, she went to the bathroom and turned on the shower to allow the water to heat. Turning to the mirror, she almost screamed seeing how bad she looked in her clothes. She would have to stay up, do some washing, and dry her clothes using an iron to press them.

She walked under the shower and within minutes felt fantastic. The warmth of the water was so exhilarating. At least for the moment, all was good and she could relax.

Moments later, she heard a loud knock, knock, knock above the sound of the shower. Surely, it must be her imagination. No one knew she was there! Her eyes closed briefly and then opened in a panic. After jumping out of the shower, she grabbed a towel and rushed for the door, since she couldn't remember if she had pulled the chain across or not.

CHAPTER 23

She looked through the spyglass, trying hard to see outside and who was knocking on her door, but all she could see were shadows. Then, she heard the sound of footsteps as they disappeared in the distance, leaving her heart pounding so hard she couldn't hear anything except it.

After rushing to the window, she pulled a corner of the curtain to the side and glanced down into the car lot. From her room on the second floor, she saw some of the cars, but not all of them. *Should I call the front desk to see if they gave out my room number to anyone?* At first she felt inclined to do so, but knowing if she caused any problems here she might be let go, she decided not to.

As she watched a truck pull out of the lot and onto the street, she strained as hard as she might to catch any details about it, but she couldn't tell much except that it had disappeared. After looking around for some kind of weapon to use she found nothing of much value in the room.

After turning out the light, she hurried into the bed and pulled the covers over her. There she stayed for most of the night, unable to sleep but for minutes at a time. Being tired and unable to sleep felt terrible, but it was something she had experienced many times before. Late in the night she finally drifted off to sleep.

She found herself on top of a mountain with a beautiful 360-degree view of the world around her. The purest white clouds illuminated by the sun were shining all around her to the point of glowing and radiating their own light. She has never seen such a sight.

Even before she saw him, she knew he would be there somewhere. Sure enough, as she turned around, the blond-haired man with the big, beautiful, sincere smile stood there to greet her. "Beautiful isn't it?" His hands pointed to the views around them.

"Yes, it is." The more she studied it, the more beautiful it became.

"And I see you're learning quickly now."

"What do you mean?"

"The more you perceive objects as beautiful, the more beautiful they become. You'll also learn that the more you expect occurrences to happen, the more you'll see that they do happen."

"Maybe I'm a slow learner."

With an amused smile, he put his hand on her shoulder. "You've been learning for a very long time and not only in this lifetime, but in many lifetimes before. Each time, you get closer and closer to having a deeper understanding. While the works that you do each life impact the next life, it is only after you learn to control your dreams that you can you really advance."

"That still sounds impossible."

"That's exactly why it's impossible for you. Not because it is, but because you think it's impossible." After walking around her, he continued, "Dreams can show you the best answer to a current problem. When the mind's free of earthly restraints, it's very powerful and creative."

"That's easy to believe, since I often think of problems and sometimes know the answer after I wake up. It's kind of like sleeping on the problem."

"Your past is the knowledge you use to make decisions. Floating back in time's easy and done without much effort at all."

"I think everyone has at one time or another thought they lived before as someone else."

"Yes. Let me ask you a question? Would you rather see your future or your past?"

Thinking on it, she says, "That is hard to say."

"What if I told you they are one and the same?"

"What? How can that be?"

"I'll answer that when you're ready. For now, you have to learn the third step."

Still not knowing exactly what the third step is, she thought of another question she wanted answered. "Can I ask you one question?"

"Sure."

"It's strange, but many times lately I've seen people or items that glow or stand out in front of me as if to draw me to them."

"Yes, yes, the work of your angel, the enlightened ones trying to help you. Because you're vibrating on different levels entirely, the glow you see is the only way they can help you. You see . . . light's the purest and simplest form of energy and love. It's the easiest way for them to direct your path."

Jacquelyn started to ask about the third step, but the sky faded away and she woke in the darkness of the hotel room. All remained quiet, and for the next hour she contemplated all that she has learned.

After finally deciding to get up, she cleaned the room and left for the ridges again. As she enjoyed the early morning sounds, the walk in the cool mountain air felt invigorating and helped to clear her head. While the sights of the early morning were special in many ways, she looked at all objects in a different way, finding the beauty in all that she saw.

Upon hiking to the cliff she now called home base, she waited for the sunrise. It soon appeared, and was just as beautiful as she imagined, filling her heart with incredible joy. In almost no time, she saw images of the angels. She watched something very different in the images this time. Her angel wasn't still and patient this time. Instead, her angel kept looking over her shoulder. Sometimes she turned all the way around. What could that mean?

This movement repeated several times until the full sun made her image fade away. She knew her angel was trying to tell her something, but what was it? Concentrating on every movement, she soon understood that her angel was telling her to watch her back and to be careful. She was trying to warn her.

She immediately hiked down the mountain and didn't slow down to enjoy her surroundings. She didn't even think of Farmer John's place, let alone exploring it as she considered earlier. After rounding the last bend and seeing the town in front of her, she started to relax, but then fear came upon her again. She needed to be careful as she walked the street since she didn't want to be seen.

She quickly went to her work and completed the rooms as fast as she could. After finishing the last one, she rested on the bed for a while and waited until time to go to the tai chi class that she had planned on attending. After all, the notice for the class has been illuminated by the light of her angel.

The flat walk to the visitor center was comfortable walking as she studied the many sites along a side trail to the entrance of the national forest. She remembered seeing the visitor center before like every other tourist who has ever been to Gatlinburg.

She found the group meeting in a small field behind the center where she counted about twenty people in a semicircle around a young Asian-looking man. Knowing she had the right group, she entered them from one side and dropped to the grass like most of the others there.

Without moving his head, the man moved his eyes to one side and studied her before scanning the people in the group. "Thank you for coming. I hope I can teach you something that will be of interest to you and will encourage you to want to learn more."

The few that were standing slowly joined the rest of the group. Many also followed the teacher's example of crossing his legs in front of him. "If you have any questions, please feel free to ask. For those that know very little about tai chi, it'll be interesting for you to know a little of the history, but I promise not to make this a history class." With a small smile, he looked around the group. "Tai chi chuan is really easy and simple, but it also takes a lifetime to perfect. In addition, the only purpose you can use it for is to teach others about the wonderful flow of energy that fills the universe. You'll learn how to get in contact with that energy, and how that energy enlightens your body and spirit."

Watching him speak, she noticed he had a halo of colors around him. At first, she thought she had a problem with her vision and started to rub her eyes.

"There are many stories on the origination of tai chi chuan, but the one I think is most correct is the one developed by Chang San-Feng. While even the accounts of his learning are questioned by many, it's my belief that he learned from the Shaolin monks."

"What exactly is tai chi?" a young impatient girl asked as she raised her hand.

With a slow but dignified smile, he turned toward her. "Tai chi chuan is hard to express in few words. While it's a form of martial art, it's also a form of healing and meditation. It can be a way of supreme expression and a way of reaching enlightenment. Think of it as an art form that cultivates and encourages not only emotional and mental growth, but also the needs of the body. You'll learn that the principles of body movement are in direct proportion to the energy flow that occurs in the body. The energy flows along certain meridians within the body. If it's disrupted, the body will be injured. It's said that Chang San-Feng became so advanced that he did remarkable feats. The legend is there, and it's up to the individual to believe or not to believe. Even today, there are examples of his legacy in Tibet. It's said that he lived in the mountains where it's extremely cold and was able to walk around in his bare feet."

Several of the people in the crowd gestured to one another in disbelief of what they heard.

"Also, it's a well-documented fact that the descendents of his disciples there still walk around in the mountains and never wear shoes. The legend is much greater nevertheless."

Knowing that he must have their attention, he surveyed the crowd before he studied Jacquelyn who was, in turn, watching his every move while concentrating on what he was saying. "It's said that he walks in the snow and leaves no footprints in the snow. In fact, it's said that he generates so much heat that he usually ends up walking on dry land. His heat not only melts the snow, but also dries it up instantly."

Jacquelyn followed every word as this story intrigued her into wanting to know more. It's almost as if she was hearing words she had heard a long time ago. The more she heard, the more all of it came back to her.

"Remember one test you can use when you find a truly holy man. You'll always see that he knows how to generate heat. He has learned the principle of generating energy from within his own body. He doesn't take from the world, but gives unto it. Even today, you'll see monks again in Tibet and other places that need almost no food or nourishment."

While the crowd listened to him, the teacher indicated that he could tell almost everyone only wanted to see the tai chi movements and learn the graceful form of exercise. Thinking he taught about as much as they could absorb, he stood. "I think you'll like the training today. I'll be here to answer any questions you have for me later."

As he stood in front of them, he offered one last instruction. "It's always important to practice as slowly as you can. That's the only way you can fully understand the movements. There's no end or beginning in the movements. You have to start by relaxing and cleansing you mind and soul. We'll work on building up the good energy as soon as we empty the bad."

Jacquelyn watched the movements and followed all of his instructions. The more she listened, the more she appreciated all he taught her. The energy in her felt indeed very good. Tai chi felt so familiar to her, but she couldn't figure out why.

After the class finished, she stayed on the grass and waited for everyone to leave. When the last one waved goodbye, the teacher turned to her. "I can tell you have a question. How can I help you?"

"You said it's possible to build up your own energy directly inside of you. How is that possible?"

"That's the one piece of knowledge that almost no one can show you, but you have to learn yourself. It comes from an inner awareness of yourself and the universe that you're a part of. Many great masters talk of enlightenment and this journey takes a lifetime to complete. When you know exactly how to do it, you'll be on a plane that's well above those who can understand you."

Jacquelyn replied in a soft respective voice. "I think I understand, but I want to know more."

"I'm walking back into town and perhaps we can talk some more as we walk."

"Yes, I would like that. You know, I assumed I was the only one walking today." The walk felt good, and she asked many questions. She had so much she wanted to learn. Nevertheless, one thing she knew for sure, this had to be the third step she needed to learn. She felt sure of it.

CHAPTER 24

While concentrating on the events of the day, Jacquelyn thought about the angel she had seen in the morning who looked over her shoulder. Almost in a mimicking way, she copied the movement. In the distance, she saw someone walking fast in their direction. "I have to go," she yelled to the teacher as she turned to her left and ran down a back street of downtown Gatlinburg.

Being too scared to look back, she ran faster, knowing someone was chasing after her. She pushed herself to put as much distance as she could between them until she finally saw the back entrance to the hotel. A quick glance over her shoulder sent shivers of terror down her back. He was gaining on her. Thinking it would be bad to give away the place where she worked, she decided to keep moving.

She saw a small restaurant around the corner and after chancing another quick glance where she saw nothing she rushed inside and quickly found a booth. Minutes later, she rushed straight for the restroom in the back where she locked the door and prepared to stay there for a long time—forever, if need be.

Where is my angel now? She really needed him, or was it her? Funny, this was the first time she actually thought about the gender of angels, and she suddenly wondered if they have genders at all. She remembered how she was saved at the truck stop by a man walking out of a truck, and how she had first been shown the way to the mountain ridges in the dark. She even remembered how she had been saved from the agent at the cabin who tried to take advantage of her.

The door rattled as someone tried to turn the handle and open the door. Then, it remained silent for several seconds until she heard an older lady. "Are you okay in there?"

"Yes, I'm fine . . . just not feeling too good. I'll be out in a second." Jacquelyn knew she had little choice but to venture out soon. She would have to be cautious.

Once inside the restaurant eating area, she saw several people, but no one she recognized. After moving to an empty table she adjusted her back to face the entrance. She saw a blue jean jacket on the seat next to her that someone apparently had forgotten when he or she left. She reached over and picked it up. The scent coming from the jacket registered a very unique smell. She recognized the smell of the cologne in a heartbeat. It came from the man who had helped her before, and she knew it.

She ran to the register. "Do you know who was sitting at this table? He left his jacket."

"Yeah. He just walked out."

Jacquelyn ran out the door in a flash, but she saw no one on the street. Instead of walking back inside, she decided to walk back to the hotel. The manager smiled at her as she walked in and handed her a key. He looked like he wanted to tell her something, but the phone rang. She waved at him in appreciation and walked to her room for the night. While it was early and too dangerous to be out on the street, she wondered what he wanted to tell her, but thought she would find out tomorrow morning.

As she opened the door to the room and turned on the lights, she saw a ghost from her past sitting in the room waiting for her. "Hello, Jacquelyn. Come on in. The office manager was good enough to give me a key so I could wait for you."

"Shawn, how did you find me?"

"It wasn't too hard. You left many items in your room indicating you liked this place. Since you told many of your friends how much you wanted to live here one day, I anticipated you'd show up here and be on the main street at some time."

"I want you to leave me alone."

"And leave you in a place like this with no money. You know it's only a matter of time before you come back, and I think we need an understanding."

"An understanding . . . ?"

"Well . . . you know . . . we can't have your mom getting the wrong impression, now can we?"

"You mean about how you can't keep your hands off me?"

"You think that you're so damn cute and special that you can do as you please. Well, I've some news for you. It takes money to make this world go around, and it's not like I'm asking you to do something you haven't done before."

"What do you mean that I've done before?" she yelled back at him trying to understand what he was accusing her of.

"Don't be so innocent. I've seen the videos of you. When we helped you move out of the house where you used to live with Vincent, I found the tapes he made. So only you, Vincent, and I know what kind of porno star you really are."

"I don't know what you're talking about. I've never posed for any videos or photos. My ex-husband always wanted me to, but I never did. I want you to leave me alone, or I'll call the police. My mom's such a fool." The anger in Jacquelyn's voice reached a fever pitch.

"I don't think you want me to show these videos, and oh yes, these photos of you to your mom."

Shawn started across the room toward her but never made it. The door swung open, and it looked like Shawn saw a diesel truck about to hit him as he stepped back from the oncoming attack. "What are you doing here?" His voice sounded deep but shaken at the sight of Jacquelyn's mom in the doorway.

"Doing something I should've done a long time ago—taking care of my daughter."

"I'm not sure what you heard, but I can explain."

"You're a fucking jerk," Jacquelyn inserted, walking over to her mom and wondering what would happen next.

Her mother's voice suddenly turned as cold as an arctic blizzard. "Shawn, while you're busy going through Jacquelyn's belongings, you should've been more concerned about your own junk. It's very interesting what I found in the workshop."

"You have no right going through my things."

Jacquelyn listened hard, trying to understand what was going on as her mom opened her purse and handed Jacquelyn some photos. "These are photos of me!" Jacquelyn screamed as her face flushed with heat while she studied photos of her in the bathroom and in bed. "You've been peeping on me and photographing me!" She couldn't believe the nude photos she saw.

"It appears that he's not the only one taking photos of you. There're more taken of you while you were married to Vincent. It's very obvious that you were drunk or drugged during the filming. The police have the rest of them, and they are ready to press charges against Vincent and Shawn."

"This is nothing but lies," Shawn yelled as he headed across the room for Jacquelyn's mom. "You've got no proof."

"Get out, Shawn. It's over," Jacquelyn's mother screamed as she prepared to defend herself from an imminent attack from Shawn.

"I'm going to smash your head in for what you have done, you bitch!"

As he headed for her, she lifted up a small transmitter she wore. "Did I forget to tell you that you're being recorded?"

Realizing that she had been wired and that someone was probably listening somewhere, Shawn attempted to bolt past her and head for the door. "Screw you, and screw your daughter." His face turned white with anger, and he turned to cuss one time too many as Jack reemerged.

Jack stepped forward and jerked her knee up quickly with deadly accuracy to his balls. She knew it hurt, since she had put all of the energy she had into that blow. He stumbled back as she kicked him again, but this time it was as if she was trying to kick a football through the uprights.

He yelled. "God damn, girl." He lifted his hand to strike out at her, but he moved too slow as she dropped back and placed a full soccer style kick this time to the inside of his knee, which dropped him to the floor.

She knew he had to be in pain, but wanted no more of it. "Fuck you!" he cussed as he got up. His eyes looked wild, but knowing the police might be there any second, he stumbled out of the room.

Closing the door, her mother smiled. "He'll not get far since they're waiting for him."

Jack slowly reverted back to Jacquelyn as she watched her mother cry. "I'm so sorry, Mom, I've tried to tell you so many times."

"I know, and I guess I'm a silly old fool who will not listen to the signs around me. I didn't want to believe it. The prospect of being alone is very scary, and I think I was hoping that he did love me. I'll admit I was a fool."

"Does this mean we'll have to go to court?"

"Maybe, but I don't think so. I'm sure he'll try to work out something with the district attorney. The main concern is that he's out of our lives now for good."

"Mom, I hope life will be okay for you now. There'll be someone else out there for you. I know it."

"We'll see. I was worried about you. It's going to be good to get you back home."

Back home? Jacquelyn hadn't considered moving back. "Mom, I think I'll stay here. It's time for me to start my life over also, and this can be one of the greatest places on earth—really."

"Do you mean living in a motel room?"

Jacquelyn laughed at her surroundings. "Well, this isn't exactly what I mean. I'll find a real job here and a good place to live. This is kind of temporary."

"I don't have a lot of money to give you, but I can help a little."

"All I need is a little. I'll pay you back as soon as I get a good job."

"I think you need to come home and let me take care of you for a while. Shawn will not be there to bother you anymore. I promise you this."

"I understand, Mom, but I need this time here to get over all my problems. Please understand how I want this very much."

"I think you've made your mind up on staying. We'll talk about it more soon, but here . . . take this." She handed Jacquelyn a credit card. "Use what you need, but let me know how much you use. I trust you." With tears in her mother's eyes, she gave her daughter a very big hug and held her for a long time.

"Thanks. This means a lot to me. What about the photos of me and the videos? I never posed for any photos for Vincent."

"From what I've heard from the police, they think he may have used a date rape drug on you which prevented you from remembering anything. Do you remember the dreams you talked about of being photographed against your will?"

"Yes. I remember." Like a feeling of nausea came over her, it all makes sense now. "So, it wasn't a dream at all, and that really happened to me."

"Yes, honey. I'm so sorry. It also explains why Vincent was so intent on getting you to see him. He wanted the videos back before they were discovered. He thought you had them, but Shawn had them all this time. It also appears Vincent sold some of these tapes on the Internet. The police are looking for him now."

"I thought Vincent was still in jail until I saw him here the other day."

"You saw Vincent here?"

"Yes, on the street looking for me."

"He was released from jail two days ago. He managed to get released on a retrial hearing and hasn't been seen since then. I'm not sure if Vincent and Shawn ever compared notes or not, but I'll contact the police before I leave and let them know he's here. Are you sure you want to stay?"

"Yes, I'm sure the police will have no problem finding him here soon, and as you said, he's probably in contact with Shawn and knows that he's being hunted right now."

"I really hate to leave, but I need to get back to Atlanta. The police are still doing some work on what to charge Shawn and Vincent with, and I'm sure Shawn will try to get into my house to get his stuff, if he has a chance. I'm sure I'll have to sign some papers. If we need you, I'll call you.

Also, if the police need to get in contact with you, I need to have a number to reach you with."

"I'll get a number for you, Mom. Thanks again for everything." Her mom gave her another big kiss and several hugs before heading out the door.

After several hours of reflecting on what had happened to her, she began to relax more than she had in a long time. The prospects of having her nightmares over with felt so good. As the night turned chilly, she walked over to the window, where she saw many people walking the street. She thought it would be good to walk along with the tourists and see the town one more time, but now in a new light. She would look for a place to live and a good job tomorrow.

All along the sidewalks couples walked and held hands. The amazing excitement she experienced in their eyes showed how much they were in love with each other, and obviously happy to be alive. They sent her good feelings, but at the same time brought her bad feelings since she was still there all alone.

She passed the pizza shop where she had first met Tadd. The same great smell drifted out of the shop that captured her attention the first time. It smelled so very good. After venturing in and checking to see if he was around, she slowly assured herself that he wasn't. It felt so strange how she missed him and the good time they had there.

Almost ready to give in and order a pizza, she changed her mind and prepared to leave when she overheard a couple of girls talking by the counter. One tall girl in her late twenties and with vivid red hair was dressed in a little bit of a funky style, but still fashionable. She looked like her dad must have money and still be footing the bill for her. She didn't look like the working type, and she didn't wear a wedding ring. The other girl looked smaller and much younger. If not for her blonde hair, she might have passed for a sister of the redhead. Whoever they are, she thought how great it would be to be able to afford such nice clothes.

The redhead laughed and appeared to be having a great time kidding the other girl. "I bet you have several books on kama sutra hidden at home somewhere."

"No, that's more your fantasy than mine. I'm just a sweet young innocent girl, you know." Batting her eyes and obviously having fun with the joking back and forth, she continued, "Can you believe they're going to let someone do a lecture on it here?"

"Really! But I've heard the kama sutra master is like really good looking."

"What I've heard is that he's a monk with a hood over his head to keep everyone from knowing who he really is."

"They say if you really want to know what true love is, this is the way to fly. Anyway, we'll see tomorrow night at seven at the conference center." Both girls give each other a quick high five and reach for their pizzas.

Jacquelyn made a note of the time and location of the lecture. She had heard of kama sutra like many people, but knew so little about it. If it was a way to find true love as they said, she would definitely be there.

Thoughts of her having her mom helping her now and Shawn not being able to harass her anymore felt very comforting. Life definitely looked better for her. Feeling secure in her future, Jacquelyn walked around the streets for a while and enjoyed the magic of the streets. She eventually ended up back at the motel and went to bed as soon as she entered her room.

After sleeping deeply into the night, the world turned white again as she almost knew it would. While smiling at the blond-haired man, she said, "Everything's looking much better, and I've learned so much, but I still have many questions."

"I think you'll learn the more you learn, the more questions you'll have."

"I keep hearing about the four steps to finding true love. Can you tell me what they are in clear terms so that I'll understand?"

"In due time . . . you'll learn all the steps, but you already know much about the first two steps. The third step is the one you're learning now. Creating your own energy is very important, and you're much closer than you think. It takes concentration and the ability to control the flow as it radiates out of you."

"That really seems impossible."

"As long as you think so, it will be. You must be able to shut out the entire world both internally and externally. All must be emptied from you. Only then can you create your own energy. This energy can control not only your day life, but also your dreams as well."

"My angel really helped me today, and I'm very thankful for that."

"I'm sure she's glad to help. The angels, hum, the enlightened ones, care very much about you, but it's up to you to ask for help and to be able to accept their help. The fourth step will be shown to you as soon as you master the third. It's dangerous for you to learn it before that time." As he turned around and walked away, the room turned darker.

Waking instantly and knowing it would be light soon, Jacquelyn decided to get up and dress. Her favorite time of the morning was coming. The early morning air invigorated her soul as usual, and finding the trail was easy. She almost didn't need her flashlight at all. After coming to the fork in the path that led across to Farmer John's cabin, she decided to take it. She couldn't see much through the trees, but knew he had a large plot of land with a garden.

The aromas drifting from the property smelled very nice and pleasant. She felt sure she smelled roses and many other flowers as well. The scent remained light but powerful at the same time. She also recognized a scent she remembered from before, but couldn't place it at that moment.

Back on the main trail, she soon reached her ridge and waited to see the sunrise as she practiced yoga while she waited. The positions were hard to remember, but she had enough of them memorized to keep her busy and make her feel good. She then switched to tai chi as the sunrise started. Graceful and ever flowing, it helped to clear her mind. After concentrating on nothing but herself and the moment, she felt a newfound peace. Deep within her she felt a glow, a sensation she had never appreciated before.

She tried to increase the glow inside her, but it only flickered and died. Try as she could, it wouldn't return. The sunrise offered a solid swatch of bright orange extending across the horizon. She saw no clouds to reflect any interesting features. She had hoped to see her angel this morning to thank her, but she saw no angels. Perhaps all was as it should be; after all, everything was going good in her life.

After returning to the hotel, she completed her tasks as fast as possible so she could head out and look for some better work. Thinking it would be best if she waited to tell the manager of the hotel her plans after she had a new job, she waved at him as she walked out the front door. "I'll see you later."

While passing by the jewelry shop that Tadd owned, she tried hard to look inside without being noticed. He did look good, and she felt sorry their relationship had started so badly, but she saw no point worrying about it, especially since he had a girlfriend anyway. A slim girl a little older than Jacquelyn walked out of the shop and placed a sales sign in the front window. Not wanting to be noticed, Jacquelyn kept walking down the street.

The day passed with no prospects of a better job, but she knew she had only begun to look. Thoughts of the lecture on kama sutra were on her mind as she walked toward the conference center in the middle of town. It could be interesting.

After walking into the building, she found a sign pointing down a hall. No one was in the building, and it looked deserted. As she walked down the hall, she heard voices and realized she must be heading in the right direction. While passing one door, she noticed the same sign on the door. This was the place.

As she opened the door, she estimated that about fifty people were in the room who were standing around and talking. She saw almost all women, with the exception of only a few guys. It became obvious they were there either with their girlfriends or with their wives. In a few minutes she spotted the two girls who she had seen at the pizza shop the night before. They dressed in very nice clothes that were somewhat weird, but still nice. Since they chatted away just like the night before, she still couldn't tell if they were best friends or sisters.

After seeing a group of three girls on one side, Jacquelyn decided to join them. "How long do you think it'll be before this gets started?"

Smiling back at her, a heavyset girl smiled. "It shouldn't be long. We're waiting for the instructor now."

"That's good. Do you know much about this meeting? I overheard a couple of girls talking about it yesterday."

"We've all heard the instructor's a kama sutra master of some kind. What he has to tell us will be very interesting I'm sure."

A figure in a dark robe soon entered, and everyone instantly hushed as his presence overflowed into the room. Without even seeing him or hearing him clearly, Jacquelyn knew he had walked in. As he stopped in front of the audience, he raised his hands to indicate they should all have a seat. Without any discussion, they all obeyed his directions.

His first words flowed with a powerful sense of control. "I'm so glad you're here tonight." While looking at the hood covering most of this man's face, Jacquelyn wondered why he was so secretive about his identity. "I have a lot of information to cover tonight that I hope you'll find interesting. Many people only think of one part of the book when they hear about the kama sutra. There's much more to it, I promise. If you're here hoping to only learn about erotic sexual positions, you'll be disappointed. If you want to learn about the rules of love, moods, atmosphere, and the fulfilling nature of a divine relationship with that one and special person, this is a good place to start."

He looked straight ahead and never at any one person. His accent sounded English, British English, although she remembered seeing on the poster that he was from India. "If you have any questions, I'll be glad to answer them for you later. Since I have a lot of information for you, it might be good to hold your questions and see if I answer them during this talk."

The intensity in the room grew as everyone waited for him to begin. "For those who haven't heard a lot about kama sutra, I think a little of the history will be in order. Kama's a concept based in Hinduism, which spread through Buddhism and Jainism to mention a few. Karma is associated with the expression you often hear on TV as: Do good things and good things will happen to you. Or . . . do bad things and bad things will happen to you."

Jacquelyn heard a slight rustling in the audience and the attendees acknowledged his opening statements before he continued. "If you do unkind acts, you receive spoiled fruits, which are called papa. For good deeds, you receive sweet fruits called punya. If you want to become a good person, do good acts. If you do bad acts, you will become a bad person. You become the way you act."

The crowd remained quiet and listened as he continued, "There are three kinds of karma. The first is sanchita karma, which is all the old karma in your past that hasn't been resolved. The prarabdha karma is the part of the sanchita karma that is to be dealt with in this life. The kriyamana karma is the karma that's being created currently. This is what will affect your future."

A short pause in his speech gave everyone time to concentrate. "When we get into the kama sutra, we're dealing with the rules of love. With over 1,000 chapters and 64 arts to the kama sutra, there's much more than we can discuss tonight. It's a way of instruction to teach a wife to be a good wife and a husband to be a skilful partner. In learning the kama sutra, the following arts also have to be learned: singing, playing instruments, dancing, writing, drawing, flower arranging, arranging beds, taking care of teeth, playing musical glasses, cooking, sewing, reading, and about several hundred more activities."

As Jacquelyn noticed many in the audience leaning forward to take in everything he said, she now wished she had taken a seat in the center of the room where she could see the speaker better. The ideas he talked about were the ones most girls would love to have in a mate, but she had heard all these comments before.

He continued with more information as he explained, "The kama sutra's covered in about thirty-five chapters, which are found in seven different parts. The first four are on love in general and man's part in it. There are ten chapters devoted to sex, which give a very in-depth discussion regarding it. Also, there are five chapters on how to obtain a wife. Two chapters are on the proper conduct of a wife. Six chapters are on seduction, and the last two are on relationships with other people."

Jacquelyn thought the lecture was beginning to sound like a history lesson, but she still found it interesting. Also, there was something in his voice she recognized as he continued. "The writer of the way of the kama sutra is a man named Vatsyayana. He believed there were eight ways to make love and eight different positions for each way. That was how he arrived at the 64 arts of making love. The chapter on making love is the most well known and referred to in the kama sutra. Only about twenty percent of the book is contained in this part, however."

The lecture continued for about two more hours, and the more he talked, the more questions she had. She prepared to ask many question after he finished, but with everyone else there also raising their hands to ask questions the chance of her getting to ask a question wasn't going to be very good.

One girl stood and asked a very pointed question Jacquelyn was interested in also. "I have the same dreams often, and I wondered if you knew why certain people or activities are repeated over and over in our dreams?"

"There, of course, could be many reasons, but I think it may be because of the way karma works. The sanchita karma works in not only your day-to-day life, but also in your spiritual and dream life as well. It's a way of reminding you of events yet unresolved. When you face it in the present, it may get resolved, which is what is known as the prarabdha karma."

Jacquelyn knew she had to talk to him since she had so many questions about her Dream Master. Until now, she didn't really have anyone with whom she could openly discuss the nightly presence of a Dream Master in her dreams.

As he finished, he added, "The energy that's transmitted becomes more refined and passionate as it accumulates within you, bringing pleasure and enjoyment both inside and outside the body. When you reach this state, you will feel as if you and your partner are one. When you discover the goodness within the other and the fulfillment that awaits you there, the study will be well worth the effort."

With these last words, he stood, turned around, and left. Somehow Jacquelyn knew she would find him to ask more questions; she knew it. He had the answer to finding out the fourth step she needed to learn.

CHAPTER 25

Back at the hotel, Jacquelyn received a key and quickly went to her room. As excitement ran through her mind she digested the information she had learned. She needed to find a better job and buy a car, but even though those events hadn't happened yet, she did, however, feel confident that all was moving in the right direction. A hot shower would definitely be great right now.

The shower was in fact very good, but as she lingered in the shower, the phone rang. Wondering who it could be she ran across the room while still wet. "Hello." While waiting for someone to respond, she heard nothing. "Hello," she repeated, but she still heard nothing. The line went dead.

Jacquelyn's heart raced as many thoughts ran through her head. It wasn't her mom as she first thought it might be. She picked up the phone and dialed the front desk. "Did you put a call up to my room?"

"Yes, I did."

"I didn't hear them say anything. Did they say who it was?"

"No, they were looking for a Jacquelyn that works here. I assumed it's a friend of yours. They'll probably call back."

"Thanks." Damn, someone knew where she was now! Taking her master key with her, she changed to another room and turned the lights off as she crawled into the bed. The next day she would have to leave.

Sleep didn't arrive quickly, but it did come as she examined photos taken of her. She saw hundreds of them around her, and in all of them she was totally nude. She felt embarrassment, debasement, and then anger. This was a total violation of her. She also could see sex toys on the table in front of her. These were the kind of objects her ex-husband always tried to get her to use, but they were too kinky and weird for her. It made her feel like she was a whore in the worst way.

A sudden image of Vincent sent a new wave of panic through her. With the presence of her ex-husband coming into the room she ran out and kept running and running. *Where is my angel now*?

When she woke soaked in sweat and hyperventilating, she rushed to the bathroom where she washed her face. As she turned off the water she heard the sound of heavy footsteps outside her room. Her heart raced as the steps went on by her room and disappeared. It was still late, and she knew she needed to get some sleep, but true sleep never came as time came for her to go to her sunrise. That was the very best part of her day and it felt like something she had to do, no matter what.

As she hiked up the mountain, she smelled the freshness of the mountains, but as she passed Farmer John's cabin she studied the unique difference in his flowers. He even had left on a light which glimmered through the trees. One day she would have to take a closer look.

While the cliff looked the same as always, it now felt as if she owned this place. It was her special place. She started the exercises she had learned from the yoga and the tai chi masters. All was in order as she watched the sky start to come alive. Low clouds were everywhere, and the colors in the sky were all over the rainbow. The more she concentrated on them, the more vibrant they became. When she thought it was the most beautiful scene she had ever seen, it became even brighter and more vivid.

It wasn't long before she could make out her angel again who was sitting and looking peaceful with her eyes closed, as if in deep concentration. Is that her message for the day—that she needed to concentrate?

As the sun started to melt the cloud's fantastic color, Jacquelyn remained and concentrated on the world in general. Then she slipped into thinking of nothing but her inner energy, not forcing it, but letting it grow naturally. It felt warm and powerful, giving her a strength that she didn't know she had. It felt as if it came from within as it kept building and building.

As it grew, she felt it needing to be directed. If it stayed inside her much longer, she felt like it would make her explode. Thoughts of her mom drifted across her mind, and she knew that her mom had many problems now. With these grounds for concern, she felt the energy leave her, and she knew it flowed out of her and to her mom, wherever her mom was at that moment.

It was soon time to go back to the hotel and get her work done, since she had to find a new job and move today. She felt ready to handle the challenge before her, and she knew she was close to discovering the fourth step now.

After finishing her work, she walked toward the trolley stop. At first she didn't see them, but then there wasn't a doubt. She ducked into a shop. Her ex-husband and the rental agent from the cabin were walking and talking together with both of them acting disgusted. How do they know each other, and what were they doing together here?

After finding a rear entrance, she sprinted along the back street. She didn't want to go to jail for trespassing, or give her ex-husband ammunition to use against her. How was she going to hide out all day here? Vincent and the rental agent were close to the trolley station, so she couldn't go back there any time soon.

After going into one store, she worked her way up to the second floor and found a good place to watch the street. It might be a good idea to see if she could follow them. Something inside her told her it would be better to be the hunter than the hunted for a while.

Her waiting paid off an hour later, when she saw them walking down the street together. It was obvious that they were looking in all the shops and talking to many people on the street. Yes, they were hunting for her. Somehow, her ex-husband had made contact with this rental guy. Thinking about it, she realized it would make sense that if he thought she was here, a rental guy might know something. The rental agent might have told her ex-husband he had seen someone fitting her description. She wouldn't doubt that her ex-husband was offering him money for his help.

As far as the sexual arrangements made by the rental agent, she felt sure he would lie about that. She could even see her ex-husband laughing about it if he did hear; he was such a pervert. She watched them working the far side of the street from where she hid. Apparently they had worked her side of the street on the way down.

Once they passed by the store where she hid, she began to follow them as they continued to make their way down the street looking in all of the shops along the way. After they reach the end of the street, they walked into a parking lot and got into a car. Jacquelyn makes a mental note of the name of the rental company on the side of the car as she watched them leave.

Jacquelyn instantly walked to the trolley pick-up station. She had thought all was good, but now she had Vincent and this rental agent to contend with. There was a warrant for Vincent's arrest, but she didn't want to have the real estate agent involved and get herself in trouble. She hoped that it would only be a matter of time before the police found him here. Surely it would be over soon. She wanted to get on with her life and do what she really dreamed about in her heart. While she had come to Gatlinburg to find true love, the only guy she had met so far was Tadd, and he already had a girlfriend.

The trolley made many stops along the way where it picked up and let people off. Sitting on the seat and watching the scenery was interesting for her as her mind drifted, and she quit paying much attention to the various stops. Then, almost in Pigeon Forge, the trolley made one of its scheduled stops, and her fear resurfaced. Vincent and the rental agent were at the stop, and it looked like they were planning to get on the trolley. She had to get off if they got on.

Realizing there had to be a warrant out for Vincent based on what her mom had told her, she knew that she needed to call the police as soon as she could, but she froze as she worried about the night she had been caught by the rental agent, or caretaker of the cabin. Since she didn't need to go to jail for trespassing, it might be best to keep a low profile until Vincent was caught.

While ducking low and keeping a watchful eye, she prepared to jump and run, but fortunately as the two men were about to get on the trolley someone yelled at them. Since the trolley wasn't able to stay there waiting, it pulled out, leaving them at the station. After looking over her shoulder, she saw someone getting out of a truck and walking toward them. She wasn't sure, but she assumed that had to be her angel again helping her out.

A young woman on the seat across from her started smiling at her as Jacquelyn recognized her from the kama sutra meeting the night before. "How are you?" the girl asked.

"I'm fine, thanks. Didn't I see you at the kama sutra meeting last night?"

"Yes. How did you like it?"

"It was very interesting, but the instructor was kind of strange, I think."

"You mean with the hood and all. I think that it's his way of giving respect to the culture or profession or whatever you want to call it. It did make him appear more mysterious, and if I was going to teach the kama sutra, I wouldn't want everyone to know who I was. Are you going to the advanced class later?"

"I didn't know about an advanced class."

"I heard that he might have one."

"You know all that he said was good, but without the right guy I don't think any of it will do me much good. Somewhere I need to find the perfect guy, and so far that hasn't happened. Sometimes I wonder if such a guy exists."

"If you ever come up with a simple way of finding him, let me know. I have considered the same for a long time myself."

After arriving at the stop Jacquelyn wanted to make she stood. "I hope to see you later, maybe at the next meeting." She jumped from the trolley and moved fast to get off the street. It would be hard to look for a job while looking over her shoulder all the time, but she had planned to do what she could. Somehow she needed some time to figure out what to do. She knew her ex-husband couldn't stay long because of the police hunting him. The rental agent she could deal with later if she needed to.

CHAPTER 26

While walking the streets, Jacquelyn hoped for the best in her job search, but still found nothing of interest from anyone there. It was always the same story. She was given many applications and told to complete them and bring them back later. Every time she ventured out on the street she worried about seeing Vincent and the rental agent again. She did see one place where she thought about staying. It wasn't too great of a place, but would provide some security for her for a while.

Since she had to get her belongings at the hotel in Gatlinburg, she decided to head back that way on the next trolley. Somehow, she would make it through one more night, and especially if her angel would look out for her.

After walking through one of the discount malls, she stopped at the food court and decided to have a quick snack and a coke. When a girl slid into the seat across from her, Jacquelyn recognized her within a few seconds. It was the girl who had been working in Tadd's jewelry shop.

As she was finishing her snack Jacquelyn looked over at the girl and noticed that her eyes looked very red, and as if she had been crying. With compassion in her heart and curiosity, Jacquelyn wanted to know what was wrong. "How are you?" she started with an honest smile.

After smiling back, the girl replied, "I'm fine, and you?"

"I'm fine. Didn't I see you working at a jewelry shop in Gatlinburg the other day?"

"Yes, I'm working some there to help a friend. He has a good shop."

"I'm very impressed with the quality of the jewelry there. Many of them I've never seen before anywhere else."

"A lot of the jewelry Tadd sells comes from India."

"India, that's interesting. I think I've heard somewhere that they do great work with jewelry."

"It's going to be a shame to shut down the jewelry shop."

"The jewelry shop's shutting down! Why's that?"

"Tadd's going to move back to India. That's where he lived before he moved here."

"I thought Tadd was from here. Wasn't he born here?"

"His father was born here but he married a woman from India. Tadd was actually born in India. He spent most of his early life here, however. He's half Cherokee Indian and half Indian from India. That's an interesting combination to say the least. I hate seeing him go, but I want him to be happy. He's a good friend and we have a lot of common friends."

"Why is he going back to India?"

"Tadd's a very complicated, special individual. The last few days have been hard on him. He met someone that made a big impact on him, and he has been looking hard to find her. He's now convinced that she left town. I know Tadd loves it here, but he has a mother still living in India, and this was the last straw to make him want to go back there for a while."

Remembering the call she overheard, Jacquelyn asked, "Is that his girlfriend Shannon?"

"Shannon? He doesn't have a girlfriend named Shannon." A slow laugh followed a look of relief which changed her mood. Then, she started giggling, nearly uncontrollably. "He has a sister named Shannon."

"A sister? Tadd has a sister! Oh . . . my gosh! That explains the necklace she was talking about." Jacquelyn covered her face as the embarrassment sent by a wave of heat hit her.

The girl suddenly had an acute interest in Jacquelyn. "How do you know about a necklace for Shannon?"

"I heard her leaving a message the other day on his recorder."

With a great big smile, the girl whispered, "You're the girl he has been talking about?"

As she lowered her head, Jacquelyn nodded and added, "I think I really screwed up. I thought he had a girlfriend and used me. To tell the truth . . . for some reason, I thought he might have several girlfriends around."

"You know, Tadd has been looking everywhere for you. That's all he has done since you left. He told me that he got very drunk. It wasn't until late that night that he realized that he had made a big mistake. For some reason, he thinks that you're the girl he has been looking for most of his life."

"He thinks that I'm someone special! I'm just me: a common girl."

"It's too bad. Tadd has either already left this afternoon, or he'll be leaving early tomorrow morning. I've not been able to reach him on his cell phone all day."

"He's already gone." Jacquelyn felt her heart sink, as she now wished she had not thrown her cell phone away.

"I'm not sure. I've been crying all day about it. Tadd's very broken hearted. He feels like he missed his one chance to find his true love."

"I'm sorry also that I made such a bad mistake, but I don't know if I'm that special person for him. We just met."

"Tadd talks often about a dream that he has. He has a special man in them that had talked him into coming back to the mountains. It's a mysterious blond-haired man that always appears in white settings."

Jacquelyn couldn't believe what she heard. Tadd had the same Dream Master. All she could venture to say is that it sounded very interesting to her.

The girl found her phone and started dialing. After looking over the top of her phone, she held up a thumb to indicate they would work together. "We're going to find him. Shannon, this is Alex. Have you heard from Tadd?" After a long pause, she continued, "I found Jacquelyn and I'm with her now. If you hear from Tadd—please have him call me." Her face drew tight, and she started to cry into the phone as she replied, "I understand."

Jacquelyn moved over closer to Alex. "What's wrong?"

"She thinks Tadd has already left."

"Maybe it's not supposed to be since we only met for a few hours. I'm sure he'll be fine."

"Who knows? I think I can use a drink. How would you like to come to my place for a while so that we can talk some more?"

Jacquelyn thought why not, since she didn't have anywhere else to go. "Maybe I can for a little while, since I'd like to know more about Tadd. He seemed like a very interesting guy."

Jacquelyn soon learned Alex lived in a cabin up on the top of Ski Mountain which looked directly down upon the town of Gatlinburg. Having a place like this would be great, Jacquelyn thought, and if she stayed in Gatlinburg making a new friend would be fantastic.

Jacquelyn asked, "What are you going to do if Tadd shuts down the jewelry shop?"

"I guess it'll be shut down quickly and the entire inventory shipped to India. I'll be busy for several months doing that. I have many friends here and will do something different after that, but what are you going to do? Tadd mentioned that you had just arrived here and was looking for something to do."

"Right now, I'm still looking, but I hope to have something soon."

"Maybe I can help you. Give me a call in the morning, and I'll see if I can find something for you."

"Thanks. You've been very kind, and this wine's very good."

"Tadd loves wine, and I would guess that this one may have come from him. He always gives wine as presents," Alex added as she apparently thought of Tadd as she bit her lip as if in pain.

"I'm sure you're going to miss him. It seems like he was a good friend to you."

"Yes, he is and will always be."

"I've been thinking of his wine collection lately and trying to understand how he became so interested in them."

Alex smiled. "This is a subject he's talked to me about many times. To Tadd wine has a very unique energy in it. It's different from all of other foods out there."

While Jacquelyn wanted to hear the full story, she glanced at her watch. "I hate to run, but I need to be heading to the hotel where I'm staying. It'll be great if you can help me out."

After Jacquelyn hurried back to the hotel and got her key, she first went to the assigned room, and then, as in the previous night, changed rooms again. She knew this night would be her last there, especially after finding a friend who would help her the next day.

CHAPTER 27

In spite of being extremely tired and nervous Jacquelyn had a hard time falling asleep because of all the events happening to her over the past few days. While she could see all the good, there were still a lot of problems she needed to deal with.

Sleep, however, did come and her world again became a vivid glowing white, but the setting looked much different from before. Jacquelyn walked on a beach where the sand was bleached a pure white, and a familiarity about the place told her that yes she had been there before.

She soon saw a man walking along the shoreline toward her, and even before she reached him, she knew it would be her Dream Master, the same man she had seen so many nights before. "Where are we?" she asked when he came in range of her voice.

"This is a place I thought you'd love to see again. It's beautiful here, isn't it?"

"Yes, I think I recognize it, and I was here before, but . . . I'm still not sure where it is, or what the date was when I was here."

"Do you remember I told you one time that your past and your future are one and the same?"

"Yes, and I've been thinking about that and I still don't know what you mean."

"You've been learning a lot the last few days, and now it's necessary for me to try to explain some facts to you so that you'll understand. We've a lot of beach to walk, and

I'm sure you'll have many questions to ask me along the way."

After turning to walk with him, she felt a deep relief as she thought she might finally be getting some answers. "This place is beautiful. Have I been here before?"

"Yes, this is where you lived the last time you lived with your true love."

"I had a true love here?"

"Yes, and this is Greece, which can be a very romantic place."

"What happened to us here? What happened to him?" Jacquelyn had so many questions.

"Since then, you've been looking for him, and he has been looking for you."

"Really, that's interesting."

"It's not the first time for you, and it's up to you if it'll be the last. One of these days, I do think you'll both get to a point where you'll both go on to the next level. I'll do all I can to help this be that time. You've had many lives together, and there have also been many times you couldn't find each other. Sometimes you were separated by times in history, and other times you were too far away from each other physically to make contact. Then, there're the times that you were so close and didn't make contact."

"Why do I not remember all this?"

"In a physical state you're very limited in your ability to see different times or dimensions, but your soul remembers everything. That's why you recognize this place. In your spiritual state, you can travel as you wish. That's why you need to learn to control your dreams, the manifestation of your spiritual state, and make them work for you."

Jacquelyn understood parts of his statements, but also became more confused on others as she listened. "You say we've met on several occasions before. Can you tell me?"

"Let me ask you a question first. Do you remember other dreams you have had during your life? I mean the ones where you thought you were someone else and living a different life."

Thinking about the question, she remembered many dreams where she had been living in other places and was a totally different person. "Yes I do, actually. I remember them being very interesting, but also weird at the same time. I never could figure out what they meant."

After putting his arm around her shoulder as they walk, he continued, "You were dreaming about what you can remember of the past lives you have had. And . . . the only time you get these glimpses of this past is in your dreams and when the energy's right." He paused to face her. "Finding true love isn't so much about the person as it is about being in the state of mind to be able to accept him and give love as well. Do you now understand the four steps in finding true love?"

Jacquelyn thought about what she had learned. "I know I have to eat right to build up my energy in my physical body."

"Yes, that's a very basic part of what you must do."

"I also know about becoming one with the world of beauty around me. The beauty brings much love to me, but I've learned that I also make the world beautiful in perceiving it that way."

"Yes, you're learning much and very quickly. As you learn, more information will be presented to you because you'll be ready to receive it. And the third step is what?"

"This I'm still working on, but I think it's how to generate energy internally on my own."

"This step's not easy and takes a long time to master, but it's totally required to make the last step."

"I'm still not sure what the last step is. How do I learn it?"

"To find true love, which is between you and your mate or others in your life, you have to be able to let your love flow freely with no restriction or demands. It must be totally unselfish. You'll meet one more teacher tomorrow who will teach you about the importance of unconditional love, but there's another part to it. You also have to be able to receive love without demanding it, and by taking all that's offered gracefully and thankfully."

Jacquelyn listened to everything her Dream Master told her, but couldn't get one main question out of her mind. "Why are you telling me all this?"

"When you want something so intensely that it consumes your every thought, you simply have to ask, and the entire universe will help you, that is, if what you're doing is in the name of love. You and your love of all ages are close to seeing each other and meeting here. That's why I entered your dreams and have been trying to help. There'll be many people in your life that you think might be him, but when you do finally find him you'll know it, and he'll know it also."

"You know I've felt like many forces have been helping me. I have you at night in my dreams, my angel in the clouds at sunrise and sunset, my teachers, and my guardian angel that keeps getting me out of trouble."

"My job as a Dream Master, as you like to call me, is to connect your spiritual life with your physical life. The enlightened, the angels, are around and reveal themselves in many ways. The teachers are there to guide you, and they always have something to teach you if you're willing to ask. The real guardian angel you have there is a man who loves you and has for thousands and thousands of years. He always is in the right place at the right time. However, like two ships in the harbor at night, unless the lights are on, neither of you will ever see the other boat passing."

Jacquelyn thought of the stranger who saved her at the truck stop and the truck horn at the cabin where she was being pushed into prostituting herself. She had thought of him as a guardian angel, not as her true love looking for her. "I never realized I had someone actually looking for me before."

"I know. In learning the final step, all will become clearer to you. The two of you still have much to learn. You'll be both teacher and student to each other. That's the way of human development. As I said earlier, you've been chosen to advance, and by doing so you'll have the ability to lead mankind into a whole new world of possibilities." With this the blond-haired man turned and waved over the top of his head before vanishing into a white mist being blown in from the sea.

While watching him disappear, Jacquelyn yelled to him, "Will I see you again?" There was no answer as the beach remained white, and the clouds shimmered beautifully above her while she rested on the sand. She had so many thoughts in her head. How was she going to find this stranger who always showed up at the right time? Smiling to herself, she knew he must be close or the whole universe wouldn't be trying so hard to help her.

It was several minutes before she finally realized she was still on the white beach by herself. The Dream Master had left, but all was still there. She had all kind of visions around her which included images from her past and her future. While everything became clearer and so exciting, there was nothing from her current life however. She suddenly realized she couldn't see her current life because it was incomplete. That life was what she was making of it, and her future was still being decided.

After waking up from the dream, Jacquelyn watched the sun coming through a window blinding her. She had slept late. Afraid the sunrise was already over, she decided to take a slow shower and still go out for a while until it was time to clean the rooms. She would have to let the manager know she was leaving today since she could not stay there any longer.

After making it to the lobby, she handed him the key. "Thanks again. I slept very well last night."

"We're going to have a big crowd coming in tonight. I thought I would let you know." The manager smiled but retained a gentle compassion.

"That is okay. I think I have a place to stay. I'll talk to you about it after I get back."

"Okay, that's good." The curious look on his face suggested to Jacquelyn that he knew she was leaving.

The walk down the street was interesting with all the shops moving into high gear to get ready for the tourists. Even this late in the morning, Jacquelyn constantly watched the street to make sure she wasn't spotted. It was this keen awareness that made her notice a group walking in front of her that looked like a wedding party. Someone was getting married.

An unexpected fear suddenly came upon her. For some reason, she thought she was being watched, but since she wasn't sure from where, she felt the best course of action was to blend in with the crowd and follow the small wedding group to the top of a small hill where a tiny wedding chapel awaited them. As everyone found a seat, she scurried to the back and waited.

The service looked absolutely beautiful. The groom and bride appeared very happy as were all the people watching the service. No one asked Jacquelyn who she was, or which side of the family she was associated with.

The preacher finally began to speak. He looked to be a short, heavyset man in his late sixties, but with a big robust smile. While he was almost completely bald, he looked very clean and pleasant. From apparently years of preaching, he spoke in a very clear voice that carried well even without the use of a microphone. "I have performed many marriages in my lifetime. It's the most important day in these two lives, for sure as they declare one proclamation. They have found their true love. But . . . what is true love? I've been asked that question many times. Since the bible has an answer most people know, it would serve us well to examine that answer again at a moment like this." He then opened his bible and started to read. "I'm reading from first Corinthians where it says that love is patient, which I think means it's not demanding. Love is kind, which is why so much importance is placed on serving the other. It also says that love is not envious, boastful, or rude. It's something that's given freely and openly because you want to make the other person happy, and not only for what you get in return. It's not something that insists on its own way and is irritable and resentful. Love bears all things, believes all things, hopes all things, and endures all things. For with faith, hope, and love, the two are much more than singles, making love the greatest force in the world."

The whole church echoed a subtle amen as the preacher closed his bible. "He'll be there and sustain her, and she'll be there for him and sustain him. However, I think there's one more part that I want to add. This is from a plain old country preacher that has, as I said, performed many weddings. Some of those I've married are still happily married, and I hate to say that some aren't. The one item that I think makes the difference in these marriages is commitment. For love to grow, it must be secure. Within a marriage, there can be no time for doubt or second-guessing. True love shall last forever and ever."

"How true your words are," Jacquelyn said to herself. The fourth step she needed to learn was becoming very clear to her. The preacher kept speaking; however, she had had heard what she needed. As the ceremony was ending and the groom kissed the bride, she decided to make a quick exit through the back of the church.

A girl holding a basket of flowers greeted her as she opened the door. After handing one to Jacquelyn, she smiled and said they were special flowers from a friend that grew them. The girl's smile was very contagious as Jacquelyn recognizes the smell at once. It was the flowers from the cabin she often called Farmer John's place. She noticed something else in the smell. It had the scent of a man's cologne in it, the same scent she had recognized before. It wasn't a fragrance after all, but the smell of the flowers he grew that she smelled on him.

Looking at the girl, she asked, "These are very different flowers from anything that I ever remember seeing before. What kind are they?"

"I'm not sure. They come from the perfume garden behind his house."

That was all the answer she needed to know. She knew where to find him now.

CHAPTER 28

While walking down the street, Jacquelyn focused her eyes straight ahead as her mind raced but stayed alert on her destination. The fragrance she had smelled wasn't cologne, but the smell of exotic flowers from his perfume garden which had become embedded in his clothing. The man she was looking for and her angel were one and the same and she knew it. Having no idea what she would say after she got there, she hoped for insight from above to lead her.

The trail ahead of her felt like an old friend as she now knew every turn. Almost everything in her path was exactly as she remembered. After making the climb, she felt great. Her energy was high, and the anticipation was more than she could stand.

While taking the shortcut quickly brought the cabin into her view, she stopped for a minute to survey the area before crossing the ravine toward the field behind the cabin. Everything looked manicured. It was easy to see that he put a lot of effort into the yard around the cabin, which had three levels. While she entered from the back side, she knew there had to be a road to the front of the cabin from somewhere.

Without hesitations, Jacquelyn quickly knocked on the back door. She heard no answer, so she waited. After thinking she should go to the front door, she started to leave the door, but she suddenly heard some noises inside. Someone was at home after all.

The door opened promptly, sending Jacquelyn into shock—standing in the doorway was Tadd. With both not knowing what to say to the other, the two look at each other for a long time, but finally . . . Jacquelyn broke the ice. "Ohhhh my God. I didn't know this was your house!"

Still trying to figure what was going on Tadd stared as if in a trance. "Why did you come to the back door?"

"I didn't realize this was your house. I knew you lived up here somewhere, but we came a different way, and it was dark. I smelled your flowers from the trail over there, and I wanted to come over and—"

"I've been looking for you, and I had assumed that you had left." Tadd stopped her from interrupting him by raising his hand. "The other night I was afraid that I made you upset or something. I promise I only put you to bed, and I never bothered you after you went to sleep."

"I think I believe you now." She tried to regain her composure. "The smell of your flowers is what attracted my attention. The fragrance is incredible."

"Thanks! I really like my perfume garden, and it's a special hobby of mine. Would you like to see it?"

"Yes, I'd like to very much." She finally allowed her eyes to come directly in contact with his. With the initial embarrassment over, there would be time for questions later.

After walking into the cabin and up to the next level, she started to recognize it from her time there before. As she walked by the wine cellar, she only smiled at how happy he had been telling her about his wine collection. She turned to Tadd and smiled. "I'm not sure I even thanked you for the wine the other night. It was very good."

"You're welcome, but perhaps we drank too much the other night."

"It's my fault. I should've known better. I don't drink that much since being this small it only takes a very little for me. I have a confession to make. I overheard a phone message that someone was leaving on your recorder after I woke. I was sure you had a girlfriend, and I even imagined that you had many girlfriends. I didn't want to be another notch on your bedpost."

"So, that's why you left. I wish you had given me time to explain. Anyway, if you will let me, I'd love to start over. It'd be great to get to know you better."

"Yes, I'd like that. In fact, I'd like that very much." A rush of heat flooded her face. "I also talked to a girl that works for you yesterday. Alex told me a lot about you. It appears that you've had a very interesting life."

"I think many people have led interesting lives. All people are different and have something to give you, but you have to take the time to listen to their stories."

The flower garden looked beautiful in many ways. She saw a definite order in its design. With the smell beyond belief, perfection was obviously the goal in every part of the garden.

"Tell me about the flowers? Many of these I've never seen before."

"I've been collecting various flowers for years. Many of these flowers exist only here in this garden, where I've cross-pollinated and grafted them. The seeds produced here I've crossbred as I continue to try to create new smells. This is something my mother taught me how to do back in India."

"Every morning I walk by this place and go to the top of a ridge over there to watch the sunrise." She pointed in the direction behind him. "And in the evening, I go over there to watch the sunset. The smell of the flowers has always intrigued me, and that's why I had to stop by and see them."

"So, you really didn't know this was the back entrance to my place?"

Thinking that she needed to further explain her actions, Jacquelyn explained, "I know this will sound really weird, but I was thinking my guardian angel lived here. It's as if my dreams have lured me to this spot. I've been in many close calls, and my guardian angel has always showed up at the right moment."

Tadd laughed. "Well, I'm glad someone thinks I'm an angel."

As they walked around the corner of the house Jacquelyn noticed a black truck sitting in the driveway. While looking harder she recognized it as the truck of her guardian angel. The shock in her voice became very apparent as she turned to Tadd. "Were you in Chattanooga about a week ago?"

The question appeared to puzzle him. "Yes, for a quick trip to get some plants I needed there. Why do you ask?"

"I was at a truck stop when the men giving me a ride began to give me some trouble."

"Wow! You must be the girl I saw running from a truck. I remember that. Since it was easy to see what was going on, I thought it was best to follow the two out of the truck stop. When I returned, I didn't see you, so I assumed you were okay."

After rushing over to him, she gave him a big hug. "I really owe you for that. It's not too many times that you can hug your guardian angel."

He smiled. "How well do you know the mountains?"

"I've been here several times, why?"

"If you're not doing anything today, I'd love to show you around a little."

"Sure, I'd love it. This place is beautiful."

"I have to make a few calls first, but it'll only take me a minute. Perhaps you'd like some tea while you're waiting. I promise I'll only take a few minutes."

"Okay." Jacquelyn watched him walk away before she went into the kitchen where she could smell the tea. She carefully searched through several drawers hoping to find a teacup. After locating one she poured herself some with a color that looked fantastic and emitted an intoxicating aroma. This was a kitchen she could get used to. Now knowing that Tadd was from India, she fully expected him to be a very big tea drinker. It would be so interesting to know more about which teas he liked.

As he walked out to meet her, she noticed that he had on a new shirt. "If I knew you're going to dress up, I could've changed also." She hoped he enjoyed being teased.

"I think you look great, but I know how girls like to shop, so we might visit a new store my sister just opened first. If there's anything else that you want to see while we're out, let me know."

Jacquelyn felt extremely happy as they walked out to the truck, where he opened the door for her and made sure she got in okay. That small gesture confirmed his good manners and something she really looked for in a special man. As Tadd jumped into the seat next to her, she had to ask him to grant her one more request. "Do you mind letting me hear what the horn sounds like?"

With a look of curiosity on his brow, Tadd honked the horn three short times. She had heard that horn before; it was outside the cabin where she was caught trespassing. Now she knew without a doubt that he was the one there also. She started to tell him about it, but decided recounting the incident would be too embarrassing and decided to tell him later.

After backing out of the driveway, Tadd turned on the radio and a country love song began to play. Tadd apparently knew the words very well as he sang along with it. With his voice sounding smooth and mellow, she loved to hear him sing. When he realized that she was smiling at his singing, Tadd started singing the words directly to her. Jacquelyn loved and greatly appreciated Tadd's serenade, since it was something no one had ever done for her before—at least not in this life. "Where are we going?" she finally asked.

"I just changed my mind and thought that we should start with a secret waterfall that I know about. It's small, but impressive, and there're some interesting places for you to see along the way."

Within minutes, they located the trail entrance and started their hike. He was right, since the secluded forest was so beautiful. As they strolled along the trail that was easy to walk, Tadd reached over and held her hand in his. His muscular hand made her feel like he had the strength of the world in it, making her feel more secure than she ever had in her life.

After an hour of walking, they reached a beautiful waterfall. Tadd led her over to a rock to rest for a minute, while he explained. "This has always been a special place of mine, and I think I always assumed that one day I would have a special person to share it with." As he talked, his focus locked in on her eyes, and even with all the beauty around her she couldn't see anything but his dark brown piercing eyes in front of her. Since he was so close to her, she thought he was going to kiss her. He even glanced slowly down to her lips as if he was contemplating it. His eyes lingered there for a long time. As he looked back up, Jacquelyn realized she had not been breathing.

When her lungs returned to normal she sucked in the sweet smell of the forest and looked around her. "This is a lovely place, and the kind of place most people can only dream about seeing."

"I agree, and in fact, this place is in my dreams very often. Even while I was away from America, this place always found its way back to my dreams. It's the place I know finally lured me back here."

After talking for a long time and realizing the depth of the feelings they had for each other, they hiked back to the truck and rode toward town. Tadd told her more about his sister's new dress shop. Since Tadd no longer planned to leave, he suggested they go there together and tell her the news.

"Alex told me the woman on the phone I assumed was your girlfriend was actually your sister."

"My sister will get a kick out of that, and by the way, she's a half-sister. My mom still lives in India. She never came back to the United States with my dad. That's one reason I travel back and forth so much. My dad came back and remarried."

After entering the shop, Tadd flashed smiles and waved at his sister, who looked much like him. After finishing with a customer, she rushed over to meet them. "Hello, sis," Tadd said as he pulled Jacquelyn next to him. "This is Jacquelyn, a new friend of mine. She thought you were my girlfriend."

"I'm not that desperate yet," Shannon said with a loud laugh. "However, it's great to see that you're not leaving now."

"You have a great looking shop here." Jacquelyn smiled as she looked around. The shop wasn't very large, and more of a boutique with very expensive clothes in it. The décor did look very elegant and gave the whole place a feeling of importance. It was obvious how much love had gone into its design.

"Thank you, I hope the customers like it."

An outfit on a mannequin caught Jacquelyn's eye. "That outfit's beautiful."

"Yes, I think so too, but it'll look much better on you than it will on me. What size are you?"

A small look of embarrassment passed across Jacquelyn face "I'm a size four, but I really cannot buy anything right now."

After pulling a size four from the rack, Shannon handed it to Jacquelyn. "Try it on, and let us see what it looks like."

At first she was going to refuse, but it looked so very beautiful that she decided to slip it on and see. Besides, she also knew Tadd and his sister wanted to talk for a minute. Her trying on the outfit would give them some time.

After walking into the dressing room, she quickly undressed. Since it felt embarrassing for her to not have better clothes, perhaps she could use her mother's credit card and buy herself one nice dress. After all, she would need nice clothes to wear to some job interviews. As Jacquelyn prepared to leave the dressing room she felt great in the simple black dress which offered a style she loved. When she opened the curtains, Tadd and his sister were waiting for her. His eyes were shining with approval. "That looks great on you!"

The attention slightly embarrassed her as she blushed. "I don't know. I don't have anything to wear with it."

Tadd's sister gave her a big smile. "I'm way ahead of you, girl. I think you'll find everything you need in here. Come with me."

"I can't. This is too much."

"Tadd has already given me his credit card, so don't worry about it."

Jacquelyn started to protest, but saw Tadd winking at her as her heart melted.

"Thank you. You didn't have to do that."

"I know, but I only do what I want to do, and I enjoyed that. Now, if you'll allow me to do one more thing for you, I'll feel like I made up a little for the other night."

"You have nothing to make up for, really."

"Okay, but I have one more stop I think you'll enjoy. I'll have to leave you there for a little while, but I think you'll enjoy it."

"Where is it?"

"Very close to here. It'll be a good surprise." He took her hand again, and walked her back to the truck after saying good bye to her sister.

After stopping shortly down the road at another strip mall, he got out, walked around and opened her door. She studied the front entrance of a spa of some kind as Tadd walked to the door and opened it for her. Now what, she wondered as she heard him ask the receptionist if they had time for one more customer before he made his way across the lobby to see an oriental woman he apparently knew.

The oriental woman smiled broadly at him. "I think so."

"Good, this is Jacquelyn, and I'll let you take care of her."

A spa treatment for her was more than she could imagine. "Tadd, this is too much, really."

Stepping forward quickly, the oriental woman took charge. "Honey, you're going to enjoy it here. We'll take good care of you."

As he left the spa, Tadd waved at Jacquelyn. "I'll be back shortly."

CHAPTER 29

Several hours later, Tadd returned with a big smile on his face. "How do you feel?"

"I feel like I've died and gone to heaven. That was incredible. I don't think anyone has ever done anything like this for me before."

"I hated having to leave you, but I had a few tasks I had to take care of. I see you were in good hands since you look like you're radiating with energy. Oh, by the way, are you hungry?"

"Yes, a little bit. It's been a while since I've eaten."

"How would you like for me to get some food and prepare you a meal. I hope you like the way I cook. I like eating a little differently."

"What do you consider different?"

"Don't laugh at me, but I eat foods that are full of life, that make you happy, and fill you with love and peace."

Jacquelyn thought about laughing, but decided not to since it would be too hard to explain. "That's the way I've been eating, or at least trying to eat for the last few days. I met a man on the cliff above your house a few days ago who acted as a teacher for me. What he taught me is starting to make sense."

With a slight chuckle under his breath, Tadd asked, "Was he a kind of hippie looking guy in his sixties?"

"Yes, do you know him?"

"I'm afraid so. He's been teaching me for a long time. He has a way of getting under your skin."

"It's very interesting that since I've been here, I've met many teachers who have taught me many important truths. Do you know about the four steps in finding true love?"

"Yes, it's been part of my training for a long time. The first three steps are hard enough, but the fourth one's the one that's the most important."

Minutes later he quickly pulled in front of a small store and dashed in to buy the food they needed. When he returned to the truck, he showed her his purchases before he asked, "Is there anything else you can think of that we need?"

She glanced into the sack where she noticed he had many different kinds of fruits and raw vegetables. "I can't think of anything." During the peaceful drive back along the mountain stream from Pigeon Forge to Gatlinburg it felt like she had known Tadd for most of her life, rather than the few hours they had spent together. Everything fit perfectly. "Do you have a lot of dreams?" she asked as they were driving.

"While I have many kinds of dreams, and some of them are very interesting, it's trying to understand them that is important. It's an entirely different world in the spiritual world than it is in the physical world. In fact, I've spent most of my life studying other cultures, philosophies, and traditions, and I've learned that many of them have a glimmer of truth in them. It's these rare precious stones of knowledge that I always search for."

"That's interesting. Can you tell me what you dream about the most?" Jacquelyn felt totally at ease with Tadd, and she felt like she was able to ask questions without any hesitation at all.

Confirming that he trusted her also, he began, "I think it would be the one where I was living in a different world and in a different time. Some of the places I've visited so many times in my dreams that I know them by heart."

"I've had many dreams like that also. Last night I was on a beach with white sand and beautiful clouds around me; even all of the buildings were white."

"It sounds like Italy or Greece, where all of the buildings are white."

Jacquelyn felt the shock of his words penetrating her soul. "Yes, it was Greece . . . actually."

"I think I've had the same dream about the same place many times. I'm always walking the beach there, and I think I was married until I died at an early age. In my dreams, I'm constantly thinking about how hard it is to die and not grow old with her. It would be so good to see her walking on the beach again. In my dream, I'm persistently looking for her."

"Tadd, I know it sounds strange, but . . . I think I might be that girl. Do you think that's possible?"

"You never know, but I'll tell you what I think. I feel like I've known you for a very long time."

"It's interesting to hear you say that, because I was thinking the very same thought earlier." With this understanding she reached over and squeezed his hand.

At Tadd's home they went straight to the kitchen and started preparing the food. They ate the raw vegetables as soon as they prepared them, and both felt their energy increasing as they ate. They knew that what they were eating was good for them.

After finishing the food, Tadd asked her to follow him outside to his garden. There were several large comfortable chairs in the garden, and Tadd pulled two of them close together while they glanced around the garden, confirming just how beautiful it really was. The more they studied the plants and flowers in the garden, especially the flowers, the more beautiful they became. It was almost mystical how enchanting the moment became. Jacquelyn and Tadd also recognized how the second step of the four steps was working for them.

"Have you learned the third step of building up your energy?" Tadd asked her.

"I'm having problems with it, but I've felt it at times. It's very hard to hold for a long time."

"When you reach the third level and generate the energy internally, you have to be able to direct the energy somewhere. If not directed, it will not flow . . . and if it does not flow, there's no reason to generate more."

What he said made sense to her since her only concerns before had been that if she generated too much she would explode. "I was thinking that might be a reason. How do you direct it, and for what reasons do you direct it?"

"That's what you learn in the fourth step. If you don't mind, I need to take a shower. Enjoy the scenery in the garden and more food if you wish. It will only take me a minute to freshen up." Before getting up, Tadd leaned over her and gave her a small kiss on the top of her head.

After he left, Jacquelyn looked around the garden, loving every bit of it. Life was very good. When she felt a little thirsty she decided to go inside to the kitchen and get something to drink. It felt unreal to think that a single guy would keep his house so neat, but even this made her more attracted to him. After entering the kitchen she poured herself some water and glanced around. Everything was so well organized. When she saw a door leading to his small office, she decided to venture in. It was almost the same in there as well. Hanging on the wall, however, was one item she didn't expect to see. The color she remembered very well as her mind went back to the last time she saw it. There was no doubt about it.

She took it with her as she walked to Tadd's bedroom where she waited on him to come out. About ten minutes later he opened the door and saw her standing there. She flashed a smile, but obviously indicated she had a big question on her mind. "I think I saw this monk outfit the other day at the center. I couldn't see the guy in it because the hood hid his face. Do you lecture on kama sutra?"

While smiling back at her like the kid who had just been caught, he held up his hand as if to say yes. "When did you see the lecture?"

"I think it was yesterday. You're a man of many surprises."

"I didn't see you there. It would have been interesting if I had only known you were there. It's easy to see that I'm much better at giving advice than following my own advice to others."

"Why do you wear the hood to hide your face?"

"It's for the same reason I never make eye contact with anyone in the room. The power of the kama sutra is very powerful, and I don't wish to make contact with the wrong person. It might give someone the wrong impression."

"I think I understand. Where did you acquire your knowledge?"

"My mom's from India. That's where I've studied for most of my life, and this subject has intrigued me for a long time. I really enjoy teaching what I've learned, and I hope that one day I'd be fully able to share my knowledge with my special love."

Jacquelyn studied Tadd in the pullover jersey and gym shorts he wore. He had no hair anywhere except the top of his head and looked rugged and very masculine, but housed a tender loving soul.

Tadd walked over, held her hand and led her to the bed where he indicated for her to sit. He went to the center of the bed and climbed in, where he crossed his legs and assumed an Indian style. As she watched him, he instructed her to turn around and face him. "The fourth step's where you have to learn on your own—more like we have to learn on our own, I guess I should say."

"Are you sure that I'm the one you want to teach?"

"Yes, I'm more sure of this than anything in my life."

Reaching over to her, he held her left hand in his right and her right hand in his left. His hands felt warm, smooth, and gentle. "What I know from what I have read is that the actual completion of this part's different for all couples."

"I can be a very good student," she said, waiting to see what Tadd had on his mind.

"First, we must totally empty our bodies and souls of all thoughts and energy. Into this union, we can only bring you and me. It must be absolutely and totally pure. Do you understand?"

"I think so."

"Good, this is what I want you to do. I want you to concentrate on your little toe and tighten the muscle on it as hard as you can. Then, let the other toes join in. Slowly allow the foot and ankles, then the legs, then the stomach, and eventually with every muscle that you have do the same. Hold every muscle you have in a complete strain, squeezing every bit of energy out of it as long as you can. Then . . . let the energy and the force release from you. Just let it go."

Jacquelyn did exactly as he asked her to do. The release felt incredible, and it was as if all of her burdens had left her.

"Now, do it again and again, and until all the bad energy's out of you." After doing the same exercise with her a few times, Tadd continued, "Now that the body has all the bad energy out of it, we must do the same with our minds. It's done much the same way. Concentrate on all of the bad in your life, all that causes you misery and distractions, as hard as you can. Don't miss any of them, just as you didn't forget any muscles before. Hold your thoughts as tightly as you can. Then . . . simply let them go."

Jacquelyn understood what Tadd was asking her to do, and it worked to some extent, but she had trouble releasing the thoughts of her ex-husband who was still hunting her and the rental agent that was with him. She decided to tell Tadd about being caught trespassing, but he didn't reply at all for some reason. She wondered why he didn't ask more questions. She even told him how embarrassing it had been for her. She then told Tadd a lot about her abusive ex-husband. Being a patient lover, Tadd continued to work with her and teach her what he knew and how to cleanse these thoughts from her mind.

"Now, repeat this mental exercise over and over until all's clear, and there's nothing else in your mind that's bad."

She obeyed his wishes, and each time it became easier and easier for her to release her thoughts. When she finished the last time, she opened her eyes and saw Tadd looking at her as she said, "That's really good for me. Thank you."

Tadd looked at her for a few more seconds until he moved off the bed and struck a match he used to light several candles. He kept lighting them all over the room as the twinkling light show became more and more romantic.

When Tadd went into the bathroom and returned with a small basket of flowers, the room quickly started to smell very special as she recognized the aroma of Tadd's flowers. After inserting the flowers in a small vase, he placed them between them on the bed.

"Building a bouquet is like creating life. Each one's different and special." He picked up a rose, placed it in the center of the vase, and turned his hand over to indicate that it was time for her to add to the vase. She picked a flower and placed it next to his. It was slightly lower, but a good complement to his. With each choice he made, she complemented him. The vase grew more and more beautiful as they assembled it together. When they finished it, Tadd placed it on the nightstand beside the bed.

He assumed his position again in front of her. "It's now time to create our own energy. This is why the third step is so important to learn properly. Inhale in and feel the energy as it builds inside you. Don't draw it from anywhere but your inner soul. There it's pure, and it's not contaminated with anything from the outside world."

Jacquelyn took long breaths of air as her rhythm remained smooth and easy. The energy flowed in, and she knew it. As she breathed in, the energy exploded inside her and felt hot and powerful, but when she breathed out she felt the energy flow out of her. Mastering this breathing exercise felt fantastic.

Upon opening her eyes, she glanced at Tadd and saw him inhaling and exhaling. With his eyes closed she allowed herself a few minutes to watch him breathe. Even in the dim light of the candles, he started to glow. Then, she noticed that as he breathed out, she breathed in, and as she breathed out, he breathed in. She also noticed the aura of the energy flowing between them. As it flowed from one to the other, it gained energy and refortified each time. They were totally becoming as one.

Tadd opened his eyes and smiled at her. After taking her hands to his lips, he kissed them slowly. His lips felt warm and moist, and even with his lips kissing her hand, he never removed the focus of his eyes from her eyes. They glowed like a burning ember in the night where all the candles sparkling in the room reflected off them at once.

After raising her hands, Tadd pulled them over his shoulders and placed them on his back. With his hands now free, he caressed her shoulders before he cupped both of his hands under her chin. With the skill of a surgeon, Tadd worked the fingers of his hands to her neck and massaged her, barely touching her skin at all.

"That feels good." Her heart didn't race, but it did beat hard.

Tadd moved closer to her as she felt his breath which was so very clean and fresh. His presence became even more powerful from being so very close to her. His lips remained only inches from her lips, yet he kept his focus on her eyes as they penetrated into her very soul. "Your eyes are beautiful," he said as he continued to study them.

"Thanks, you have great eyes also."

His lips glazed her lips, but then he briefly departed. His eyes focused on her for a few seconds as he hesitated, but then he kissed her again softly, but with slightly more pressure than the time before. It was a quick kiss, as if he was testing the waters with each kiss. Then, he moved to her cheek and kissed it delicately. He backed up again to survey her face one more time before he reached over and kissed her with an unrestrained passion. The warmth and moisture of his lips penetrated all remaining resistance she might have had.

The transmission of energy between Tadd and Jacquelyn accumulated within the depths of both and produced intense states of pleasure and expanded their knowledge of each other. Their connection was one they both knew would last a lifetime and beyond. They knew how lucky they were as they realized the happiness and joy that comes from living in a state of true love—one only a few will ever experience. Their union wasn't just physical bodies making love, but something much more important. They were being transformed into one body. Suddenly, the entire universe became involved in the union, which extended all the way across time and space.

The night continued with no loss of energy or passion. In fact, the energy level increased all night. She never remembered going to sleep, but only waking up lying on his chest feeling more fulfilled as a woman than she could ever remember.

After looking into his face, she realized he had been watching her for a while. She felt a new heat radiating from her due to his intense stares. "What are you looking at?"

"A woman who is glowing in love more than any woman I think on the planet."

"Well, I'd have to say that you're the reason for that."

"When you want something so intensely, all the universe will help you to not only find it but achieve it. I knew all along it would help me find you." Tadd sat in the bed and looked out the window.

"What are you looking for?"

"I think there'll be a very good sunrise this morning. Would you like to join me?"

"Sure."

"I have something I need to take care of. The place on top of the ridge where you go is also one of my favorite places. If you can go there and wait for me, I think you'll be very happy."

"Why? Do you have another surprise for me?"

"Yes. I think it's the best surprise I could ever give you."

CHAPTER 30

Tadd watched Jacquelyn walk to the trail leading to the top of the ridge. He didn't have much time to cross to the other side. The calls he had made yesterday to line this up went through his head. He knew he had to be careful.

While working around to the other side of the ridge across from Jacquelyn was a long hike, and for most people it would have taken all morning, Tadd was there in almost no time. The distance across the ridge was about a half mile, which he hoped would be a safe range.

After making it to the place he was trying to reach, he surveyed the area before making his presence known. They stood there, waiting for him as he approached them. All was as it should be.

"Hello," he yelled as he walked on the ridge to meet them.

"It's about time you got here! I still can't figure out why you wanted to meet here at this time in the morning. I know you like sunrises, but I think I'd rather be sleeping." The real estate agent shivered slightly. "This is Vincent, by the way. He was with me the other day, but I didn't have a chance to introduce you then." The rental agent pointed to Vincent.

Tadd didn't take his hand, but stood there looking at him. "I heard you have some information that I need to know."

The agent glanced at him with a big question on his face before proceeding, "Vincent has offered a big reward for information on a missing person. I think she's here in Gatlinburg. Vincent's afraid that she'll run again. This girl is the one I think I found spending the night in one of your cabins the other night. She got away before I could get the cops there. Vincent thinks that if we can have her arrested for trespassing, it'll give him time to talk to her and hopefully bring her to her senses. He's willing to pay for all damages that she may have caused also."

"That's a very interesting story." Tadd sized up the men and heard all he wanted to hear. "It's too bad that it's not all true."

"What do you mean?" Vincent snapped at him.

"Vincent, the girl you're after is on the other side of the ridge over there. If you had wings you could go over there, but from what I've heard, you're no angel."

"What, you know her?" the agent yelled.

"Yes . . . and she told me about you last night, and about how you tried to force her to have sex with you."

"Is that what she said?" He looked like a balloon about to explode with his anger making his face redder by the moment.

"I don't want to even hear what you might have to say. You're fired. I can handle my own rentals."

Vincent stood on the ridge trying to see where Jacquelyn was before he turned to face Tadd. "You think you're pretty smart, don't you?" He slowly removed a knife from his coat. "You know, this knife is sharp enough to skin a bear, and I'm sure it'll work on you."

"There's something else you should know, Vincent." Tadd produced a large knife of his own. "The land you're standing on is Cherokee land. That's a little known fact, but here the law's according to our customs, and punishments are decided here. I could even scalp you, and it'd be perfectly legal."

"I don't think so. There're two of us, and only one of you."

"Really!" Tadd whistled loudly and then moved his arms around to point to all the surrounding forest, which suddenly came alive with sounds and motions. "In these woods you never know what might happen."

The two men started looking around, watching the commotion and trying to figure out what was going on as a large black object suddenly rose in front of where Tadd had been standing. A thundering roar shook everything around them as the grunt of the largest bear either had ever seen stood in front of them and on its back legs.

The bear grunted again, making the whole ridge vibrate as a result of its powerful voice. The bear jerked its heads to one side and stretched its mouth open to reveal large savage looking teeth. The men panicked as they looked to see what had happened to Tadd. How could he have gotten away so quick? They had nowhere to run as they were left standing on the edge of the cliff.

"Drop down to a fetal position," the agent yelled at Vincent. Both dropped quickly and hoped for the best. They felt the bear hovering above them, but they remained untouched as they trembled at the apparent thoughts of being eaten alive. "Oh God!" They both yelled.

As quickly as it started all suddenly became quiet again. When they looked up, they only saw Tadd standing there. Tadd pointed at the rental agent. "Your time here is over, and I don't ever want to see you around here again. These cabins that my father left me aren't to be used in such a manner as this." He then pointed at Vincent. "And . . . as far as you, there's a warrant out for your arrest. I think you'll like it much better than being breakfast here. Of course, if you think you can skin a live bear, my hat is off to you."

"What kind of warrant?" The agent glanced at Vincent.

"The bitch is crazy and making up lies about me. I taught her how to live and have a good time and this is the way she repays me."

Tadd tried hard to control his anger, which was boiling inside of him. "I don't know how you live with yourself. How can anyone drug their own wife and take nude photos of her."

Vincent glared at him. "No one can prove that."

"They found the photos you took. It's over."

Vincent's face froze. "I'll see you in hell."

"I'm sorry to disappoint you, but you'll not find us down there with you." He placed his knife is his pocket. "Your blood will not be on my hands." He smiled. "But . . . you know a bear has to eat."

A roar echoed from along the ridge again, as both men turned to see if they could see the bear. Looking back, they noticed that Tadd had disappeared, and they were all alone again. There's a saying in the mountains that when being chased by a bear you don't have to outrun the bear, just the person running with you. That's exactly the way it looked as the two men ran for their lives. Tadd knew they would never be back.

After running along another trail going down and up the ridge, Tadd soon saw Jacquelyn. "Hello." She flashed a large smile as he reached her. "I was scared you wouldn't make it in time to see the sunrise since it's almost over now."

"I'm sorry I'm late, but I wouldn't miss it for the world."

After thinking for a minute, Jacquelyn had a question for Tadd. "The day before I came to your house, I heard that you left town for India. What made you stick around?"

"I had someone tell me about a girl who had trespassed in one of the cabins my father had left me with over the ridge there."

"You own that cabin?"

"Yes, my father actually built it. I knew you were still here somewhere. You don't have to worry anymore about the rental agent of my cabin, or I should say the previous agent since I took care of that this morning. Also, that ex-husband of yours will not bother you anymore."

"What make you think so?"

"Well, for some reason, I don't think he likes baby very much."

"Baby?"

With a broad smile, Tadd walked over and yelled at the top of his lungs, "Babyyyyyyy." He repeated the call loudly several times.

All became quiet again as he returned next to Jacquelyn. "I have another surprise for you."

"You're a man with lots of surprises, for sure." While leaning over, she forgot about baby and kissed Tadd softly on the lips. "You make me very happy just being here."

The ground started to shake as she heard grunting coming from below them. It started getting closer and closer, until Jacquelyn jumped into Tadd's arms when a massive black terror bounced on the ridge next to them.

Tadd kissed her on the top of her head. "Jacquelyn, I want you to meet baby." The black bear slowly walked over and turned on its back in front of them as Tadd rubbed baby's stomach. "Her mother left her when she was born three years ago. She thinks of me as her daddy."

Jacquelyn wasn't too sure about the bear, but knew they would have more time to get to know each other later. He patted the bear. "Go on baby, and have a good day today. Stay out of trouble." Honoring the hand signals of her master, baby lumbered down the trail.

After looking into a small backpack that he carried, Tadd produced a bottle of champagne and two glasses. "I think today will be a special day." He poured a glass for each of them. "What shall we drink to?"

Jacquelyn only had to think for a minute to find an answer. "To this moment and to the moments to come." With this toast, the sunrise began to explode across the sky with the colors of the rainbow. The passion in the sunrise remained only a small reflection of their love which had finally come together again after thousands of years of searching since they were together in Greece.

As they both focused on the sunrise and sent their love to it, the sun peeked through the clouds and became brighter and brighter as it intensified. Not only were they sending love to it, the sunrise was returning the favor with the whole universe joining in on this moment. With Tadd and Jacquelyn holding each other close, they both had one thought on their mind. How will they make sure, this time, they would always be together?

When they sent their thoughts and prayers straight to the sunrise as it continued to brighten with each passing moment, the world, as they knew it, melted away. They both recognized the new setting, but it usually occurred in their dreams, but with no surprise to either the Dream Master walked instantly toward them. His smiled looked more brilliant than ever before. "I'm so proud of you both."

In total agreement they looked at each other and wondered what would happen next. Where do they go from here?

"I think it's now time for me to answer many questions for you. I know you have been through a lot, but I promise it's only the beginning. The next part of your journey begins now, but I need to explain a few facts to you. If you want to stay together forever you have to follow my instructions exactly. Is that understood?"

As if there were any doubt, they both look at each other and stated in no uncertain terms, "Absolutely."

CHAPTER 31

The Dream Master walked between them, turned in the direction they were looking and took a hand of both. "This is the step of faith that starts the process. It's my pleasure to welcome you to Whitestone."

They look over at each other and stepped forward together. The world remained bright white, almost blinding, but not to the point of hurting. In fact, the white glow felt very pleasing and comforting. They continued to walk, but it felt almost as if they were walking on air.

"I know you have many questions and I'll answer them as best that I can. Whitestone's a school I've developed to help those like you to enter the final step. It's not easy, but essential for almost everyone to make the final step."

They looked at each other, knowing that the number of questions they wanted answers to was almost endless. They felt like kids in a candy store, not knowing where to start or what they were allowed to have. The slow walk built anticipation—where were they going?

Tadd asked the first question. "Where are we and where are we going?"

"I think that'll be a fair place to start. We're heading to Whitestone. Like I said, it's a special school I have created to help those looking for the side door to heaven. You're leaving the world you know—the physical world—and entering a world that's between the purely physical world and the totally spiritual or energy world."

"I can hear what you're saying, but it's still very hard to understand." Jacquelyn said as they walked and kept trying to see through the bright white glow around her.

The Dream Master smiled as he continued. "In this place you can see both the future and the past, but can't control it directly. You can roam around time itself freely. While you feel like you have a physical body, you do not. However, you can manifest yourself so that others in the physical world can see you and hear you. In fact, you have already met some of the enlightened ones here back in the physical world. I'm sure you remember Kayo, who, by the way, is very fond of both of you. She'll be extremely happy to see you made it here.

Jacquelyn's eyes sparkled as she thought of seeing Kayo again. "She's here?"

"Yes and many others I'm sure you'll recognize. We'll be there very soon." The white glow softened as they walked and images of a deep-blue sky appeared above them. A soft cool breeze full of fresh scents started blowing and removed one layer of the glow at a time to reveal more of the sky above. As both Tadd and Jacquelyn glanced upwards, the anticipation continued to grow with each step.

"If you think the surroundings are perfect, you only have to give yourself a pat on the back. This is a place you create as well as all of the others who are here. You'll learn that your thoughts create everything."

"That can be . . . interesting." Jacquelyn glanced at the others to see if she had said something wrong. She didn't mean to, but knew it could be taken wrong.

"Yes, it can be indeed. That's why you need to be trained to understand your powers and how to use them properly," the Dream Master said, as glistening white buildings covering the hillsides appeared beneath the glow. While in a futurist, kind of crystalline design, each still retained a subtle uniqueness. "You'll soon learn the extent to which Whitestone has grown. While it's a very exclusive place, the numbers here are rapidly growing." He pointed to the horizon all around them as more and more buildings appeared with some of them very high up on top of mountains with winding roads leading to them.

They all stopped walking to watch the buildings appearing as the glow decreased. The pure white designs of the buildings captured their imaginations, making them want to learn more. Tadd's face showed signs of understanding, but his darting eyes suggested an increasing number of questions. "So, this is a place somewhere between heaven and earth?"

"That's a very good way to put it. It has characteristics of both worlds in it." He stretched his arms and the glow lowered further to reveal the lush green trees, bushes and grass around them. The feelings of nature around them made them breathe deeper as they took in the smells of the surroundings.

With the sights increasing in every direction, they both knew that it was being created and recreated as they watched it. They saw the Dream Master smiling at them as he approved the events coming to life around them. He lowered his hands to his side and the glow slowly dissipates all the way to the ground. "I hope you'll like this place, and I look forward to showing you around."

"I'm very interested in seeing it." Jacquelyn glanced around, trying hard to fully understand. "Is this a dream, or is this reality?" She reached over and pinched her arm to test her mind. Everything appeared so real and lifelike. If this was a dream, it was the most vivid dream she had ever had.

"It's going to take a while to understand, but this place is actually more real than the world you left. This world's full of energy and life that extends through all time and space.

The place you left is extremely limited in time, not to even mention location."

Jacquelyn and Tadd glanced at each other hoping to see if the other understood, since the whole situation was hard to comprehend.

"We still have a long walk." The Dream Master pointed to a tall mountain with many large buildings stretching up above them. "Please feel free to explore the area around you as we travel. You'll find the new abilities you've acquired to be very invigorating."

As they walked along the path, Tadd was the first one to ask. "What exactly is this place?"

"That's an interesting question, and I'll do my best to answer it." He stopped along a small stream and rested on the grass, indicating for them to have a seat as well. "Coming from the material world, you can only reference information based on what you know. So, I'll start from there. In that world, you know of a beginning and an end. You are born and then you die—end of story." He studied them closely to see if they were following him.

"Are you telling us that in this place, we'll never die?"

"Precisely. This is an alternate way to get into heaven—a side door, so to speak."

"Is that possible?" Jacquelyn blinked her eyes.

"Yes it is. Now, it may not be the easiest way, and I'll explain that later, but it's the way some prefer, and is, in fact, necessary."

"You said that you established or built this place, this school. Why did you do that?"

"That's another good question, and one that isn't so easy to give in a short period of time. Please bear with me as I tell you a story. It'll also answer many other questions that I'm sure you have in the process."

Tadd and Jacquelyn made themselves comfortable on the lush green grass. They held hands and glowed as if they were but only one person.

"Before this place existed, it was nothing but an open path leading to the side gate to heaven. There were no signs pointing in the right direction or teachers who could help. Yes, there were others here roaming around looking and trying to find their way for sure. And . . . some found their way to the side door and entered. But . . . there is where the problems exist. On the other side, it's so beautiful, so complete, so pure that once there, you never even think about returning. In that world you know everything about the future and the past—there are no secrets."

The Dream Master lowered his head, as if in deep thought. "I also assume that it's fear that keeps many from returning; a fear of not being able to find their way back. For them to return, they lose that perfect knowledge of the universe. When they make a single change in this world, they no longer know the future because it changes also."

"I'm not sure I follow all of that, but it sounds like we have much to learn." Jacquelyn said, as she smiled at Tadd.

The Dream Master smiled at them and continued. "The school I created here floats between the two worlds. You can be in the part that knows the future and the past but not able to change or interact with it, or you can interact with it but not know the past or the future. You cannot do both."

Tadd rubbed his chin. "I think I understand to some extent, but I'll have to admit that this is very hard to totally grasp."

"There have been many civilizations across time and space that managed to advance and advance until they eventually became perfect, knowing all and becoming pure. If there's nothing left to learn, to experience, to anticipate, or a reason for existing—well it's a very pitifully, slow, but ultimate death."

"Eventually a way was devised to correct this problem. A new world was created. One where the physical body was allowed to die and the spirit, the energy force was allowed to start over, but with very little knowledge of the previous life. This way each life can be unique and interesting. However, over time there are those that advance and continue to do so. These are the enlightened ones."

Jacquelyn smiled broadly. "I guess that must be us, since we are at this place."

"Exactly. The energy in you is growing stronger all the time. In this school you'll be in a controlled environment. You'll learn that all of your past needs to be made perfect. You have a lot of work to do, trust me, but along the way you'll also see others that need help to grow. You'll know which ones. You'll be like the teachers you remember from your own past. I'm sure you have others you want to help advance with you such as your mom, and Tadd's sister. And there are others, like the girl who worked for Tadd, who can be added to the list. You will understand more as you grow."

"So, our teachers are here as well?" Jacquelyn's voice couldn't hide her excitement in seeing them.

"Yes, they're all here and looking forward to seeing you again. There's one more fact that's extremely important for both of you. You were able to find your way here at the same time, and if you hold on to each other tightly you'll be able to one day enter heaven together. Most of the souls here that are waiting to enter the side door don't for that very reason. Their soulmate's not here yet, and sometimes it never happens. They stay here . . . always looking, and always hopefully waiting."

"That's a very sad and scary thought," Tadd said.

"Yes, it is and that's precisely why I'm here. My love arrived here before me and discovered I wasn't here so she went back to find me. The dark forces of the world are hiding her from me, and they're determined to keep her hidden."

Jacquelyn and Tadd felt the pain in his heart, knowing that he must have looked for her for a very long time. "Why is it so hard to find her?"

"The dark side also has the ability to change history and the future. As fast as she establishes one, the dark forces erase it, but I know she's still out there somewhere. I can't go further until I locate her. I'm sure your previous lives of being so close to finding each other and making it here played a large role in my helping you make it."

"We're very glad you did, but I can only imagine what you must be going through." Tadd and Jacquelyn felt his sorrow.

"It's not for you to worry about. You have a lot to learn, and it's time for you to get started." He stood and walked on in front of them.

With even more reasons to be excited, Tadd held Jacquelyn's hand as she followed behind him. "I'm so glad we're here together." He reached over and kissed her hand after he pulled it up to his lips.

The walk on the path climbed past increasingly beautiful surroundings with the vivid colors radiating all around them. It took a while, but they soon recognized it at the same time. As soon as they imagined or felt any need at all, their thoughts became instant reality. They started testing their new powers and reacted differently on each new creation.

Tadd decided it would be great to give Jacquelyn some flowers and remembered a special one he had been working on for a long time in his garden. They appeared directly along the path, filling the air with the fragrances he had been hunting for. As he admired them, he started to think of the different pollinations he wanted to try. He decided to try his new powers and see the future, but nothing materialized. This puzzled him.

The Dream Master smiled as he apparently understood. "Remember you can see the future and the past, but when you do you can't interact with it and make changes. On the other hand, you can react with the world, but when you do, you'll not be able to see the future. I know this is hard to understand and it'll take some time."

As Tadd thought hard about this and knew he had a lot to learn, Jacquelyn's mind wondered back to her past. What would happen to her in that world? She even doubted if she would want to see the future. However, it was a question she knew she had to ask. "What happened to our bodies after we came here?"

"That's a question I thought you would ask eventually, and one of the first one most people ask. Your life will continue as it's already predestined to do. However, after your body dies this time, there'll be no soul there to wander the universe and look for another host. It's easy to see your life and all past lives any time you want."

"You know, I'm not so sure I want to remember it."

"I can fully understand that, but to move on you need to face that past and make it perfect. I'm sure Tadd will help you every step of the way. And you also have all the teachers here at Whitestone."

The scary parts of her past crept into her mind. While it was only a second, it was long enough to be created. Vincent started walking down the path toward them. "Oh no!" she yelled.

When Vincent's image faded almost as quickly as he appeared, Jacquelyn's eyes darted around looking for him, but he was nowhere to be seen.

The Dream Master turned around and walked over to her, placing a hand on her forehead. "This is one item you'll need to control. Like I said, this is a safe haven for you. Everything bad you create, we'll quickly erase. The others here will help you, and you'll help others over time."

Finally, the giant entrance to the school standing at least sixty feet high was visible ahead. The entire building was a soft pure white and gave the appearance of Italian marble. When the Dream Master lifted his hands, they glided open. "I hope you like your new home."

"I'm sure we'll love it." Jacquelyn leaned forward with her eyes glancing wildly from one side to the other. The entrance hall looked huge and glowed from even more white stones covering the floor, the walls and the ceiling. Whitestone was definitely a well-chosen name for this place.

On the back side of the hall were two large staircases which started on the far sides and joined in the center three floors above them. They were also made of the same white marble.

As they entered the hall many people rushed to greet them. It was teachers they recognized instantly like Kayo, the professor from California and the Tai Chi teacher. Tadd also saw many people he recognized from his past. They all rushed toward each other as they exchanged hugs and kisses. These were followed by many others as the large hall became crowded with people.

When the doors behind them closed, they immersed themselves into their new world. A number of old girlfriends from her past rushed to her as their giggles echoed around the hall. It felt so good to Jacquelyn that she cried in joy. This had to be the best place ever.

She turned to see Tadd talking to many older men who appeared to be teachers he had talked to many times before. He had a radiant smile as he continued to greet them.

Then, they both turned to each other and quickly covered the distance between them. His hand reached to the back of her head and held it firmly as he covered her lips with his. "I love you so very much."

"I love you too."

The chatting from around the room ended as the crowd listened intensely to their conversation. Tadd turned to the Dream Master as a thought crossed his mind. "We never officially became married before we made it here. Is it possible to get married in Whitestone?"

The room remained quiet as all turn to the Dream Master to hear his explanation. "Marriage is an interesting subject. It's something man has created through the use of laws to control the population, and it has many different meanings for everyone. The true union of a man and a woman is that moment they become one in mind and spirit. In your case, the only item left is for someone to tell you—you may kiss your bride."

Tadd and Jacquelyn glanced at each other as they understood his meanings. They had found their true love, and that was all that really mattered. However Tadd continued to have a puzzled look on his face. "From the life where we came from and eventually die, do we actually get married?"

"The ability to see the past and the future will soon be part of your new life here. Just remember, if you see it you'll not be able to live it, and if you change it, you'll not be able to see it. There's also one word of caution, if you decide to go change your past, you might not be able to find your way back to here."

"You make it sound like a very large risk." Jacquelyn said as she looked at the Dream Master for answers.

"Yes, it's a very big risk, and one I don't like to see anyone take unless it's absolutely necessary. However, I do think we need to celebrate your union and a wedding party would certainly be in order. Come let me show you more of Whitestone and then we can plan that party."

As the group walked up the stairs, the Dream Master smiled, but those who had been there for a while knew what he was thinking. His beloved wife wasn't here with him, and the chances of his finding her almost didn't exist.

While they all knew the Dream Master would do everything he could to keep other couples from making that same mistake, he would never stop looking for her. One day there would be a final battle that he would lead against the dark forces, but today—he would celebrate one very important victory.

The End

278